BLOOD AND FIRE

D1741922

BLOOD AND FIRE

by

LORNA PEGRAM

LONDON
VICTOR GOLLANCZ LTD
1978

© Lorna Pegram 1978

ISBN 0 575 02410 0

MADE AND PRINTED IN GREAT BRITAIN BY
THE GARDEN CITY PRESS LIMITED
LETCHWORTH, HERTFORDSHIRE
SG6 1JS

*For my youngest son Crispin
and in memory of my parents*

PART ONE

"AND NOW, JESUS," said her mother amiably, "we kneel here at thy footstool to ask thy blessing on our journey to Leytonstone about our Father's business. May we be channels through which the healing river of thy blood may flow. . . ."

"Amen," said her father.

"May we set stumbling feet upon the path to righteousness. . . ."

"Amen."

"And may the bus be on time despite the recent trouble with the 145B."

A faint reproach, a not quite hectoring note, tinged Mrs Carr's friendly tone. Last Sunday they had been made late for the Holiness meeting. It was a mercy that they had only been soldiering at the home corps, but today they were specialling in another division and must arrive on time. Posters announcing in red print topped with the Salvation Army crest that Major and Mrs Carr and Penelope (age eleven years) would lead the meetings, were posted confidently outside the Citadel. The letters 'DV' at the bottom were in smaller print, perfunctory; for they were on the Lord's side and convinced that He was on theirs. It was just a matter of communication. This was how He worked: in a not very mysterious way, showing by small and frequent miracles an order in the universe and an intimate grace upon their lives. All three members of the Carr family knelt at his footstool on the polished lino by their individual section of the three-piece suite. Two or three times a day, every day, they would move with a practised swivel from sitting on their chairs to kneeling at them to bring things to the Lord in prayer. All sorts of things, from the colour of new curtains to the international situation.

"We thank thee, Lord, for Mr Chamberlain's promise of peace in our time. . . ."

9

"Amen."

". . . but be thou in all their councils. For without thee as their personal Saviour, how can men guide the world aright?"

The Sunday-bright October sun fingered a shiningly clean room and pried into their closed eyes. Penny was resting her face on the arm of her chair to escape the feathery smell of cushion, and often rose from a word of prayer with a stigmata of Lloyd Loom's wickerwork engraved on cheek or forehead. The taller adults could rest their elbows on the seats and join their hands in a modified praying position which supported their chins on knuckles. Mrs Carr shifted her bust more comfortably into the crooks of her bent arms and continued, "Thou knowest, Lord, that Penny will support us on the platform even though her homework is not finished. Grant that she may give and receive blessing —for we remember thy promise that, Lo! a little child shall lead them—and that because she labours in thy vineyard she may escape punishment at school tomorrow."

"Amen," said Penny fervently. She kept her head carefully still as she liked the Lloyd Loom pattern unblurred; a criss-cross weave deeply etched in red blood.

"Amen," her father murmured after her, and cleared his throat to hint at alternative interpretation. She should have done the algebra on Saturday rather than go to the library and get nose-stuck into two romances. Mother took the hint and passed it on promptly.

"She needs thy guidance, Lord, not to neglect her studies for idle dreaming. Let not this lamb stray from thy flock we beseech thee, as thou art the Good Shepherd."

Images remote from the small suburban room floated continually through its placid appropriate arrangements. Flocks of sheep browsed, vines sprawled with a bloom on black grapes, floods of river—sometimes clear water and sometimes a crimson stream of blood—washed over its fawn tidiness. Pungent metaphor was the language of their lives and the child had learned, not just in speech but mind, that the homeliest acts and objects were cryptic with otherness as well as robustly real in themselves.

"Thy love is boundless as the ocean. Keep us in thy bosom all day through and bring us safe unto our home at night and safely gathered in unto thy harvest at our lives' end. Amen."

Mother bustled upright and at once began chivvying towards

departure. She tied her bonnet's big bow of moiré ribbon deftly to the left of her chin at the looking-glass in the hall while marshalling practical needs. Though the Carrs owned nothing, and every spoon and tea-cloth in their Quarters was listed and checked annually on an Inventory and would be left behind when they got their Marching Orders to another field of battle, her painstaking care treated all material things as though she held them on trust from God as well as the Salvation Army. Even dusters were ironed.

While Father checked that the gas was off at the main, Penny saw that the back door was bolted. Mother looked into her purse to make sure that she had change for bus fares and collections; Father was always giving money to beggars so she managed it. Then she led the way down the thin garden path. The edges of the little lawn were cut sheer as stone and there were no weeds at all.

Their path took them close past the kitchen window of their nearest neighbour and they turned their eyes tactfully away towards late roses straggling off the trellis on the other side.

Since her husband left her, Mrs Parker always had a cigarette in her mouth and a bottle of drink in her shopping-bag. One night there had been a drama of gas. Prying from their front bedroom, Penny had seen Father on his knees beside the gas-cooker which had failed to take Mrs Parker to the Heaven Father prayed to. Saved from gas, she had refrained so far from getting saved spiritually; putting up lace curtain instead. "Not yet ripe unto harvest," Mother explained charitably. Father closed the green-painted gate they shared carefully.

The Banjo lay open and empty in a Sunday morning doze. It was a cul-de-sac and called after the instrument, and exactly the same shape. The Carrs' Quarters were on the corner of a curved row of six at the top of the swelling circle, and two more rows, straight, faced each other across the narrower handle end which led into the street. It was all paved, with two square greens where tuning keys would be, at the street end; which made Banjo children rich in playing space though not in much else. Rent-books called it the Dagenham Slum Clearance Estate. At this time on a Sunday, only scrawled chalk hopscotch numbers and a forgotten top testified to its usual busy activity. Last night all the playing children had been called in as usual to have their baths. On Saturday evenings smoke rose even from summer chimneys as the coppers were lit and games were punctuated by cries through the dusk from one door after another. The fact that the smallest child from each family was dragged away first, but had first use of the bath water, helped to confirm Penny's certainty that there was a divine justice in the universe and a price to be paid for all privilege. The copper was the only way of heating more than a kettle-full of water and fathers carried a fresh hot pail upstairs to add for each person. Fathers naturally had more but grubbier bath water and stayed up latest.

Each of the Carrs carried a Bible, a Song Book, a clean handkerchief and five tiny licorice sweets about the size of an ant, recommended for public speakers. All three were dressed in uniform of symbolic colours, a blatant witness to which side they were on in the battle between good and evil which raged perpetually. Penny was only a Junior Soldier of the Lord but in the thick of the fight all the same. Its ground was the world and your own soul: that was easy to believe, she felt its forces warring. An ambulance went past and she wanted to lick her finger and hold it up—a sure magic against catching a fever. But such superstitions were the Devil's temptation. Though her parents were walking in front and could not see, Jesus could see everything all the time. It was awkward to have such an all-seeing eye on you; but in return you had a Rock in so personal a Saviour against o'er-whelming floods. The blind was lowered at the corner house where her friends the Lock twins lived—was their grandfather dead then? For a time after a stroke he had sat in the sun, dribbling and daft, among their games. Yesterday in a bedroom smelling of illness and roses he had made no response to Father's prayers. In a world so full of threat Penny decided to propitiate all available powers by a complicated twisting of fingers into the sign of the Cross, combined with a surreptitious pagan lick.

"Now," said Father as they turned into the proper road, "we'll save steps and time if we cut the corners. Remember how to steer by two landmarks, Penny?" Reared on a farm, Richard Carr had taught his daughter to plough a straight furrow through winding suburban streets. The skills transported from such a different landscape made the little plough-shaped party even more conspicuous. In their odd costumes they had to keep crossing and recrossing from one pavement to another, making the straightest possible line towards the High Street. A newspaper boy on a bicycle shouted at them, "Salvation Army, all gone barmy". Penny took her eyes off the next lamp-post so that their furrow wavered.

"You must learn to take no notice," scolded Mother. "It's testing your faith and you should be proud of the uniform. You must stop minding being different."

It was easier for the grown-ups, upheld by their own certainties in a community where people kept themselves to themselves. Children locally were both closer and less tolerant, and some of their mockery was cruel. In order not to mind she was beginning to be prepared to be different, even from them. Meanwhile she wore her red for the Blood of the Lamb, yellow for the Fire of the Holy Spirit, and blue for the somewhat nebulous Consecration she had not quite got the hang of, with head high anyway. A peaky little pale-faced head, with unfocused-looking eyes, a soft over-large mouth, and limp fair hair held back with a high white bow.

"Don't carry your hat by the brim: it pulls it out of shape," Mrs Carr scolded as the little procession approached the bus stop in Beacontree High Street. Penny obediently changed her grip to the elastic band, encouraging the black velour to spring up and down like a yo-yo.

"Don't do that, it stretches the elastic."

They had the street to themselves, gaudy shop-fronts shuttered, even the Picture Palace closed to repel a glance into its wicked foyer.

The 145B was, as a suitable miracle, on time. They went up-stairs to enjoy the view. The Sunday streets, so early and empty, looked cleaner than usual; as though they too had their baths on Saturday. The occasional news-stand brightened the corners with placards for Sunday papers. Though newspapers on Sunday were forbidden, Richard Carr allowed himself to glance at the boldly scrawled word PEACE repeated, with CHAMBERLAIN or MUNICH scattered too: optimistic words bright with relief in the pale perfidious sunshine of the first Sunday in October 1938.

"What are you doing for the recitation?" said her father, checking his introductions.

"Straighten out your skirt, dear, do," hissed her mother from the seat behind. "You'll get creases."

"Robert of Sicily," said Penny, obediently bobbing up and

sitting down again more straightforwardly. "Brother of Pope Urbane," she murmured on, to practise and because she liked titles. "And Valmond, Emperor of Allemaine. . . ."

"Shush," said her father. "Cissie: are you going to do the Dedication or would you rather I did?"

"Whatever you like, dear."

"It would rest your throat before the Address."

"Yes, all right, thank you, dear. I'll conduct the meeting up to then."

Dedication was the ritual which corresponded to the Church of England's Christening.

"Good. Then I'll start them on a chorus to let the parents get off the platform and you can take over, Cissie, for prayers and testimonies leading in to your Address."

"Yes, dear," said Cissie; "and do stop leaning on the window, Penny, or you'll get your face dirty and your bow all flattened before we've even started."

As the bus approached their destination, they joined in a word of prayer without kneeling, not to draw too much attention. They need hardly have been so considerate: even smokers had not dared to smoke under the blazon of their witnessing uniforms, and nobody so much as coughed while the Carrs murmured together with heads bowed. Dogs and news-vendors possessed the streets; they possessed the upstairs of the bus; and a humble but extreme confidence possessed them utterly.

When they spiralled down the stairs to the bus stop, Cissie added an invocation to her daughter.

"And eat up everything for goodness' sake. We're billetted on some people we don't know who are quite well-to-do. Don't make a fuss even if it's rice pudding." When you conducted meetings for the day at a corps not your own, you had meals with some local family. This was usually one of the services to the Salvation war rendered by Salvationists who had not given their lives to full-time officer-ship, with its prescribed poverty, but had other and better-paid jobs during the week. So another familiar paradox—for the Carrs had a high reputation and often went Specialling—was the mixture of awe and superiority with which one honoured, while accepting their hospitality, people with cars and things. They were proud to entertain you; you were impressed but also distinguished. As the Specials trod the winding bus stairs in single file, Cissie said, "I'll fluff out her ribbon when we get to the Citadel." She had a good view of the collapsed bow from above and behind her daughter. Her husband helped them off, chiding gently, "As long as her spirit is strong, dear, her hair ribbon hardly matters." The pavement was defiled with fallen leaves, bus tickets and dog dirt. Cissie stepped round the hazards capably, insisting, "No need to arrive with a droopy bow all the same."

The Citadel at Leytonstone, like most Army halls, was heated by a round stove free-standing at one side; closed except when being fed with coal through a fierce mouth at the top and when having clinker removed from a fiery opening at the bottom. But invisible hot air always hovered above its black-leaded top; made the Flag waver; might be the Holy Ghost; was certainly a mysterious emblem of fire; moved when you changed your viewpoint; disappeared in summer; still haunted, pentecostal.

"O Christ of pure and perfect love, look on this sin-stained heart of mine.
I thirst thy cleansing grace to prove, I want my life to be like thine.
O see me at thy footstool bow, And come and sanctify me now."

The Carrs sat in a row along the front of the platform with the corps officers and the local Sergeant Major. A little curtain between the reading stand at the front of the platform and the Mercy Seat beneath it hid their knees and avoided anything dreadful like showing your knickers to the congregation in the body of the hall. The Band was on the platform, ranged in a half-circle behind them, so that Penny was surrounded by its rasping sweetness of sound. Her childhood had marched to the blare and flare of flags and cornets. The crisp warm sound of a brass band nourished spiritual fervour in a physical way. It was like new-baked bread: the crustiness of cornets only outer; inside, the soft dense chords of tenors and euphoniums, the rich harshness of trombones, the warm hollow of the bass drum at its heart. High above everything, the flugel horn would sometimes float a sweet, melancholy descant; as airy and ethereal as the Holy Ghost.

Uplifted by the music, Penny counted the metaphors. Now that Miss Tucker was teaching them figures of speech at the new school, she was interested to analyse the rich, blurred vividness of their jargon and discover such imagery not universal, everyday.

> "O drive Thy foes from out my soul
> Whate'er it cost, howe'er I bleed."

That was three more. It was a good band, the harmonies in a slightly minor key quivered movingly and the notes had a tremulous round quality. The united noise embodied the spiritual, physical mixture to which she was already addicted. Between songs, usually during prayers when most people should have their eyes closed, bandsmen all opened the valves low down among the silver tubing to let out condensations of saliva. So bands inevitably sat in bright tunics in a floor-circle spattered with the dribblings of their bright instruments. To a person accustomed to it, this in no way detracted from the angelic sounds they made. Spit was anyway a substance almost as mystical as blood: in games it could make you immune from being caught and in friendship it could seal the swearing of an allegiance only a little short of blood-brotherhood. You used it too to prove you were not lying. Combined with the shape of the Cross, it was invincible.

> 'O pour on me the cleansing flood,
> Nor let Thy side be cleft in vain.
> 'Tis done, I feel the precious Blood
> Does purge and keep from every stain."

It was comforting to bathe in the warmth of blood and brass bands and know oneself saved, in the safety of the Citadel.

After the song, Father with a licorice ant tucked between gum and cheek-membrane, rose towards the front of the platform and gestured to achieve a dignified approach of the Dedicating family as the echo died away. The Flag was removed from its resting-place beside the stove and carried to hang above his head while he received a white package of baby; mercifully sleeping and silent.

The Flag. Made of a coarse stuff, it always flew like a sail at the head of weddings and funerals and the march from the open air meeting to the hall every Sunday. Its bright rag flapped in front of the band and ranks of officers and soldiers. The yellow splash in the centre was for Fire, the red surrounding it for Blood; the outer edge was blue for Purity—or was it Purity? Certainly the motto was plainly inscribed: Blood and Fire.

Penny followed the ceremony in her book.

"In the dedication of this child you now declare your willingness for the Lord to take possession of her and you wish that she shall always and only do His will. You must be willing that she should spend all her life for God wherever He may choose to send her, and not withhold her at any time from such hardship, suffering, want or sacrifice as true devotion to the service of Christ and the Salvation Army may entail."

Father eyed the parents solemnly over his bundle of baby, and Penny felt that her own life was tiresomely lacking in hardship and sacrifice of a suitably dramatic sort. The white wool in her father's hands began to squirm and a stifled yell issued from it, relieving the moment of too great solemnity. Major Carr inserted the tip of his little finger in the baby's mouth, shifted his left and holding arm surreptitiously against a sudden but not unexpected dampness, and raised his voice:

"You must, as far as you can, keep from her all intoxicating drink, tobacco, finery, wealth, hurtful reading, worldly acquaintance, and every influence likely to injure her either in soul or in body...." It was, thought Penny, an awful lot to be kept from. The baby seemed to share a sense of protest, or had discovered the misleading finger-tip unsatisfactory: it set off into that rhythmic crying which racks the whole small frame and uses all of every breath only to make itself heard. Father rocked and continued:

"... to be a faithful soldier, giving all the time, strength, ability and money possible to help in the salvation war." The baby, impressed or exhausted, gave up competition while Major Carr prayed. Penny read on in her book that if there were any other children in the family, the officer might ask them:

"Will you do all you can to help your sister to get saved, be good, and prepare for Heaven?" The children will then answer: "We will!"

That was one of the benefits of being born into the Salvation Army, thought Penny: almost as soon as you knew you were not safe, you knew you could get saved. Being a baby must be awful, she looked sympathetically at the dedicated one out-crying the united chorus. Being born flung you instantly into light, cold, hunger, solitude, at the mercy of everything and everybody, after the safety inside your mother. Other dangers loomed and threatened as soon as you began to understand things. Dark, death, disapproval, dogs which bite, Father Christmas with his nasty habit of creeping with a big sack when you were asleep: these were earliest. Also loss of love, dreams of witches, being tickled, taking risks. 'Safe' was a suspect word to children, its sound of a permanent condition must be a lie. "It's quite safe," they said when urging you on to openwork iron bridges across railway lines, towards the edge of the murderous sea, at roads full of traffic, or into toppling boats on the pond in the park: all of which were obviously not safe at all. But 'being saved' was more specific and believable. You needed only a sense of sin and true penitence.

Penny got saved at the earliest allowed age. At four, she had lied about eating up her breakfast bacon when she had actually given it to the cat. She felt convicted of sin in the morning meeting and made her way crying to the Penitent Form. It smelled of wood and vinegar with traces of Brylcreem and salt from the sweat and tears of former penitents. Cat-clawed guilt brought her by way of sin to Salvation. As soon as she had confessed and promised a true intention not to tell lies again, she was pronounced saved. All sang heartily while she hiccuped from crying, "There is joy joy joy, there is joy in the Salvation Army", and she knew that her little soul had been washed in the Blood of the Lamb and become white as snow. It sounded messy but moving, and she felt happy and redeemed.

Sin, being essential and having so consoling an outcome, held thereafter a certain fascination. She wondered what grown-up seekers whispered to the salvationist who was dealing with them at the Penitent Form. And it could be no accident that all the best stories of redemption, from olden times or weekly testimonies, began with dramatic quantities of sin. Like 'Robert of Sicily', the subject of her recitation.

It went well. After a wobble of nervousness, her voice rang out across the attentive congregation and became quite poetic in the poetic parts.

It was a good story, with a good Message. Telling stories well, all with good Messages, was what made a good speaker at meetings. It was the mode of all her parents' preaching, and seemed to Penny an inevitable style of perception and of communication. Everything which happened was an illustration of something else. First you perceived it, then you narrated it as vividly as possible, and then you drew out the meaning: that was the natural progress of every piece of experience.

Before the Address, Mrs Carr instigated a session of prayer and testimony. People in the congregation, moved to speak, did so spontaneously; standing up. There was rarely either silence, or two people talking at the same time. This indicated a providential orchestration; the prompting of the Spirit cued them like a conductor. They too told stories of personal experience and God's action which made them joint main characters. For the group, the exercise was satisfying. "Hallelujah!" they would often chorus, recognising the climax.

"This week, Lord, when I was travelling to business on the train, I was moved to speak to the fellow-occupant of my railway carriage. He was revealed as a soul in torment: a man of good education who had lost all through drink. I thank thee, Lord, that by the time we reached Liverpool Street Station, that poor creature had found Salvation."

"Jesus saves!" someone agreed.

"He does, he does," endorsed other voices.

From different places in the hall, voices answered each other and an instinctive rhythm built up.

"God be praised!"

"Amen, amen!"

The Holiness meeting that morning was proving to have a very good atmosphere; and when Cissie launched her Address, she looked and sounded confident. Penny, who had heard it before, smiled modestly when a touching illustration from her earlier childhood was invoked, but occupied the rest of the time alternately worrying about the total blank which numbed her mind whenever algebraic symbols were presented to it; and being a female version of the Scarlet Pimpernel, who might say "Demme", which was a good-hiding offence for her, but save people all the same. She did believe in saving people but had begun to question whether the Army had exclusive rights. The fantasy was broken by the stir which heralded an end of the Holiness meeting and the onset of behaving well at the Harcourts' during the break for dinner before the afternoon's Band and Songster Festival.

"Here we are then," said Mrs Harcourt. "Do come in." The house was superior but not dauntingly so: double-fronted but only semi-detached. Mr Harcourt was in private, not uniform; but he might have just missed the morning meeting to see to dinner and then come to take them home from the meeting. The car journey, though brief, was thrilling. Officers eschewed worldy possessions such as cars, but Penny enjoyed rare drives in them with sinful enthusiasm. Mr Harcourt was a square, quiet man with a big moustache, shaggily concealing his mouth as though to compensate for a lack of hair which revealed too much of the top of his head. He drove confidently but was conversationally reserved and left the talking to his wife and daughter.

They were jolly, and in uniform—both sang in the Songster Brigade—but subtly different from full-time officers like Penny's parents in looks and manner. They wore their bonnets in a faintly rakish way over shorter curlier hair and the daughter might use just a hint of make-up. Make-up was certainly condemned, but only officers were actually forbidden to cut their hair; though a bun in the nape was preferred style for all. Still, these days some whose daily life was In the World had bobbed their hair without too much censure from their Sunday comrades at the corps. It was hard to know whether or not they had succumbed to a perm or Marcel Wave, with their twin evils of deception and making oneself attractive to men. That was between them and their Saviour, Cissie announced with dogmatic tolerance when Penny had voiced suspicions about young women at their home corps. Mother recognised unhealthy fascination: the child did so long to have a mop of tousled curls like all the best heroines of school stories instead of her own dead-straight ear-length bob.

Sylvia Harcourt's hair might well be natural, Penny decided admiringly when she took her bonnet off. The youngest visitor was invited to leave her coat in Sylvia's room. Sylvia must be about twenty, quite grown up. Her bedroom was glamorous with frills of lavender-sprigged material around a kidney-shaped dressing-table to match the curtains and white wood-work, itself unusual in Quarters, where brown paint was more practical. Carpet on the floor, bedside lamps and a fitted wardrobe added to the luxury: it was almost as exotic as one of the windows in Harrison Gibson's furniture shop done up to look like a real room.

Sylvia was kind as well as pretty, it appeared. She tossed her wavy hair and smiled at Penny in the triple looking-glass.

"I take off my tunic for dinner, to keep it clean, and it's not comfy for cooking. I like *your* uniform."

"It's Goodmayes Singing Company," Penny explained gratefully.

Though senior uniform was universal and trimmings to denote rank specific, different corps devised children's garb freely; competing, especially in Singing Companies, for more ingenious interpretations of the symbolic colour scheme which was obligatory. Penny's was unusually fancy. Sylvia pulled out a kidney-shaped stool at the dressing table. "Would you like to do your hair here? Use anything you like." The glass top was gay with bottles and jars and a big drum of powder with a puff of silky swansdown perched inside. Penny accepted the strange decadence of sitting down to look at herself in comfort and from three angles and investigated the enticing clutter. Sylvia leaned across and unstoppered a bottle.

"My new perfume," she said: "Try." And before Penny could resist temptation the sultry wicked smell was dabbed on to her wrist. She sat sniffing—she saw herself—with shocked excited eyes. Encouraged, Sylvia touched the little girl's nose with the fluffy powder puff, watching her in the mirror. Her cheeks reddened with natural rouge: she looked almost pretty for a moment. Then sneezed at the tickly fronds of powdery feathers. They both laughed as Penny wiped off powder and blew her nose. "That will be a lesson to me," said Sylvia, biting her lip in shame though with mischievous eyes still shining. Following nice Sylvia downstairs, Penny thought how cleverly the Holy Ghost kept you on the right track; that her conscience should warn her by a sneeze against the wicked worldliness of wanting to be beautiful.

Mrs Harcourt was a bustling little woman with small features, once as regular as her daughter's, now slightly fudged by fat. Her face still showed oval bones but had spread like a cooking bun into a rounder shape, around a small neat nose and bright brown eyes. Her movements were quick and perky in the kitchen at the final preparations for a big roast dinner.

"Can I help?" asked Penny politely.

"No no, dear, I said to your mother, I said, you're all working at the meetings, just you have a nice rest while you're here. Your Mummy and Daddy are in the dining-room, you go and have a nice sit down."

But something was flustering her and Penny hung about as Sylvia took an apron off the hook on the back of the kitchen door and tied it over her uniform skirt.

"Michael with Dad, is he?" said Sylvia, stirring gravy. Mrs Harcourt gave Penny a troubled glance as she said: "No, he's not, he's not down yet. He really is too bad. When I told him we'd got the Specials coming."

This family problem sent Penny tactfully out of the kitchen to find her parents in the dining-room. But in the hall she heard a sound and looked up to the stairs. Through the banisters an astonishing sight approached her level. The first things she registered were bedroom slippers and pyjama trousers, then a dressing-gown, and—as if this were not shocking enough—the sheets of a loosely gathered newspaper swept against the banisters at her eye-level. A Sunday paper! Work of the Devil! And it seemed almost the devil incarnate who neared the foot of the stairs when a hand with a smoking cigarette in it was revealed.

"Hallo!" said this monstrous apparition, surprised. "Who the Devil are you, then?" And continued to come down, though not to her level, even when he reached the hall floor. Speechless, Penny stared up at a tall young man. He took a puff of his cigarette and stared back at what was to him clearly as unexpected an apparition. She was wearing a crimson silk blouse with long full sleeves gathered into a cuff at the wrist and a white silk rope draped across where her bosom would be eventually. This—like dressing-gown cord—was bunched at each side into a trefoil, drooped in a double loop across, and dangled loose, hanging from the right side of her front with two fringed bobbles at the end. The young man inspected this arrangement curiously.

"What on earth are you wearing?" he said.

"It's my uniform," said Penny with dignity.

"Yes, but those amputated daisies: what do they signify?"

She looked disapproval. "You're not dressed at all, so I don't see why you should criticise."

"Fair enough," he said cheerfully, folding up his newspaper.

Briefly reprieved from the attacking encounter, she observed him. His face reminded her of a picture of Mercury she had once seen. Its winged eyebrows, lobeless ears, wide forehead creased with arching question-lines and bright eyes under emphatically curved lids gave him a faunish, fleeting look. His chin either actually receded or was tucked in and pointed: certainly the overall shape of his face was a steeply narrowing wedge. A mocking mouth completed the features, set in a sarcastic grin. He seemed older than other teenage boys because of an air of confidence in his shocking behaviour. He clapped a sudden hand to his untidy hair. "Oh God," he said, "you must be part of the visiting lot. My mother will be livid—I'd forgotten all about your coming to lunch. Hell." His disgrace was lightly taken; so far as she could tell its main effect was to add swearing to his other blatant sins. He shrugged and straightened his dressing-gown. "Oh well," he said, "too late now, or I'll ruin Mum's Yorkshire pudding as well as the social occasion. Let me escort you to the dining-room."

He dumped the newspaper untidily on the hall-stand, stubbed out his cigarette, and offered her his arm. She drew back slightly and he tilted his head and straightened the rejected arm to reach forward and shake the hanging piece of her silvery-silk cord critically. "Isn't it an awful nuisance getting in the custard?" he asked and went past her.

"Oh Michael, really," his mother greeted him.

But "Hallo," he beamed, "You must forgive my dress—I get up late on Sundays."

"Major and Mrs Carr," said Sylvia in a warning tone but with a tendency to giggle, "my younger brother Michael."

"How d'you do," said Michael. "Is the person in the hall yours? The rather young person with big eyes and sort of epaulettes on her chest?"

He turned—he had been blocking the doorway—and called: "Come on in, Angel." Then disappeared into the room. Following, Penny heard him say to her father easily: "She wouldn't tell me her name, she was far too shocked. Let's get a proper look at you, Nameless."

"This is our daughter Penelope," said her mother in a putting-down voice; and Mrs Harcourt glowered at him while arranging the table.

"If you'd sit here, Major Carr . . ."

Michael ignored the attempt to quench his defiant non-conformity. "Put angry little angel-eyes where I can see her, Mum. Popping out of nowhere in the hall there. Thought she was a figment at first. Hey ho. The guilty soul of a deep-dyed sinner is prey to the vision of innocence in a child's eyes." Perhaps that was the most shocking of all: that he should use their language mockingly while unrolling his serviette with an acted sigh of shame which should be real.

"He's going through a difficult stage," murmured Mrs Harcourt.

"Very difficult," he agreed.

"Penny did a lovely recitation at the morning meeting," said Mrs Harcourt after an awkward pause. "Pass the sprouts to Mrs Carr, Michael."

"Did she now," grinned Michael, obedient only about vegetables. "Was it deeply moving?"

"Yes it was," said Sylvia. "It was jolly good."

"I might as well admit I can't take the dreadful style of those evangelical poems. 'Bad language' shouldn't mean only swearing."

Penny said furiously: "Longfellow, actually." She pricked her fork into the tablecloth.

"Don't be pert," said her mother.

"*Hiawatha*? Gosh!" said Michael. "How did he come to join the Army?"

Father took the fractious tableful of people into firm conversational hands, "Not *Hiawatha* in fact, but one of the *Tales of a Wayside Inn*. Less well known but probably superior work. A pity most people associate Longfellow only with the innovation of *Hiawatha*'s verse structure."

The critical young man looked at Major Carr with new respect; Penny looked at her father with old admiration. He was much more intellectual than most Army people and read theology and wrote poetry. That was why he was in the Editorial Department at International Headquarters and not a corps officer. It was through his encouragement that she had taken the scholarship to the grammar school; many Salvationists feared that too much

24

education would take their children away from simple faith. "Be good, sweet maid, and let who will be clever" had been written four times in Penny's autograph album as a heavy hint of where danger was seen to lie. But Richard Carr did not accept such arguments: his faith was too strong to avoid risks. His certainty and Cissie's fierce maternal pride that the child kept being top at school overcame misgivings. Though Dick was a dreamer, and she complained that Penny took after him, 'always stuck in a book', it was with a proud, showing pleasure. It was she who dismissed financial arguments and flouted the Banjo custom of not letting children take the scholarship because they must start earning at fourteen. "We can manage," said Cissie. She was a good manager.

"What lovely light Yorkshire pudding," she now said firmly to Mrs Harcourt; and that end of the table filtered off into an exchange of recipes while Michael and Major Carr, opposite Penny, turned to politics. Mr Harcourt made predictable conversational overtures to her.

"And how do you like school?"

"I'm not really used to the grammar school yet. We do Latin."

Father nudged a warning glance in her direction: not to show off.

"That's nice," said Mr Harcourt. "You must be a clever little girl."

"You want to watch it, Angel," said Michael. "You might get disillusioned like me."

"What's disillusioned?" asked Penny with interest.

"Why are you disillusioned?" asked Major Carr with concern. He was still subject to critical comments at the War Cry office about sending his daughter into the hazards of higher education. The bad-mannered youth in a dressing-gown might offer daunting evidence in his own person. But Penny noticed that Michael became more polite, quite shy and somehow younger when Father treated him as a grown-up than when his mother treated him as a child. Now he flushed and straightened at the table.

"Oh well, you know. I started work last summer. Clerking in an office is a bit different from the sixth form at George Monoux." Father was impressed: it was the best boys' school in the entire area. But the remarkable young man seemed cross to have been deceived into being personal and explanatory. "So it's a bit of a blow to hear that what I thought of as a revelation of pure spirit is only a rather clever little girl," he said. "Beastly idea. Arriving with false credentials. It's the light in the hall; filtering through the stained-glass sunrise, it can turn a scholarship-swot into the illusion of an angel. My mistake. No, blame the fellow who designed the tops of suburban doors."

People chewed and swallowed; then Father started again on politics in his gentle, stubborn way, refusing to waste time.

Sylvia whispered, "Don't let Mike upset you, does he? He's always like that. He's only teasing; not you: Mum." Sharing Father's predilection for more than small talk, Penny shook her head impatiently. "He's not Army, then?"

"He's an agnostic. Whatever that means. Dad's Church." Penny made a mental note to look up agnostic in the dictionary.

"And look up cynic while you're about it," said Michael, laughing into her eyes. Though startled, she saw that his were blue and merry and not unkind. "Now, as I was saying," he turned back to her father, "war's inevitable, it's only a matter of when. So pacifism is no justification for Munich. It was just a sell-out, we needed time to prepare for war and we're preparing. That's all."

"I think you're wrong," said Major Carr. "War solves nothing and is, in my belief, evil in itself. 'Thou shalt not kill', I take it literally. You should hear Doctor Soper—I often go to his talks on Tower Hill at dinner time. I agree about the evils of Nazism, but can't condone answering one evil with another. And war to me is abhorrent."

Michael leaned back to examine him more carefully. "You'd be a conscientious objector, then?"

"If necessary. Yes. But it's only fair to tell you that in my job I'd be exempt."

Michael laughed. "Yes, of course. As an officer in the Salvation Army I suppose you count as a minister of the gospel?"

"Yes. That's right."

"It's a hell of a funny branch of the ministry for anyone with your views on war!" Michael grinned. "Do you still speak of 'Firing your cartridge' when you contribute to the collection?"

"Yes," said Father in the quiet, carefully level tone which showed disturbance or anger. "All our military allusions prove rather than disprove my point. The only war I can believe in

26

fighting is on the spiritual plane. The salvation war is against the powers of evil, not against people, not even against sinners. Only the sin."

There! That should show him, thought Penny. But:

"The world's due for change," said this bad-mannered Michael. "Perhaps a war's needed."

"Needed? That's an irresponsible remark." Father looked stern, becoming bad-mannered himself. So the young man must be interesting. "Reform may be overdue: there I'd agree. But not through war. Social progress can't justify guiltless victims. I presume you're a socialist?"

"Of course," said Michael. "You?"

Mrs Carr said with a firm intention to defuse and a false, critical smile: "I always vote for the candidate, myself. I read up about them and choose the best man." Michael ignored her; pinned Father: "You live in a poor area. What d'you do about the exploitation of the working classes there?"

Mrs Carr was stung into an anger of her own. "We earn less than most of our neighbours. Some of them work at Fords! Of course they're all communists there!" She sniffed crossly.

"Now, Mummy," said Father warningly, and turned back to Michael. "The Army's social work has always done a lot for the down-and-out, as you know, and the depression causes more hardship. We do what we can. But to our minds their souls are more the concern of Our Lord and Saviour Jesus Christ." It was, you had to face it, a more impressive title even than Robert of Sicily's. But Michael snorted contemptuously.

"Pie in the sky," he condemned. "Victimised by the capitalist system all their lives, they can hope for a Mansion, but later. If they settle for hell here, and your preaching, they'll avoid the fire later. While the bosses boom."

Penny rushed to Father's defence. "Nobody's starving in our Banjo and bodies anyway are born and die and the soul's only in them for the time of their lives so it must be saved for eternity."

While parents shushed her, Michael's scowl twisted into a smile. "I like 'the time of their lives'," he said.

"The Army's not political," said Father, with a certain emphasis against emotional female intrusions from any direction. "You must agree it would lose even its social-work's value if it were to take such sides as you're doing. There's no need to bring in the nature

27

of Man and Eternity to argue that." He peaked his eyebrows at Penny not to speak until she was spoken to. She felt snubbed but Michael smiled amusement at her before returning with evident relish to airing some practised grievances against his disapproving family and their guests. "Very well then, let's shelve the issue of whether a man's spirit—soul if you prefer—can develop best if cramped into an assembly line. Repetitive unrewarding work can't be the ideal way, even with your beliefs, to spend the time of their lives. What are you doing about it?"

Mother interrupted: "Daddy's always giving away money to people, even drunkards and people who've brought it on themselves. He'd go without himself rather than let even people like that go hungry."

"All right, mother," said Father. "What other changes than social did you have in mind when you said war could be needed?"

"The Empire," said Michael with gloomy relish; and handed round sprouts again. Penny's ears were so pricked she was forgetting to eat at all, let alone everything, so as not to disgrace the family with her faddiness in front of their hosts. Empire Day meant to her a small coarse Union Jack on a splintery thin pole to wave; and the ceremony seemed always to come after needlework. Or needlework perhaps was something to do while you were waiting for occasions to begin. Anyway, she recollected the little soft packet of talcum powder sewn into a tiny pillow to keep your hands from perspiring and spoiling your section of the sheet you hemmed in groups.

"Imperialism in India for instance, what a history of shame that's been. Not to mention the Black Man's Burden throughout Africa. Painting the map red in native blood. It'll all have to change." Fascinating; though Penny relinquished Empire Day with reluctance. Few things were so comradely as stitching sheets with friends; a hill of white cotton, valleyed with shadows, shifting on the desks between you.

"Our work in India has made marvellous headway," Father was saying. "Ours were the first missionaries to live as the natives not as the White Men. Back in the Founder's time, Army officers went out with nothing but their faith."

Michael said: "It didn't occur to anybody that the Indians might have had more than enough gods to be going on with? White

28

men in red white and blue uniforms with brass bands must have been all they needed!"

As you turned the crunched-up sheet in hemming, its landscape altered. Mountain peaks flattened and new plateaux formed. Though the white table-cloth in front of her remained flat, Penny became aware of a serious shift in the look of it. She located this in a change of mood (a silence knifish, a forked crossing of glances) at what Michael had just said. Father's face looked whipped and also clenched as when he sometimes slapped her face. She exploded with furious loyalty. "Stop being rude to my father!" When father pushed his uniform cap back on his head he looked more gay and handsome than any sight; when she cried the smell of his handkerchief was the deepest comfort and reassurance. "How dare you sit there in your night-clothes and smoke and swear and be so rude to Daddy!" She literally saw red.

"Penny," warned her father.

But: "Stop sneering and being stuck-up," she shouted.

In the embarrassed hush, Michael said, "Sorry", with a serious face, holding her eyes until the red faded and she saw his blue gaze honestly ashamed.

Father cleared his throat and said in a carefully moderating voice, "We are having a discussion. You don't understand, pet. But that's no excuse for being naughty and I think, if Mrs Harcourt agrees, that you should leave the table. If you're not grown-up enough to take part in a serious argument without shouting you shouldn't be with grown-ups at all. So, Penny—"

But: "Don't make her," said Michael abruptly. "Please. It was my fault. Pa!" he invoked Mr Harcourt urgently, "you agree with Major Carr, don't you, about all the good the British did in the colonies?" His expression was both keen and pleading. Looking at his father, he reached across the table to put a restraining hand on Penny's wrist.

"We'd have a job to survive if we lose the Empire," said Mr Harcourt. Penny sat very still under the hand on her wrist, while all seemed doubtful, in the balance, war and the Empire and whether she would be sent away from the table in disgrace. And more.

"Wasn't that a lovely Dedication," said Mrs Harcourt, determined to change the subject though far from certain what it was. "I did like your prayer, Major." She sent a smile down the length of the table which included a warning to her son in its extreme revelation of teeth and glittering of eyes.

"Oh God," he said. He removed his hand from Penny's wrist and brushed some crumbs towards him to cancel the previous gesture. "Not another poor little devil having the world, the flesh and the Devil abdicated on his behalf before he's had a go at them, even?"

"It was a girl," said his mother firmly; "In Fact." Facts were always invoked with a hard emphasis of authority; usually as an attack on faith. Mother still flushed if anyone mentioned Darwin. Men from apes, indeed, when God created Adam from the dust as the Bible plainly said. 'Scientific' was an alarming word in the Carr family. Absolute to most people now, it seemed essentially the opposite of 'religious'. Mother fought its arrogant assaults on God by ignoring anything which must be, therefore, wicked. But Father read late into the night to accommodate its insistent certainties into his faith; fearing ignorance ineffectual as well as being over-come by curiosity and argumentativeness. 'Proof' and 'fact' had become too loosely used imperatives. Penny knew about this from Science at school. She looked anxiously; but Mrs Harcourt's in-tonation of "in fact" about the baby had been only carelessly imperious. She was on Father's side against her odd, airy, shocking son. Who said in renewed perky insolence:

"A girl! Worse! At least for all the baby boys of her genera-tion. All right then, if you insist, deny the Devil; but what's wrong with the World and the Flesh for God's sake? Stop squirming, Mother, I'm not swearing at the minute. I mean actually for your creating God's sake. Or isn't He supposed to have made the world and become flesh?"

Father quelled and rescued Mrs Harcourt. "The Army service is rather different from the Church of England ceremony," he said, "for just such reasons. I'm rather in sympathy with your son, Mrs Harcourt, about the lip-service so many disbelievers pay in such rituals."

Oh good, felt Penny; though why she was relieved to find her father and the quarrelsome young man in agreement was puzzling.

"Were you dedicated?" he asked her.

"Of course. Weren't you?"

"Probably." He glanced at his mother, a gentler look. "But am not."

30

Mrs Harcourt said excusingly, "He got a lot of ideas at school."

"Dangerous things, ideas," said Michael.

"Don't be rude to your mother, son," said Mr Harcourt; and coughed shyly but wiped the extreme edges of his moustache with a manly flourish of elbows.

"They learn a lot at these schools nowadays," Mrs Harcourt apologised comfortably. "Ideas."

"But I only express them so rudely since having to leave."

"Yes, he minded that. He wanted to be an artist," she confided, as though it were at once amusing and impressive. "Of course we told him there's no money in it, not a proper job. Out of the question," She fiddled with her side-plate and smiled.

"Quite," said Michael. "Still, everything else is open to question."

"An artist! Like that Picasso!"

"Shut up, Ma," said Michael, reddening. But Major Carr said: "I can understand the disappointment."

"Resentment," said Michael. But Father continued steadily:

"I often feel that artists are closer to God than any except the Saints. And some were saints."

Penny looked adoringly from her father's familiar face to the face beside it. It had seemed so sophisticated when surly; but Father's gravity and kindness had unmasked it. The flush which made his eyes more blue made her own skin startle to scarlet, and caused a quiver in some nerves below the breast-bone usually associated with the feeling before tears gushed or the climax of a brass band rhapsody. When the chords were in a minor key. She forked her greens out of cold gravy. Perhaps if she ate them more mysterious pains could be escaped. It anyway helped, to focus imprecise emotion upon the nastiness of cabbage in her mouth.

Mr Harcourt was saying: "Whatever he does won't be for long. They're bringing in conscription so they must expect war."

"Or may hope that a show of strength will make Hitler climb down." Michael had joined Major Carr against his father and his own former case, she noted. That was fair, like Banjo bath water. Mrs Harcourt and Mrs Carr busied to stack plates, indicating with eyebrows that their daughters should accompany them into the kitchen. "Oh do stop arguing you men," cried Mother with mock-annoyance to disguise real. "Always arguing!" She tilted her head at Penny to help clear away.

31

"It's not an argument, dear, it's a discussion," said Father with the deliberate patience which was his nearest to annoyance with her. She left the room with a high colour and stack of plates. Penny looked questioningly at Sylvia, who pursed her lips and shook her head and demonstrated that she could manage the cruet and bread board by herself. Penny was left with the men.

"Are you a pacifist, too, young lady?" Mr Harcourt included her kindly.

She nodded fervently. "I can't kill spiders even. And think of destroying a baby which might be going to grow up and be a great author."

"Is that what you're going to be when you're grown up?" asked Michael in his teasing way. "What authors do you know anyway?"

"Shakespeare's my favourite," she said at once. "Who's yours?"

"Baudelaire." She had never heard of him and looked away, defeated.

His father was saying quietly to her father, "Mike would be in the first age-group to be called up. It's not just a discussion to us, you see."

"No," Father replied as gently, "and the child would be evacuated with the school. They were having practices before Munich. No, I do understand."

A sighing hush of separate but shared fears united the four people accidentally at one table whom speech had seemed only to divide. It resonated beyond their little place and moment.

Recently, when Penny had been washing at the kitchen sink during the News, she had heard from the living-room a wailing sound so terrifying in itself—up and down, up and down—that she had rushed in to stare at the console without drying her face. Mother, instead of being cross, had taken the towel and wiped her gently while Father explained with a whitish look that it was the siren to warn of air raids in the unlikely event of war. The sinister, despairing sound was proved by this calm explanation and Mother's hands to be as fearful as it seemed. Its memory wound through the silence now, while each looked at the others and then away, as if ashamed—not of the thoughts Mr Harcourt had prompted, but of the future itself and the earlier idle exchanges which, in its light, seemed neither truthful nor intimate enough. Pictures in the papers of wars still far away no longer evoked distant sympathy but pangs of home-fear. Refugees with bundles of belongings looked too like the school crocodile rehearsing evacuation in their straggling lines. Foreign soldiers grimacing through wounds infected the faces of the spruce tidy soldiers you saw—more often now—on foot or in lorries. And they had always disturbed Penny. Father's pacifism taught that they had chosen an ungodly trade and the colour of their clothes seemed cruel as well as ugly. Conscription meant that Michael would become one of them.

The grown-up women came in with the pudding. "Why, Penny, you're crying," said Mrs Harcourt.

"Leave her alone," said her father, as she bit her lips but could not stop the spurting tears. The thought of the bad but fascinating young man shut into hard khaki was somehow more than she could bear.

"She must have got over-excited," said Mother doubtfully.

"Pop up to my room," said kind Sylvia.

In the strange pretty room, Penny sat at the dressing-table to observe in three mirrors these peculiar tears. They dried under her scrutiny. She had always taken it for granted that your body was yours but not you. You occupied it more intricately but in much the same way as clothes or a room; you could after all see it change as what looked out of its eyes essentially did not. She looked now into her own eyes but could not see what she felt in any of the three angles of Sylvia's mirror. Frowning and bending closer until her breath misted the glass, she thought that she would see Michael again with these seen eyes and was suddenly ecstatic. Sylvia came in with a cup of tea to this radiance and laughed her own sympathetic expression away.

"I don't know," said Sylvia. "My brother seems to have cast a spell on your family. It's all fixed about this afternoon. He's getting dressed and you're going for a walk in the woods."

"Who? Just me and Michael? What about the meeting?" It was almost too large a miracle; almost alarming.

"He said did you have to go to meetings? That was a challenge I expect, to make them prove you didn't. He said he wanted to talk to you. He can make himself very charming." Sylvia flicked at the counterpane disapprovingly.

"What did Mummy say? I don't think he charms her."

"No, she looked a bit taken aback. But your father seemed to give way as if. . . ." The older girl looked puzzled.

33

"Well I never," said Penny; and thought that that was true enough.

Sylvia did her hair and put on her tunic again to go to the Festival while Penny watched. She felt calm and empty as though all her inside had been sucked out and left her as light as a shell of thin bird's egg. Something floated in her airy centre not unlike the idea she had of the Holy Ghost. That her father had recognised something outside the ordinary was more significant than her own mood which was often fickle, intense, uncertain.

"I like your father," said Sylvia. "He's nice." She nodded. Sylvia put on her bonnet.

"And he just agreed that I could miss the meeting? It's funny."

"Yes, it seemed funny," said Sylvia. "I wonder if it was right? But then it all seemed funny, really, and as if he was just recognising something very funny."

Penny took a deep breath and gave her reflection a short desperate stare in the mirror; as though it were the face of someone she was saying goodbye to without knowing if she would ever see again.

Once alone with him, she felt sick with nerves and tongue-tied. Uneasiness spurred her to affectation. "I do love walking through leaves," she said.

"Hey, but Ha'penny!" said Michael mockingly, "what about spiders? Suppose you trod on a lot of hidden little spiders, walking through leaves? You do look soppy sometimes."

She felt the pink flow into her cheeks and the prick of mortified tears.

"Do you have to wear that awful bow?" he asked.

She untied it with one hand, stomping on ahead of him through leaves, with the other hand sulkily in her coat pocket.

"Race you to that gate," called Michael as he sprinted past her. After a second, she started to run after him. By the time they reached the gate they were out of breath, and less nervous.

"That's better," he panted. "You're quite fast."

"It's not fair in these shoes."

"No, but your hair looks much nicer now." He turned her to a new direction and they set off in step. "Well, then, let's talk," he said. "Tell me about yourself."

"What?"

"How old did you say you were?"

"Eleven."

"Jesus."

"Would you mind not blaspheming?" she said.

"All right. But I can't think how old eleven is. It doesn't seem very much." He picked his way with a kind of graceful clumsiness, one foot set down more directly in front of the other than was usual, so that he moved with a positive but unsteady gait. His body bent as though boneless or at least double-jointed: wrists and ankles appeared looser than other people's; more frail but more flexible.

"Eleven," he complained. "Watch out for spiders, won't you." He looked cross, sneering. "So why is Shakespeare your favourite author? And what have you read anyway?"

"Hamlet's my favourite," she said. Though thin and long-legged for her age, she walked dogmatically: a staunch left-right, left-right, influenced perhaps by all that marching behind the band. In sensible lace-up walking shoes with squarish toes, she kept up with his longer stride simply by keeping on forward while he turned and swayed and skirmished through the wood.

"Mine too," he said, "Is that something you do a lot? At eleven?"

"What?"

"Keep having favourite everything?"

She considered. "I suppose we do. Yes. My friends and I."

"You have favourite colours, I suppose, and teachers, and songs and things? Who's your favourite painter?"

In an effort to keep up, her thin skin grew pinker on the cheeks and whiter on the rest of her face. "Constable," she remembered from the Special Offer edition of the world's hundred greatest paintings which they got through the *Daily Herald*.

"Rubbish," he said shortly. "That shows you've never looked at a picture in your life. You're quite right, you and your friends: discussing favourites is a good way to learn about people. So then: why Hamlet?"

His veering walk and conversation began to induce elation. A long knitted scarf swung round his movements, making him appear even more air-borne and wavering than his foot-loose steps. He trod a fastidious line through trees and seemed to sway above his narrow feet with the scarf floating. She thought he matched the trees with

35

latish leaves wind-torn, blowing about like rags, above slender, swaying trunks. Everything about him seemed wayward and remarkable.

"They had Hamlet on the wireless one evening. When they made me go upstairs in the middle because it was after my bed-time, I called goodnight and shut my bedroom door loudly, but from the outside, and crept down and sat on the stairs to listen to the end. That was rather bad."

"Bad?" he exclaimed, "that was terrific."

"I meant sinful: deceitful."

"Oh I see. You have a lot of that? Sinfulness?" She did not answer, feeling mocked. "Do they keep on at you about it?"

"Not really. It's an inner voice tells you."

"Oh," he said gloomily. "Is it? Is that what it is?" He strode on with his hands in his overcoat pockets looking as melancholy as Hamlet. "You're a bit of a prig aren't you? Even for eleven." His mockery hurt. "Still, I suppose you can't help it with your up-bringing."

She felt defensive, but also wanted to cheer him up. "I do deceive them quite often," she claimed. Something—the Holy Ghost perhaps?—had reminded her of a true story which might also amuse. "Once when I was younger I was reading in bed after they'd put the light out, with a torch, under the sheet and things so they wouldn't see, only I was reading a religious book called *Netta's Mission*. About a poor crippled girl who never told a lie. When I got to the end where she died of consumption I was cry-ing like anything and I felt convicted because Netta was all white and dead and never deceived anyone while I'd lied by reading in bed. So I got up and went into their room to confess. They were a bit muddled, I think my father might have been asleep. It was funny really."

He stopped walking suddenly to look at her. "Do you still read in bed?"

"Yes, but not evangelical emotional books."

"Good for you. Right inside, d'you mean?"

"So that the torchlight won't show. Yes, like a white cave."

"How do you close the top?"

"Put the pillows over the join."

"Of course. Why didn't I think of that?" He set them into motion again with a finger on her elbow. Her navy-blue school

36

overcoat was belted and she wore long white socks which kept slipping down; she would haul one up without slackening their pace, hopping beside him not to fall behind. Even on treacherous terrain, she rarely withdrew her eyes from gazing sideways at him.

"I've never caught you blinking yet," he accused. She blinked without shifting her stare.

"Well I don't want to miss anything," she explained.

"Fair enough. What about the Sonnets?"

"What sonnets?"

"Shakespeare's, you loony. Don't you know about the Sonnets?"

"They're not in Arthur Mee's."

"Whose?"

"It's abridged or something. Arthur Mee's Children's Shakespeare. They gave it to me last Christmas."

He snorted, cheerful again. "Bowdlerised!" His moods were very sudden and total and often went the opposite way to what she could predict. It was alarming but heady. The cruelty of his teasing hit her when she was not expecting it; braced to withstand mockery, she would meet beaming approval.

"I'll give you the Sonnets for Christmas," he said. "Here! Stand still a minute, I can't light this damned cigarette."

The wind was gusty, flapping leaves and flame and her flopping hair. He made a tent of his coat and bent his head to matches that kept flaring and fading out. His face flickered golden in matchlight. She watched it with October trees behind his head and leaves at his feet; a yellow leaf of face above a leaf of flame to be remembered.

He coughed; then said apologetically to her flushed, frowning face: "Stop looking disapproving, dammit."

"Why? Anyway I wasn't. I was just making sure I would remember."

"You look so healthy," he complained. "I bet you're even an Ovalteeny!"

She resigned hurriedly. "Not any more," she said. "But you shouldn't smoke so much."

"Why? Because it's sinful?"

"I was thinking more that you might get ill." He took a deep draw on his cigarette.

"You have awful eyes," he said, turning from their obstinate candour. She closed them flushing, but tramped on heroically.

37

"Oh?"

"They go right round my head and meet at the back."

"Oh."

"Who's your favourite person?" She gave him a sideways, speculative look.

"Sir Percy Blakeney and Mr Rochester in *Jane Eyre*."

"I meant real people," he said.

She kicked a conker deliberately, then said: "Always my father I suppose." He grunted and hunched himself deeper into his up-turned collar. She decided to pick up the early conker and pulled off her gloves. Watching in a sulky way, he was forced to laugh to see the gloves bounce, then dangle outside her wrists. They were attached by elastic to the lining at the top of her coat sleeves.

"You look like Pierrot!" he claimed.

"Who? Oh, my gloves. Well, I do lose things such a lot."

"Come here, Ha'penny, let me see." He pulled at the strung gloves: they flapped and sprang back to the edges of her coat sleeves. She looked at him with guarded dignity: "Don't be unkind," she said.

"Unkind? To you? How could I be?"

She held the little conker tight between gloveless hands which looked too naked, pathetically vulnerable and wounding. He turned to walk on.

"What do you lose then, Ha'penny, besides gloves?" She continued diligently to unpick the prickly outer coating of the conker and trudge after him.

"It's because I'm always dreaming, my mother says," she offered, "and highly strung. Or is that the piano and I'm overstrung? One or the other." She looked so staunchly rooted, and spoke with such an air of sensible conjecture that he could not quench his laughter. Pleased to have pleased him, she drew level with the new chestnut glimmering wetly between her fingers. "I actually lost a new umbrella one day, on my birthday, while I was coming home from school. I was imagining Lady Jane Grey in the Tower waiting to be executed, you see, and I hung the umbrella on a park railing when I stopped to tie up a shoe-lace and forgot it. It was my birthday present."

"You were probably on your way to the scaffold."

"Yes I was. And not accustomed to umbrellas anyway."

"Were you wearing your crown?"

"Of course." He laughed happily at her, then turned gloomy again. "Do you think you're very important?"

"Well. Yes. So's everyone. Don't you?"

"No. Pawns to politicians, flies to the gods, bits of matter which don't matter. You, I and everyone."

"I don't agree," she said, shocked but certain. Smug? She remembered his hurtful condemnation.

A piece of grass which was dead but would not lie down pinged lightly against their shoes, leaned at their passing, and sprang upright behind them. If they trod that way often, the tough grasses would snap like return railway tickets, which Father bent to and fro between his fingers until the piece of green cardboard broke neatly into two. One half was always kept safe to get back home with. This walk with Michael seemed to be taking her somewhere without a safe return ticket.

"People whose view of life is based on Western Christianity," Michael lectured, "inevitably inflate the value of the individual. Precious in the eyes of the Lord. Makes them insufferably egotistical."

"But they're not selfish, my mother and father."

"Not selfish: self-centred. It's a proper pride if you assume a personal God keeping count of you like sparrows."

She looked up at bare boughs and wondered about return and journeys.

"What's your favourite sweet?" he shot at her as though it might be a trick question.

She replied precisely: "The licorice stick in a sherbet fountain." Added coldly, "Now."

"You change?"

"Often." They seemed to be waging a small war. She stopped on her sturdy legs and nailed him with eyes. "Are you cross because I didn't say you were my favourite person at the moment? You are, of course, but perhaps only now."

"Touché," he agreed, merry again. "Me and licorice sticks."

"What does touché mean?"

"That you scored a point. Why so specific about sherbet?"

"Because that's the point, the mixture. You lick the tube bit so sherbet sticks to the licorice and you get both together."

"Black and white?"

"I hadn't thought of that. Wet and dry, too. The sherbet rough

39

and fizzy on your tongue, and the strong smooth licorice inside."
He took her hand in his and swung it so that the loose glove
flapped.

"I like you, Ha'penny," he announced. "It's a bit ridiculous
but then so are you."

They walked and talked for what seemed a year or two and
spent the rest of the afternoon looking at postcards of paintings
in his family's sitting-room. He had a shoe-box full of them in
envelopes. "Constable's not your favourite at all. You'd have to
be simpler or cleverer than you are. But I've got someone in mind
for you." He snatched up envelopes and discarded them. "No.
No. Oh dear me no." He tucked one envelope under his cushion
—they sat on the floor—and he continued rummaging. "Here!
This is your chap unless I'm very much mistaken." He gave her
an envelope of paintings by someone called Turner and she looked
through them murmuring pleasure. The windy light in the pictures
on the postcards, whirling radiances, made tears prick. But everything had become highly-coloured, charged. The pattern on the
hearth-rug and the flames in the grate made her ache in some
place she could not identify. She began to feel lost. So, as if to
recover playground tricks of yesterday, to belong to children
again or still, she suddenly grabbed the envelope he had hidden
and waved it tauntingly, jumping up and skipping around the
room like a safe, naughty child. Then was dismayed to peep
inside and find rude pictures of naked ladies. And more dismayed to hear him say: "You won't tell your father, will you."
He looked worried and young. That shocked her. As if she would.

"As if I would," she cried. "No, you don't know how old I
am, do you," she accused in hurt and scorn.

"I said I didn't. Have I shocked you?"

"Thinking I'd tell my father? Yes."

" I meant the pictures."

"The rude ones? A bit. I can't think why you'd want them."

Then it was his turn to be dismayed. She could see him troubled,
looking at her, and felt it had to do with her being too old to tell
her father everything but too young to be shocked at the ladies
in the right way.

So they went through a period of distance and gravity and
then he made her say favourite bits of her recitations and he
recited some things she did not know. Then he wound up the

gramophone and played her something which he said was "my favourite tune", teasingly. She listened to a little wistful melody.

"What's it called?" she asked, unimpressed.

"La Fille au Cheveux de Lin," he said.

She thought him mocking again, his head tilted, his eyes so bright and laughing. "We don't do French yet," she said sadly.

"It means The Girl with the Flaxen Hair," he said. "I thought it might suit you."

Disappointed in the tune, she missed the first compliment of her life; until later, in recollection.

After the Festival, they all had tea together in the dining-room. Penny was quiet; after the meal the Carrs would leave, presumably for ever, for the meeting and then the bus home. She would never see Michael again. He talked quietly to Father about his sense of bitter waste at leaving school for a dull job. Not just for himself; he had not realised the drab trap of work which dominated most lives.

Mrs Carr broke in. "I hope Penny didn't chatter too much this afternoon and be a nuisance or boring?"

"No," said Michael, "she didn't bore me."

"It was nice of you to take an interest."

"Oh, is that what it was?" said Michael. "You'll come back for coffee after the meeting won't you? Won't they, Mum? They'll need a sandwich before that journey. And anyway I can't let Ha'penny here out of my pocket so suddenly. So off you go and save a lot of souls while I get the sandwiches ready and prepare to pay your Penny back for good." Then: "Good," he snorted, and lit a cigarette. But she was elated, and stared entreaty, so that Father agreed.

The evening meeting was more robust and emotional than the morning one. It wooed the spirit to get saved in a fervour of muted brass and pleading choruses. Love, the suffering love of the Saviour, was the theme. Darkness at the windows made the bright hall more welcoming and the Mercy Seat more enticing. "Love Divine, all loves excelling...", "God so loved the world...", "Jesus loves me, this I know...". There was a deliberate seductiveness in the Salvation meeting to which Penny had always responded, but that evening a new, muddled intensity suffused her.

Love had formerly been dutiful, comfortable; what passed

41

between her parents and herself. It was considerate and being looked after, prayer and gravy. This cosy and obligatory feeling was roughly what she assumed in God's love. Jesus saved from sin and Mother from getting run over or losing your gloves. There was another version of love, shadowy still, which went on in *Woman's Own* and the films she was not allowed to see and songs skipped-to in the Banjo. "Tonight, I mustn't think of him. Music, Maestro, please." This had something to do with sin; and Mrs Parker's drinking and gas oven, because her husband had gone off with Another Woman. But since she had met Michael Harcourt, it had all got confused and expanded.

"Breathe on me, Breath of God, Fill me with life anew . . . Oh take my heart, my life, my all, I sacrifice them to thy love. . . ." This had little to do with cough medicine—why had she not understood before? "He shed His Blood" . . . through such thin skin as bound Michael into one person? And "God so loved the world" . . . that he gave his son fragile body and blood? Words which had passed from tongue to tongue too often not to have become dulled as old coins were suddenly minted into brilliance by the day's sensations. God gave more than she had realised at any Easter; and no wonder Mrs Parker preferred Heaven to the Banjo when her husband left. Love was match-light, Turner-light, leaves; tough as coat-stuff and wrist-bones and frail as that French music and the flames which flickered and faded in the afternoon fire. It included in some way still cryptic the pictures which had made him blush. Her idea of love was transfigured by new experience but it was all connected: for her there were no distinct and separate categories. Her first human passion comprised religious ardour and fed back more feeling into religion. Just as sin was a requirement of salvation, the illuminating humanity of sinful Michael raised her love of Jesus beyond comfortable care. So *that* was Love? He was right ('he' was Michael): you shouldn't deny the world and the flesh. The world and the flesh might be Divine 'illustrations' like in testimonies; but God's.

When her father called on her to read the Bible, she was unprepared but ready. The used black leather lay open at St Paul to the Corinthians. At first she sight-read the familiar words automatically, more intensely engaged in fingering the creased leather covers of the Bible's skin. "*Love suffereth long, and is kind. . . . Yea, though I give my body to be burned and have not love . . ."* Now she noticed what she was reading and her voice broke as her eyes darkened in a face pale with excitement and exhaustion. "Love," she stared, *"Beareth all things, believeth all things, hopeth all things, endureth all things. . ."*. Trained to accept all incidental happenings as meaningful, Penny was overwhelmed by the significance. She read on in a trance; cliché texts felt for the first time. The effect on the hall was palpable. Several of the congregation made straight for the Mercy Seat. Her mother's morning prayer that a little child should lead them had been fulfilled in an unforeseen and disturbing way. Michael Harcourt and Jesus had somehow got mixed up. *"For now we see through a glass, darkly; but then face to face; now I know in part; but then shall I know even as also I am known."*

Major Carr had reservations about extravagant appeals for demonstrative souls gulping at the foot of the platform, and decided during this outburst of premature seekers that Penny should leave before the prayer meeting. A message was dispatched to Sylvia in the Songsters. Even Mrs Carr agreed that the dangers of spending more time with the young man who was plainly a bad influence were less than her being overwrought to such public effect. As Penny sat down again Mother whispered, "You're to go back with Sylvia before Daddy's address," under cover of a chorus. Penny stretched upwards and outwards in her seat as though exposing more of her surface to the atmosphere might help her to discern its odd qualities. They were treating her as though she were wrong but not exactly to be blamed, like a person with an infectious disease. The emotion of the congregation, Father's troubled glance, Mother's hasty tone, a stir of curiosity among the front members of the Band, the way the Sergeant Major next to Mother looked away from her eyes: no, not an infection, more like electricity. Magnetic but slightly dangerous. Was she at fault? Did she perhaps love Michael more than God? Well, she told Him in faintly resentful apology, "But I love your Son more and differently because of Michael." Nudged by Mother, who sang lustily as though to drown under-cover business in the words of the chorus, she edged crouching along the front row of the platform. People tucked their knees in to let her pass. The Band played into her ear from bass to treble and each instrument sounded unusually distinct and sweet. Everything from chords to black shoes in a twisting line seemed part of a universe which had been tuned up a key. She paused when she reached the obscurity of the back door. She felt light but swollen, like a balloon which might, with equal likelihood, either float weightless to the rafters and beyond into the sky, or burst and shrivel into a pap of wrinkled slimy skin. The chorus trembled to a quiet close.

The moist night outside the hall lit her. She breathed it in to help the balloon not burst.

"Oh there you are," said Sylvia. "Come on then."

Gazing directly upward, the little girl trotted beside her with rash indifference to kerbs and paving stones with cracks. "Look at those stars," she exclaimed.

"What about them?"

"They're so much brighter than usual."

Sylvia made an annoyed noise in the nose. "This is getting beyond a joke. Are you often let out early?"

"No." Poor Sylvia. "Do you mind missing the address?"

"It's not that. It's just—well—funny."

"I love him," Penny explained helpfully, taking the older girl's arm as if to reassure her.

"Yes, that's the trouble," said Sylvia. "I'd have thought you were too young." She squeezed the hand in her elbow briefly.

"Yes, so would I."

"How do you know it's that?"

"I recognise it from Jane Eyre and Jesus and love-songs on the wireless."

Sylvia hurried their step as though to escape something. "I'll do the sandwiches, you can talk to Michael."

"Oh, thank you, Sylvia, I'll never forget you, never." Fervent, extreme, she tripped over a shoe-lace.

"Shut up you silly," said Sylvia.

Penny looked from the gutter where she hunkered to do up her shoe. "Isn't God marvellous?" she said, "to make stars and Shakespeare and Michael?"

"Look," said Sylvia, "he's perfectly ordinary and upsets my mother with his ways and is a terrible flirt. Girls are always popping notes into the letter-box." Sylvia stood under a lamp-post with her hand on her hip. Penny flinched, finished with a double-bow, and stood up bravely.

"He's not ordinary to me," she said. They began to walk; at a distance.

"I'm sorry," said Sylvia, contrite. "You're too young. You don't want to know things like that. You've got a pash on him."

"No. A pash is what I had on Miss Tucker. Lots of girls or one?"

"Lots. But look, forget it. You're far too young."

But Penny was getting older every minute.

"I'd better learn then. I'm glad it's lots. Does he love them?"

"Oh goodness, what does it mean? I shouldn't think so for a moment. I don't suppose he knows what love is. I know I don't, and I'm twenty."

"Well I know," said Penny. "Will you really do the sandwiches, it doesn't seem fair. But kind. 'Love suffereth long and is'—wasn't that a miracle?"

She skipped at Sylvia's side, amazed at the glory of it all; the pavement lights and vacant dark they pointed. Articulate avenues of houses all led to one house, like but unlike all the rest, containing one person, ordinary and unique, summing up the nature of things for her. She was another common phenomenon of singular accidents, with a name acquired at Dedication, who defied gravity and skipped at Sylvia's side across drab paving stones sparkling with specks of micah like a distant galaxy at her feet.

"I do *know*," she said vaguely but with conviction. "Please don't worry about it."

Perhaps the training of being possessed utterly by God, as she had been taught, enabled her to make similar total surrenders more easily than those with less extreme habits.

When she arrived at him again, it was very like being saved. She did not want to talk: Sylvia had been aeons behind, they had been through that phase long before, that afternoon. When she was let into the sitting-room he stood up to kick the fire and to switch off the light Sylvia had switched on. "Hallo, Ha'penny." Then they sat in silence.

She was no longer at all shy. When you were saved you gave your heart to Jesus and felt redeemed. Now that she had given hers to a slim, cynical young man whose soul was almost certainly lost, she felt similarly transfigured. They looked at the fire which was convalescing from neglect and kept spluttering into little gaudy patches of flame and out again, like an invalid's occasional lift of spirits, until the sound of the door proclaimed the return of the rest of the world.

They brought in the smell of serge and the hot hall, put on the lights, made an occupation of briefly-held territory. His father came in with coal to feed the ailing fire and Sylvia handed round coffee and sandwiches to feed the people.

Penny moved to the fender seat beside Michael's armchair, and then disappeared. If she could not make the others go away, it seemed, she could absent herself. Occasionally she turned from the fire to glance at Michael, but it was not a look in which she sought to involve herself with him; rather, like a snap in a photograph album, to remind her of something not there at the moment. She looked from a distance of time not space; backwards at him or forwards to him. Her present seemed not to exist at all.

Michael accepted this as though it were true. He too behaved as though she were not there. He chatted to her parents and ignored her at his elbow, but in a way which seemed protective to her. It united them in a curious collusion. Mrs Carr kept peeping round Michael in the way, but failed to attract her daughter's eyes beyond his uncharacteristic gestures.

Mr Harcourt put on the wireless for the nine o'clock news. Hitler's troops had moved into Czechoslovakia during the day; the German army was advancing across the map; refugees from occupied territory poured ahead of tanks. It had been agreed, but felt different from the paper transaction of Munich. 'Ceded' sounded respectable: it had somehow concealed actual people leaving home. The Harcourts and the Carrs passed cups and handed sugar, as the calm voice continued, with a serious, gentle caution. A sense of insecurity gave the simple ritual peculiar grace. They felt the fact of war begin to creep through the safe suburban dark outside towards this little room; its wallpaper with a matching border beneath the picture rail, its suite in uncut moquette, even its fragile cups of best china. They shivered on their saucers and careful hands righted them tenderly.

Mrs Carr reached instinctively towards Penny, but Michael intercepted her, saying "shush" so gently that she found herself nodding agreement that the child should not be disturbed. She sat back puzzled to be together with the alien young man even for that second of time. Uncertainty was rare to her. In the sudden human practicality of the news she observed with unusual confusion her little girl with rumpled socks and lop-sided hair-ribbon gazing raptly into space and the loose young man casting a web of invisibility around her.

Strangeness caught them all in silence which was not embarrassed when the News was over. Though they had thought themselves uncongenial at the beginning of the day, alert to differences in bonnet-brim, income, intention and worldliness, these now seemed trivial. The world itself in measured tones but stark fact had forced them closer together. Major Carr turned to the word of prayer which preceded all journeys in unusual quietness.

The Carrs knelt beside their chairs as usual while the Harcourts bowed their heads. They bent deeply or just dipped according to inclination. Penny's view through the slit between her praying hands joined at wrist and finger-tips was of a small portion of Michael's tweed jacket. It was wide enough. Through this window she saw vividly all that her father brought to God in prayer. Refugees torn from familiar land and beloved possessions. Soldiers young, even idealistic, who knew not what they did. All victims; including those who seemed to conquer but were themselves overrun by the demand of violence. All who were separated from their loved ones. Those nearer who were, without dramatic news to prove it, lonely and uprooted in their own city's streets. Those nearer still, who though still close to human home might risk their home in heaven through not accepting it. Then he mentioned each one by name, pausing after each so that Mother could say "Amen". Brothers and sisters in the Lord who had been brought together briefly but must now go their separate ways. Young people who faced more serious separations: to be a soldier or evacuated to a safe area.

At the end they opened their eyes, blinking, and busied to put on their outdoor clothes. Mrs Harcourt bustled, Mrs Carr tied her bonnet ribbons, and Sylvia fetched Penny's things from upstairs. Michael, perhaps aggrieved at condoning prayer by even looking down at his own knees, seized Penny's hat from his sister.

"I've never seen *this*," he proclaimed. "You've been keeping things from me."

Mrs Carr frowned. "It squashes her hair-ribbon."

"Oh good."

"But she should wear it going home. October's treacherous. It's colder after dark." Penny took the black felt hat and tried to tuck the mortifying elastic band into the crown.

"No," said Mother.

"Let me," said Michael. He squashed it into a gangster shape with a homburg dent in the crown and perched it on her head at a rakish angle. She glared through these indignities. "I say, that's rather fetching, let's have a smile." She stared at a mark on the wall at her level and he was forced to say, "Sorry".

Mrs Carr bustled disapprovingly between them, picked off the hat, punched it into a proper shape and put it firmly on. Elastic band and all. She seemed to be bullying more than a school hat. Propriety seemed recovered; even the state of Europe a little more under control as she anchored it firmly under Penny's chin. Since the child held her head level, uncooperative, nobody taller could now see her face under the curve of the big brim tilted over her eyes. She marched out first without looking up as if to all intents and purposes everything was already over.

The bus seemed subdued; its light dimmer than the starry, staring night outside. With a glance of accord, the parents took the back seat on the top deck where they could sit three abreast and placed her between them.

"Well, now," said her mother firmly. "Now, then," said her father at the same time.

These introductions had the same meaning and heralded the onset of a serious talk. Daunted by speaking at once and therefore remiss in the prompting of the Spirit, they fell silent a moment. All registered the unusual silence of the bus in which people seemed isolated by the evening's news, and then returned to the family problem.

Mother said with a heavy lightness: "You got on well with the son, what was his name, Michael, then?"

Penny looked blankly straight ahead from under the brim of her velour hat and explained: "I love him."

"You mustn't say things like that," said Mrs Carr. Fraught, but controlled to kindness, she added: "You're too young to know what they mean. People might not understand."

The child looked 'no' with a distant disobedient air, signifying that she realised *they* certainly failed to understand. The parents exchanged a nod which agreed her father should take over. He cleared his throat and looked out of the window at the lamp-posts and passing trees which brushed past the upper storey of the bus,

48

briefly and luridly lit by each gas-light, and seemed for a moment defeated by his own insights. Absurdity and extremity seemed to have taken over.

He said: "We sometimes have feelings we don't quite understand ourselves. Especially if we are given intense natures."

Mrs Carr resettled her bonnet. "She always was highly-strung," she decided to agree; but tame, if at all possible, by words in common usage.

"And when these feelings overwhelm us, we're confused."

"Yes," said the child without docility. "Like love," she understood. "I don't understand but it doesn't stop me feeling it. I love Michael, you see."

"Do hush," said Mrs Carr uneasily. She looked haughtily and anxiously around the bus as though Penny had let some dangerous animal escape which must be recaged by calm people who knew how to handle it before it caused a panic. Love, indeed. The obstinate child picked at the elastic under her chin and let it slap back once or twice as though determined to hurt herself; actually only a habit when concentrating.

"How can I not know what the word means when we use it all the time? Choruses and things. The love of Jesus."

"But that's different," said the mother, shocked at last into a panic of her own.

"Not to me," said Penelope sternly, and twanged her elastic again. Though frequently self-willed, her stubbornness now had a novel serenity. She showed no tendency to raise her voice or fling herself about; sat looking straight ahead with the rapt indifferent profile of those to whom the worst has already happened.

"Listen, pet," tried her father. "Human love is as you say a beautiful thing and a reflection of divine love. Mummy and I for instance know that we love and serve God better through loving each other and you. But these very strong feelings must last and settle down before we can build our lives on them."

"She's far too young for all that," said Mrs Carr crisply, because perhaps he was speaking to her as well and she had less truck with those very strong feelings he spoke of.

"And anyway," agreed her father.

"He's not at all a suitable person," Mrs Carr finished. They looked across her head some melancholy but accustomed misunderstanding.

"What's that got to do with it?" said Penny.

Mrs Carr felt she had got the whole thing more or less under control with the word 'suitable' and shifted into the affectionately brusque manner with which she disposed of unsuitable things like poetry and passion.

"He's not a Salvationist," she said, moving around in her seat to shake off the last shred of unseemliness, "not even a Christian by all accounts, and he smokes cigarettes." She sounded almost indulgent, so great was her relief to be free of the fearful innuendos of very strong feelings. But the child held some tough thread tight.

"I thought we were supposed to love sinners and only hate the sin," she announced. "What about that Captain who spoke at last week's meeting about nursing lepers? I don't think Michael is worse than lepers because he smokes. And if he was worse or a leper I would still love him. That's what love is. You taught me that so you must see."

Nonplussed, Mrs Carr sank to a mean trick. "His mother told me he has lots of girl-friends," she said. The white profile turned to give her one bitter stare.

"Yes. His sister told me too." Penny had discovered jealousy in discovering love. Though awful, it was no argument. She now appeared to her parents inviolable, at risk, and something of a threat. Small, dogged, one sock wrinkled, her brimmed hat a little askew, her chin reddened from the chafing elastic, she stood—or rather sat—for something outside expectations; upright and ardent on the back seat of the bus. Her mother was more shaken. She said, rapidly, as though something must at once staunch this palpable breach: "You are only a little girl he took a fancy to. He'll forget all about it in the morning I expect."

Penelope turned rather stiffly to look at her and said: "I expect so too. But *I* won't."

Her strict stare broke into tears. The mother gathered her into comfort; though neither was really relieved, they capitulated for the time being. The little girl sobbed on her mother's breast and both were momentarily consoled. The man looked at them with affection and disappointment, because she had in a way betrayed him by agreeing to cry into her mother's coat.

"You'll get over it," he said, and turned his mind to the more dependable and distant misery of Czechoslovakia.

But she did not get over it or forget all about it in the morning. Long-rope skipping gave way to hopscotch and the hopscotch season to five-stones, and all street games were acrostics of love. Skipping, especially bumps, seemed its rhythm; chalk-scrawled pavements were its diagrams.

Though grown-up people tended to keep themselves to themselves in the small symmetrical houses, the Banjo was the domain of all the households' children. Nobody knew by what instinct or tradition games pursued a seasonal pattern, but it was as regular as the sun and seasons. There came a day when all the girls at the circle end, who had been in and out of the long skipping rope for weeks, or doing more and more complicated things with their individual shorter ropes on the fringe of the big skip, put together the wooden handles at each end of their skipping rope, wound the loop tightly round the handles, and forgot skipping until the correct time of year came round again. Marbles came and went; cigarette card crazes; cat's cradle with a piece of string was all the rage for a week or two. Ball games were in one week and out the next for no discernible reason. It was up and down like a yo-yo, which also took its turn.

Through all seasons, beyond public games in the paved area, smaller groups pursued more private projects in gardens behind privet hedges. In games of hospitals, witches, mothers and fathers, battles and explorations, they practised to be ill, afraid, grown-up, or in danger, with elaborate ritual. Occasional community practising—for Silver Jubilees, battles, cigarette-card auctions—took place on the greens at the handle end of the Banjo. But the most frequent use of these areas was focused on the round iron bars which encircled them between upright concrete posts. One thick bar ran around each green at a height which allowed small children to slip under without difficulty and older children to vault with one steadying hand, or no-hands, sideways, like proper high-jumping at school. Often each segment supported one child or more turning and turning in various well-established acrobatics. You could turn a forward somersault with your waist on the bar and your hands grasping either side before you were six. Later you learned to sit balancing on it and then surprise by a sudden drop so that the bar was under your knees before somersaulting backwards through the hand-polished-smooth iron. Other tricks of some risk were undertaken despite warnings that you might cut your head open. The concrete kerb surrounding the grass made this fear not fanciful, and legend, with a certain admiration, named several who had, through the ages, cut their heads open doing a double-back-somer-sault-no-hands, perhaps. Penny had never witnessed such an accident. Her imagination conjured a topped egg, spilling brains instead of uncooked white. Girls of her age gave up athletics but still used the bars. Sometimes a row of them would converse quietly while hanging upside-down-no-hands with the bar gripped under the knees. Their hair brushed the kerb as they swung gently to and fro and turned their upside-down faces to each other.

Penny's closest friends were the Lock twins, whose father was a greengrocer, and Alice, whose dad was on the railways. Once when she called with the usual question, "Is Alice coming out to play?" Mr Jackson said, "Hang on a minute, mate", and she felt proud to be mate to a man who was one to an engine driver.

Her best friends were sympathetic about the falling in love and let her tell them about it often at first; then grew bored. They had favourite teachers, of course, and sometimes a boy they would lark about with and always—for a week or so—drop their handker-chief behind when playing 'I sent a letter to my love'. But Penny's obsession outlasted their curiosity: she brought it into everything. If she could skip twenty bumps without stumbling, catch four of five-stones first go, walk all the way up top to the high street without treading on a crack, Michael loved her. They began to groan at his name, fetching exaggerated sighs and rolling their eyes to heaven. "That's the twelfth time since dinner time," they would complain. "Let's go up top and look in Harrison Gibson's and play furnishing."

But Penny, pressing her nose against the glass with the others to admire satin bed-covers and long-haired furry rugs, had a speci-fic worry to spoil the old fun of favourite colour-schemes. "When we grow up and get married . . ." would Michael agree to blue and yellow? Might he prefer Alice's cherry-red and cream, which was after all more sophisticated? She had pinched it from a film star magazine on Ginger Rogers' bedroom; but finders were none-theless keepers. Their hands made peepholes of shadow through which they peered to prevent reflections from the street in the shop window concealing the room-settings within.

"Bags I that blue carpet," crowed Connie round the corner.

"Let's have a look." They gathered in a little row.

"Blue's Penny's colour," Grace reprimanded her sister. "You can't have it if she wants it."

"I don't know if Michael likes blue."

They groaned in chorus.

"Thirteen since dinner time." They turned away, blinking into the busy street again.

Alice said kindly: "It's up to the woman to choose decorations. You have the blue carpet."

"All right."

It was as blue as the zinc bath under the mangle on Mondays: water so bright-swirling when the blue-bag had dyed it, it made her feel thirsty. Mother's hands came out blue-tinged when the sheets on the line shone with sharp whiteness from their blue rinse. She helped to carry the bath outside by its handles and tip it down the drain, a whoosh of falling water of a drowning blue which drenched the brain and whirlpooled round the grating.

"I might change to mauve," Connie confided as they set off back home abreast, a nuisance to shoppers. The others looked at her.

"Mauve and what?" Alice wondered.

"Light mauve and dark mauve," said Connie boldly.

They were impressed. Everybody felt they might reconsider their schemes, except Penny, who stuck to blue and yellow. They affected her physically, seemed more like taste or touch, she was on the whole visually insensitive and sight seemed less sensual than informative. But blue seemed drinkable and yellow was lickable, the colour of pencils and buttercups and Walls' lemon. These triangular blocks of tinted ice cost a penny for a whole one but were usually purchased by the half. You pushed it up in its cardboard casing with one frozen thumb as you licked it away at the top. Towards the end, a flavour of soggy cardboard spoiled the sharp acid of the splintery iceberg. Lingering too slowly, you might end with nothing except a pappy cone stained with vivid yellow water, stickying fingers. But it was a lovely yellow. She vowed to have a blue and yellow room one day; unless Michael disapproved.

"Michael's sister's bedroom is mauve and white. Well, more lavender than mauve."

"You told us that already." They stared with pitying but stern boredom. "Do give over going on about him all the time."

Eventually, they succeeded in shutting her up. So it was all shut

53

up. If by day she had become insufferable to her friends by talking all the time about her unique emotion, by night it had always to be suffered.

She inscribed his name on a piece of best writing paper in a lettering her grandfather had taught her. You pencilled black shading everywhere which was not the letters, so that they stood out in white bas-relief through the shadow you had made, as though carved in stone. She wore this under her night-dress next to her heart and cried herself to sleep. Once her mother looked in long after bedtime, and found her still awake. She plumped up and turned the pillow for comfort, but found it so wet that she was disturbed. Penny explained that she was crying for Michael, and admitted this was not unusual. Mrs Carr was at a loss: if not exactly naughty, it was unseemly. She decided that Daddy had better deal with it, but Major Carr was out at a Corps Cadet meeting. She made Penny get up and sit downstairs in her dressing-gown waiting for him to come in.

Sewing under the gas mantle's glowing effulgence, she stole glances at her daughter's swollen eyelids with deep shadows underneath. Hiccuping after prolonged weeping, Penny was permitted to read the *Young Soldier* while they waited. She could not tell whether her mother was cross with her or not. Nor, perhaps, could the mother. Bewildered and at first sharp, Mrs Carr began to treat her as though she were an invalid or sickening for something. She made comforting bread-and-milk but maintained the silence of reproof.

The child did look ill; Mrs Carr almost wished it were measles or 'flu. Love was not a childish complaint and she knew no remedies to doctor it.

Eventually, Major Carr being so late, the child so exhausted-looking, and Cissie herself so troubled, Penny was tucked up in bed again with the threat—made in rather a pleading or promising tone, now—that her father would have a word about it with her later. He never did.

The worst thing about being a child was helpless immobility. There was absolutely nothing she could do. She could not take a bus, or use the telephone, or risk writing even if she knew his address. She was tied down by childhood and envied those old enough to go as they pleased and make plans for themselves.

"Is Penny coming out to play?"

"Penny! Are you going out to play?"

"Yes. Wait a minute I'm just coming."

In the darker evenings they played frightened games with torches; probing through privet which threw back the beam revealing nothing, unless a glitter of hiding eyes. Was it worse to be searcher, though, surrounded by living shadows, alone? Or hidden, unfound or even unsought? Lost, behind a bush eerie, even earwiggie, while the beam of torch goes past and leaves you in the dark more frightened than the seeker. Run home, then: that's the game. Make for the tree or lamp-post which is 'home' today; where all will gather when the game is over.

Today.

'Home' had become less of an unconsidered certainty. They kept having practices for evacuation. You walked round the school playground wearing your gas-mask in a square cardboard box over one shoulder, and carrying your luggage, which must include a blanket but be portable by a smallish child. This left little room for so-called inessentials and no hope at all of keeping what had formerly seemed essential.

Once or twice they practised to the extent of walking to the railway station in a crocodile which, lined up along the platform, was ordered to make a right turn. The right-angled crocodile, now two ranks facing the track, was suitably warned not to stand too near the edge if an express train to Harwich went through. Most already knew of the danger of being dragged off the platform in the wake of the nervous clatter of fast trains and seriously believed that you might find yourself floating helplessly in the air behind the guard's van if you ignored the warning. After ten minutes or so, they walked back to the school again, humping their bundles. After school, they went home with the same burden and the additional one of reiterated evidence that what they called home was undependable and might not be transported.

One Sunday just before Christmas, Michael arrived. His advent was astonishing indeed; on the doorstep with her parents after the Sunday evening meeting.

When the Carrs were not specialling, Penny stayed at home for the evening meeting, with Alice to keep her company, and was required to be ready for bed when they returned.

"Scrub your nails till they're like little pearls," Mrs Carr used to say; so they did; and the house smelled of soap when the parents returned. Then Alice was dispatched to the engine-driver's mate on the other corner of the Banjo with nails like little pearls as well, and Penny had cocoa and went to bed. This night, pearl-nailed, they heard:

"Coo-ee. Guess who's come to see you then?" Hugger-mugger down the stairs they tumbled after an interesting game of ballerinas to find Michael and her mother looking deceitfully cheerful on the hall mat.

"He came to the meeting as he hadn't got our address," said Cissie apologetically. Well she might. For all parties.

Two little girls halted on the stairs; one reeling against the banisters, one slightly too fascinated for comfort; so this was the grown-up man Penny was in love with. Major and Mrs Carr in uniform attempted to pretend the apparition was all quite ordinary. Alice was seen off, cocoa was made, they all sat to drink it in the front room, occupied usually only by the piano. Major Carr made conversation. Michael had either forgotten, or chose not, in such circumstances, to expose, the Sonnets.

Mrs Carr hurried him away with greetings to his parents to prove this a family visit. He spoke very little. Penny not at all. When he had left for the bus, Penny's love was briefly disabled. How could she pine for him when he had in fact been there? His memory had come to represent more than he could actually embody. After a night or two, she could weep again in earnest for her hopeless love. She had, after all, failed to get his address during the uncomfortable encounter and was if anything more at the mercy of his and the world's whim. The former flashing intimacy had made no appearance, had been quenched in time or circumstance, or because her dressing-gown was ugly and her slippers had rabbits' heads on the toes. He was unlikely to come so far again to see such a person. Perhaps anyway she would have chosen to sleep with his name in bas-relief pinned to her night-dress rather than endure the improbable alternative of yoking everyday life and him into some reality at this stage of powerless childhood.

But she frowned at their distance, either geographical or more poignant when he was sitting in the front-room arm-chair. It seemed inevitable but unacceptable. Just as Heaven and earth must interpenetrate for human life to be satisfactory, her dreaming and a real Michael must be reconciled to make human love. She enlisted in a new cause with the obstinacy which exactly matched her dogged walk: stiff, broken in rhythm, but onward.

"Onward Christian Soldiers, marching as to war."

Which approached; in its specific manifestations making every-day imagery odd as well as ominous. Giant weapons photographed in the newspapers haunted Sunday's firing of cartridges; and apprehension lurked through Banjo battles. Boys zooming with arms out-stretched as aery-buzzers might stop suddenly beyond privet hedges, as a real aeroplane throbbed in the high dark.

As the days lengthened, hoops, then marbles, then hopscotch returned to the Banjo at their appointed times. With spring the pets' phase changed its manifestation. Mice had been banned last year for failing to clean out their cages so everybody decided to keep newts instead.

Newts were interesting. You had to make sure that a sticking-up stone in the water allowed them access to air as well as water: they needed both to survive. Little and slithery, with fishy tails but elbowed arms almost like people, they simply but unequivocally died if you forgot to change their water or provide a rock for them to climb. So Connie and Grace, Alice and Penny, kept their captives kindly.

One day in March the four girls were transferring them from one glass jar to another in the Lock twins' garden when Mrs Carr made an unprecedented appearance at the back gate. It was so unusual for any grown-up to visit another's territory—you sent another child with messages—that something important was signalled by Penny's mother peeping uneasily past the dustbin with her neat bun and clean wrap-around pinafore.

"Penny, dear, you'd better come home at once."

"Why?" Shock made Penny's voice sound critical; the group of crouching girls seemed frozen in mid-gesture. Mrs Carr tilted her chin defensively, holding on to the gate to prove she did not plan to come actually in.

"Michael Harcourt has just arrived out of the blue."

It was a good phrase: the colour of sky, Harrison Gibson's carpet and the Holy Ghost's blue band round the flag was suitable for his dramatic advents.

"And didn't you hear the news boy calling?" Mrs Carr was spurred to add less domestic information in a disapproving tone. "There's bad news from Czechoslovakia, that Hitler's advancing into parts Mr Chamberlain didn't say he could have. They say it means war."

What held them all so still was an instinct to resist as if physically the onslaught of events. The four little girls stared motionless as though for a time-exposure snapshot to be taken. Fathers sometimes required such breathless frozen postures when the light was bad at birthday parties. Then the moment could be transfixed for ever in the snap album. They met this moment with such a stillness, dictated not by a box camera but by the moment itself. The greenish newts panted, poised between one jar of water and another, divided between fins and gills dangerously. Mrs Carr felt the girls' immobility expressed hostility to her invasion—just another worry like war and unexpected visitors—and sniffed crossly. *She* painted her dustbin green, scrubbed it weekly, and concealed it under a syringa bush.

"Well I'll get back then," she said. "Don't be long, Penny. *I've* got nothing to say to that Michael."

Some points in time were so vividly present that they intersected eternity. Penny recognised such a moment, inexplicit but acute, when she looked up from the crazy paving of the Lock's path and saw her mother. Between "Hallo!" surprised, and "All right I'm coming", everything had expanded and turned.

But the newts throbbed on a piece of rock, with an imperative claim for priority, gasping all over at too much air. So she embraced their bodies in a damp hand and slid them into their new home of clear tap-water quickly; then dawdled up the Banjo to her own side gate.

It had been one of the first days of promising spring. Primulas blazing in pots and a canary in a cage—a yellow fidget and flutter —emphasised the stillness of old people sitting on kitchen chairs outside their front doors with their hands on their knees to catch the warmth of the sun. Their stillness emphasised Penny's sense of an unaccountable whirling of time: too much was happening at once, and dawdling hardly slowed it down at all as more sensations and thoughts crowded to fill the time gained by loitering.

"Oh, there you are, Angel," Michael accosted her uneasily with a pretence at off-handedness. "I've been waiting ages. Where the devil have you been?"

"You asked where the devil I had come from first. I've been looking after my newts."

"Poor little buggers," he said feelingly.

She worriedly touched her hair and then her face, at the astounding sight of him.

"What's that supposed to mean, that I said it before?" He seemed peeved; as though she were criticising. Though she had meant it to be significant and moving, he might think he repeated himself boringly.

"When we first met in your hall," she mumbled, aware that she must fail to communicate. It struck her suddenly that people were forced to be alone, even in their memories. With the best will in the world, what happened to them, even together, was separate, and what either knew as truth might not be shared. This depressing insight pinned her in the doorway.

"Well, sit down, for God's sake," he said huffily.

Since they last met, she had begun to grow breasts. Though still occupied with newts and the hopscotch season, these as yet diminutive appurtenances affected her stance. Flat discs of muscle had formed behind each sexless nipple. You could wobble them about, they were loosely attached; but attached all the same and enlarging. They made her move in a more self-conscious way.

He seemed disappointed in her. "You're beginning to turn into a teenager," he complained. She blushed and ducked her head. "I came to say goodbye." His brutal tone held relish.

"Goodbye?"

"I've joined up. Couldn't stand home and that job any more. I'm going overseas soon."

"Mummy said something about the war."

"Did she? Yes. It seems inevitable now."

"I was changing my newts' water."

"So you said. One can see the attraction. You're rather amphibious yourself." He looked unsuccessfully for an ashtray. Feeling in the wrong, he had to insist, "I don't think I came all this way to hear about your newts", as he dropped ash into the earth of a potted plant. He looked round the room querulously. Everything was fawn and extremely clean. "I shouldn't think we're likely to meet again," he said with apparent relief, and fixed the picture above the mantelpiece with a critical gaze. It was Holman Hunt's famous *Christ Knocking*. With his lantern and his sad, handsome face he knocked continually at the door of a heart from a commanding position above the fireplace round which all chairs were grouped and thus perpetually in sight of the pleading look under that reproachful crown of thorns. Michael said, tapping it: "Mucky colour, Hunt's. Looks as though he painted in sick, doesn't it? D'you ever see any more Turners? I suppose not. Though they're far more religious paintings than this."

She felt out of breath like an air-drowned newt; looked beseechingly across at Michael, and back to the tactful hand raised against the weedy door in the picture. Christ came better out of the comparison. Yet the colour was drab when you remembered Turner.

"Let's go for a walk," Michael said suddenly. He had not yet taken off his outdoor things; she quickly put on her best coat. He contemplated with increasing gloom this maroon garment, double-breasted and waisted, with a velvet collar. It was known as princess-line.

"What happened to your navy blue number? And that marvellous hat?" he questioned.

"They're for school now. This is my best."

"I see," he sighed, as though his worst fears were being confirmed.

Yet she sensed that for him there was some necessary relief in attack. His very visit was odd enough to demand rudeness; what was a nineteen-year-old near-soldier doing with a little girl? A long bus-ride away? They seemed to be shouting their separateness hopefully—she somehow knew he would dislike her best coat and hair now twisted nightly with pipe-cleaners into curled ends, and small unsettled breasts; but proposed them without pity. He similarly made haste to annoy with bad words and nastiness about Jesus and ashtrays. In the half-light of a March evening they stepped down the path in single hostile file but exchanged a peevish, conniving glance. She remembered suddenly the dangling, para-military rope she had worn as part of her uniform when they first met; that he had tugged at. At its ends, the wound cord was unwoven to make a fringe of separated strands; nonetheless and evidently the tassel remained, despite steaming and combing, part of the same cord. Merely untwisted below a certain tight knot.

He turned at the gate to block her way. "You still got that white dressing-gown stuff drooped across your red blouse?"

"Yes," she said, gruff at the significant coincidence.

The Banjo was almost deserted—it tended to be at tea time—

and presented itself strangely to her familiar eyes because he was beside her. Its greens seemed obtrusive, gaudy. Had she hung on that rail dreaming of Michael? Not exactly. The rail was no more constant than anything else and the Michael of her memory was not this grumpy stranger at her side.

Still; she was eased. The failure to be one with him, or even suitably in his company, was alleviated by walking, when she could at least be in step.

"Your mother invited me to tea. Well she had to really."

"Yes. You will stay won't you?"

"I don't know. D'you mind walking?"

"No, I like it with you."

She trailed her hand through dusty privet to make one white glove dirty, as though that might help. He snorted. "You must admit, Ha'penny, it doesn't make sense. I feel daft, having tea with your Mum. Even walking, with a kid."

She swopped hands so that the other glove could become dirty too, and picked some fat leaves to stain. She observed: "You are nasty sometimes." Her fingertips bit into the fleshy whitish stuff under its tense green skin and gritty coat of dust and chewed it all together.

"Yes I know. I have to be really. It doesn't make sense."

She looked at her hands and saw blackish stains. It was not evidently darker, as daylight seeped away; but colours were disappearing. "About tea," said Penny. She shrugged. "I love you, you see," she explained.

"You can't, you're too young."

"Well, I do anyway."

"Yes, I know."

She walked deliberately around the outside of the next lamp-post.

"I could write to you?" she suggested.

"God forbid. Do you still do printing or are you up to real writing yet?"

"We've been doing real writing for ages," she said sadly.

A moment of pique had become pity. She felt, for some reason, sorry for him, and stepped down into the gutter.

"What are you shuffling down there for?"

"In case someone left a marble behind."

"Of course. There you are. You can see, Ha'penny, how awful

letters in real writing from you would be. In a barracks or something. Telling me about your newts or sensitive bits you'd have practised. I don't think I could stand it altogether. D'you see?"

She was silent but agreed to step out of the gutter on to the kerb when he touched her elbow. "Are you hurt?" he asked.

"Yes, of course. But so are you and that's worse." He gave her an alarmed look. At his pause her step stuttered and her eyebrows unconsciously imitated his.

"Look, Ha'penny; there's going to be a war. I'll be away and you'll grow up."

"Yes, I was thinking that. When I get older it won't be so funny. You haven't got those sonnets on you, have you?"

"Oh God. I am sorry. I forgot."

"It doesn't matter, I could get them from the library. So what about tea then?" She shifted pace to fall in exactly with his stride.

"You're very obstinate."

"Yes."

"Good." She must be taller, she could keep up easily now. She measured him to see where she came to, a more interesting marker than notches on the back door.

"You look at me," he complained. "It's bloody uncomfortable. Over tea. I mean . . . cakes."

"Sorry," she said.

"So am I, Angel," he agreed. They limped on through a depressing dusk.

"Look," he said, "are you allowed out after dark? I mean, can you get back home on your own?"

She stopped so dead it was as if she had come to a high blind wall suddenly. He was left stragglingly a pace or two ahead of her, looking back.

"What's the matter?" he called. He had stopped beneath a lamp which then came on. A quiver of wavering light settled into steadiness.

"Yes, I'm allowed out. I can go home alone."

He called impatiently: "Come on, then."

She stared at his face, glowing as it had been in match-light and called: "No."

"I just don't think I could face it; you must understand."

"Yes," she agreed, "I do understand."

"Then let's get on with our walk and then I'll go for my bus."

But: "No," she said. The wall seemed impenetrable and since she stood so stock still, he moved to return to her, a yard or two behind him on the darkening pavement.

"Look," he said: "surely you see—"

He advanced out of the lamplight towards her. She stared at his face until it became shadow. Then, turning towards the way they had come, she called: "I do, really I do, but I can't bear it. Good-bye." And took flight towards home.

He stood for a while looking after her. She still ran childishly, fast, unwavering, as in a race. The last he saw of her were white ankle socks flickering in the dusk which blotted out her dark coat and shoes. Two hovering moth-like pale blobs flickered up and down, up and down, regularly in and out of lamp-posts' illumination and the dark between. He watched until she turned a corner, then hunched himself deeper into the turned-up collar of his overcoat and went on towards the High Street.

PART TWO

LARE BELLAMY HAD been abroad. Penny had never met a child who had been abroad before. Since the war people spoke of going overseas about soldiers; adopting, it seemed to Penny, the Army idiom: her father had sometimes been overseas before the war to report in the *War Cry* the General's visits to Territories Overseas. But overseas was different from abroad. The Bellamy family went abroad every summer just for a holiday. And in September 1939 they got home to the Grange only just in time, as France was invaded by the Germans and the village by the evacuees. It was due to this late return that they had no evacuee billetted on them. The size of the Grange might have made them liable for several.

Clare was an extremely pretty girl, with hair like a buttercup in colour and shape. Of a yellower fairness than Penny's, it clung close to her head and curved in big locks like petals slightly inward at the nape of her neck. She was lucky in having a natural wave. Among other fortunate advantages were a car in which her father sometimes fetched her from the village school; light-coloured shoes when most children's were dark to be practical; and a pleated skirt which swung even when she walked and swirled round her thighs when she ran. This emphasised her movements, which were graceful, but so confident that they seemed not vain. Penny envied but could not dislike her. Clare was a larky, unserious girl, who took lessons lightly and wheedled her way out of games. She was considered stuck-up by those few born mean and aggrieved; on the whole she was popular in the community of village schoolchildren into whose midst the London children had been thrust.

The actual evacuation, on a Friday, had begun as an extra and fuller rehearsal and ended as a nightmare. The older children had now traipsed to the station on and off for a year. This time, they actually boarded trains; trains without lights, so that smaller children screamed in tunnels. The journey was long and all the stations had their names painted out; so their route was obscure throughout its distance and as well as their destination their direction was unknown. They arrived towards dusk as dizzily disoriented as the blindfolded person turned round three times in Blind Man's Bluff and incapable of bluffing anybody. They stood about in the village hall being chosen or rejected and finally bundled like parcels into reluctant homes. Few of the unsolicited gifts knew even the name of the county or the village where they went to bed. Even their exhaustion could not save their sleep from bad dreams and their waking from dismay.

Those who clung to the hope that it was all a practice and they might go home again soon learned the worst on Sunday morning. The service in the village church began just after eleven o'clock with an announcement that we were now at war. There was then a prayer of such gravity that numb and hazy fears must flow into actual weeping. The stranger children felt less estranged but more alarmed to see older and local people wipe away tears as they sobbed. Evidently something more generally dreadful had happened than their particular dire circumstances of being away from home and nowhere.

The overcrowded school was at first haphazard; but quite soon lesson timetables and classroom accommodation had been more or less suitably organised. What no amount of skilful arrangement could overcome was the separation between the local children and the outsiders. The evacuees had the haughty, beaten air of the dispossessed and stuck together. They knew they had not been invited, and appeared hostile partly through fear of being unwelcome. The indigenous children, unnerved by adult talk of war and invasion, eyed with distinct lack of warmth the army of strangers who now dominated the playground and sweet-shop. They spoke almost another language, had different clothes and customs, and ranged themselves in sullen belligerent lines on one side of the playground; growling, "Gerroff".

Clare Bellamy was the first to cross the lines. She seemed indifferent to the glowering atmosphere of the involuntary invaders or impervious to it. She skipped across the invisible demarcation to offer Penny a perfectly fair swop of one new *Film Fun* comic for two slightly used *Girls' Owns*. Penny agreed, aware of the mistrustful gaze of her party. They all watched Clare's smile and airy wave as she went back to her side of the playground. Though you could not be certain, her gestures did not seem treacherous.

Penny was one of the oldest of the evacuees. Those whose new grammar schools were at a distance from their homes were moved from London with their old neighbourhood schools. (Instant devastation was possible; administrators stuck to pre-Munich plans.) Clare was the same age—the village school mixed children from five upwards. She did not have a close friend but flirted through the local population, always the centre of a changing group, though too elusive to be thought of as their leader. You could not call her unassuming for, though frank and friendly, she had many assumptions natural to the privileged. But she wore them lightly, twirling on her graceful brown legs in a flutter of pleats, laughter and detachment. Penny had always been weighed down by heavy hems, as all her clothes were bought with so much room for growth that they had to be taken up about four inches; sometimes doubled. Nothing ever swirled around her stolid, marching walk. She envied the twinkling girl and was attracted to her. In the second week, she stomped across the invisible line in the playground to offer a reasonable but slightly more complicated swop. Clare accepted without counting the cost; which was in fact immaculately fair.

The guarded intruders observed Penny not being tortured or even rebuffed. The occupied village children took a lead from their central character. Within a few weeks a good deal of intermixing improved the atmosphere of the overcrowded school. Teachers of both sides observed liaison across the former barrier with relief and encouraged the friendship between Penny and Clare which pioneered it.

Among girls of school age, boredom tends to make subordinates. Boys follow physical strength or glamour at games, but girls tend to gather around the one who keeps them entertained. Penny was by situation and temperament this sort of leader. Clare's authority was of a different nature; she was attractive, self-possessed and of sunny disposition. Her group was less organised: it was they who followed her, rather than she who led them. This made collaboration between the local and London children possible without conflict of loyalties. Clare was the first to find Penny's projects enlivening and could accept Penny's leadership without any loss of face. If she grew bored, she would merely drift away; if not, she obeyed instructions. Penny became more ingenious and imaginative to retain her interest.

The village had a definite though straggling centre in its one road known as the High Street. This was tarmaced all along but had sketchy pavements only at salient points. Along its half-mile or so were sprinkled school, post office, shop, hall, bus stop, forge, two slatted seats for sitting on, pub, pond, telephone kiosk and church. This conglomeration was not so much convenient as inevitable because a steepish hill led into the village, and it became very steep indeed beyond the church where it led out. The lanes which diverged from the High Street at irregular intervals on either side were all winding and climbing with high banks and each made its way only to one house or a small row of cottages.

One of the first disconcerting changes to the London children was the isolation imposed by distance and the daunting fact that any walk included some part cruelly uphill. In the first bitter winter they were largely cut off from each other as well as from their parents. So widespread a community made for strong ties and a certain aloofness. People rarely gathered all together, there was little visiting and no dropping-in. This made the imposed visitors more than usually disconcerting to their hosts, and most, without wilful unkindness, found it inconceivable to change their own ways. There were no habits of casual hospitality.

The two largest houses within the central stretch were the Vicarage and the Grange. Outlying farmers owned a hundred times more land and some local tradesmen had bigger cars, but considerable respect was paid to the occupants of these two big houses, apparently on account of their different ways. Penny found this interesting because in the Banjo it had seemed more desirable to be the same. There was no doubt that the Bellamys were different in a particularly enviable way; if only because of the indifference with which they wore their alien but insular eccentricities.

Dr and Mrs Bellamy decided that Penny was a good influence on their adorable but flighty daughter. Clare was considered bright at school but lacking in concentration; Penny was good at lessons. Something had to be done about the dearth of evacuees at the Grange and the Bellamys came to the conclusion that the Carr girl filled the bill conveniently. The children themselves were told nothing while discussions with teachers were conducted and arrangements with the billetting officer made. Wisely, from one point of view; in case nothing came of it, not to cause unnecessary confusion. But the result was sudden and a shock.

Penny was told to stay behind at the end of a school day and informed with benign complacency that she should pack her belongings when she got back to her billet as Dr Bellamy would come and fetch her to live with them at seven o'clock. Her burst of tears astonished the billetting officer, who had ended with an almost envious smile: "You'll have a lovely new home at the Grange." But Penny was overcome with sorrow that 'home', that former absolute, was changeable; could be 'new'; that her real home was made further away by such usage. Though this move was what she would joyfully have chosen, the glib announcement proved that she had now no choice at all in her own life and could be shuffled about at the whim of others. The headmistress was shocked. Hostility and disapproval replaced her confident, well-meaning expression. Didn't she want to live with Clare then? Yes, very much, she sobbed. In that case, why in the world was she crying? The headmistress and the billetting officer eyed her with pursed lips: people who do good have a right to expect gratitude, their look implied. Penny wiped her eyes as quickly as possible. "That's better," they said. She was a very lucky little girl, to be moved to so superior a position. Now, the people who had a right to complain were Mr and Mrs Cooper, who had been kind to her and taken her into their home and might feel slighted. A fresh outburst of weeping offended them. The poor Coopers! It took some time for everybody instrumental in this kindness to forgive Penny. But it took far longer for her to relinquish a queasy sense of outrage on behalf of all the poor and stupid who are, like children, at the mercy of others, even when they are being done good to.

The Coopers, an elderly, childless couple, took their weakness in the face of privilege and authority for granted. They looked with dubious indifference at the tear-stained girl. She had certainly not cared for them until she had to leave them. They accepted the machinations which removed her as stolidly as those which had deposited her; and could not understand why she minded on her own or their behalf. They had the secret strength of those in a weak position: giving up without resistance those aspects of their lives in which they were imposed upon, they maintained the rigid habits of their private life with blind self-interest. They had not modified their ways one whit at having a child forced on them.

So that afternoon they made the strong tea which she could hardly swallow (milk, though plentiful, was not to the Coopers a reasonable drink), cut inch-thick slices of stalish bread (new bread disagreed with Mrs Cooper's stomach), and sat at the kitchen table beside the window to eat their last meal together.

"You'll not forget your gas-mask then?" said Mrs Cooper kindly.

"No. Thanks."

Talking at meal times was an innovation. She looked at the laid table with transitory nostalgia. They ate in the accustomed silence, defined by the heavy tick of a big clock. A newly-skinned rabbit lay bloody in a chipped enamel bowl on the dresser. To avoid its frightening deadness and smell of blood, Penny looked out of the window.

She felt a curious remorse and regret. Perhaps it was just the disturbance of moving on again into something unfamiliar. Even her fears here at the Coopers had assumed an air of habit. At first, the softness of feather beds seemed to smother children used to firmer mattresses. Going to bed in strange houses, under a country darkness so heavy it seemed as thick as soil, sinking into a yielding substance which piled up around the edges of your body, was like being buried in a shallow grave. No lights of neighbours or lamp-posts lit the unknown landscape behind the windows; and inside, candle-flame, casting more shadows than brightness, only enunciated the terrors of the room. Once the candle was blown out, night shifted like soot in a dead grate and settled over them and their dreams with a silent, muffling, churchyard dark.

The year was sloping down to its shortest day throughout Penny's stay at the Coopers'; so each day darkness came a little earlier. She had learned to watch it, sitting after homework at this kitchen window or venturing outside to hoard the last day-light. Night like a great mouth sipped at the eastern horizon then gradually sucked more and more of the earth into its dark throat until it had swallowed everything including her. "Time for bed," said the Coopers at this point, following the animals and birds naturally, and saving paraffin's unnatural, expensive light. So nightfall shut her up in a tunnel, and she could only cower in her burying bed and wait for the small white hole of morning, which faith alone made credible, to enlarge into another day.

Each morning did indeed arrive; pulling her from the tube of night into Cooper-calling, hen-muttering, bird-clamouring breakfast. Perhaps because nights in the country were more dreadful, mornings seemed exceptionally vivid and raucous resurrections. She got up more quickly—anyway it was colder and the water in the ewer on the wash-stand had bits in it—and ran down to the bacony kitchen with so much relief that all her senses were alert. "You'm bright and early," Mrs Cooper would say with an air of satisfaction and reproof.

But never, it seemed, again. Perhaps only such bad nights bought such radiant mornings. Muddled, moping, Penny gazed out of the kitchen window and at her tea. A last supper at a place she had not liked but was sorry to leave.

The long, narrow garden was a neat patchwork of different vegetables or turned earth. At the end, a shed with a window and a door looked like a smaller cottage. Every cottage in the terrace had one; as though each family had a branch of gnomes or midgets playing house at the end of the gardens, on the edge of the field.

"I kept your label," Mrs Cooper said when the munching-time ended. "Will you need your label?"

"I don't think so. No surely. I know who I am." Penny tried a smile.

"Well, I'll keep it then," said Mrs Cooper. "You'll know where 'tis if you need it later. Dresser drawer if I be taken."

The taking of Mrs Cooper was frequently mentioned and its apparent imminence had been another worry. This and remembrance of the label and the curiously pointless intention to preserve it with insurance policies and pension books set Penny off crying again. The pathetic hoarding of this pathetic object. When they left home and London, each child had a label tied on to its person. The gas-mask was bad enough: made of black rubber dusted inside with some grey powder, it had a celluloid window to look through and a long snout of nose with metal nostrils to breathe through. It smelled of operations to Penny who had had two, one for tonsils and one for appendix, anaesthetised by a rubber mask which expunged consciousness terrifyingly in the operating theatre. The rubber-mask smell was mixed up with ether in gas-mask practices, her own panicky breathing sucked in its rubber cheeks and filmed its eye-shield with condensed breath; so she could neither see nor breathe and seemed liable to suffocation as alternative to being gassed. Yet the label was worse in a way. A label insisted that identity was extremely insecure; for no one alive, conscious, and with a memory needs to wear his name, age and address. So at best it meant you were going where you were not known; and at worst that you might not get there in one piece. If you were blown to bits the label would tell strangers that one bit was you.

Mrs Cooper pushed her plate back to make room for her elbows. "What be you crying for?" she asked, now eating was over.

"I don't want you to keep my label" was all that seemed simple enough to say.

"Course we mun keep it. 'Tis official. You ought to be happy goin' to big house. They have inside lav and all. Though mind you they'm queer folk, Dr Bellamy and his missus."

"Queer?" Penny brightened.

"Nice, for all that. Always fair, Mrs B. He be a dreamer mind."

At this her heart lifted: she and her father were said to be dreamers by practical Mrs Carr.

"Oh good. Where's his surgery, do you know?"

Mr Cooper enveloped himself in clouds of smoke before saying: "He b'ain't that sort of doctor." This remarkable pronouncement gave him evident pleasure.

"Though Lord knows why not." Mrs Cooper arched and tilted at clearing the table.

" 'Tis not for us," said her husband sternly. He guarded the mystery as jealously as his wife any official paper.

She sniffed. "You mun mind your manners," she insisted. "You munna think to understand." But seemed annoyed at the rule she passed on, and coughed affectedly at her husband's pipe smoke, clattering plates unnecessarily. Penny agreed with the implied annoyance and began to help with the clearing-away, interested in something she did not understand but proposed to. But:

"Leave that to me," said Mrs Cooper sharply; who had formerly expected help, reasonably. "They have a girl to clear away at the Grange: you'd best learn to be waited on."

So Mrs Cooper did feel slighted. But during tea Penny had relinquished her brief attachment to the Cooper household. When she tumbled down the short path to Dr Bellamy's waiting car, she waved back a final farewell, as if going further. Apprehensive and not arrived, she had nevertheless definitely departed.

The Grange was a square grey house with a central door and an equal number of windows on either side and above. Its windows had shutters—"They all do in France," Clare had said airily—which were not intended to shut but in practice could, so they assisted the problems of the black-out exotically. A wedge of subdued light slid on to the gravel of the drive as Dr Bellamy ushered Penny through the door into a dim hall. When the door clanged shut behind them they felt secretive, standing there blinking. The black-out made people quieter as though noise were connected with light; but the Grange had an unusually ample silence which swallowed the click of the door greedily.

Dr Bellamy was a large man; woolly. His hair was like a hand-woven rug made of some flecked wool, two-toned fawn and grey. His face, too, was patchy and freckled, much the same colours as his hair. Skin, too, looked soft and crumpled, like un-ironed knitting. The lines and puckers on his broad face made him look smiling. He dressed always in loose sweaters made of long-haired wools, jackets of tweed with a slight furriness, and trousers of fuzzy flannel or corduroy. So there was nothing knife-edged about him and this gave him a big, soft, doggish air. He was usually surrounded by smoke from his pipe; which increased his blurred comforting image to the point where actual contact seemed both improbable and safe. There would always be a lot between him and another person, however close they came; which made him as huggable as dogs or farm animals.

"Is that the child? Welcome and so on." Mrs Bellamy's percussive consonants hit the muffling gloom of the hall like sparks and she followed her high bright voice. Her face was the exact opposite in shape from her husband's, long and narrow like a horse.

"Hello, Penny. D'you mind if we go straight into dinner? Some pathetic little cutlets which will be beastlier cold. Julian will take your things up later. Darling, do call Clare down . . . those *poor* cutlets."

The not entirely intrepid explorer observed the customs of this new country cautiously. She knew that some people had dinner in the evening instead of at midday; but Mrs Bellamy's calling her husband by his Christian name in front of a visitor, and a child at that, was rather embarrassing: all the families she knew would have said 'Dr Bellamy'. Among themselves, parents called each other Mum and Dad or Mummy and Daddy, and spoke of each other so to their children; who were always in the same room when in the house. The need to 'call' Clare, and speaking of 'Julian' easily, indicated something more significantly foreign than a cooked meal at night. The Bellamys were not identified by their relationship to Clare, as Penny's were to her. Mothers and fathers must be only one of their games.

When Clare danced into the dining-room, she greeted Penny and her parents from much the same distance: it was obvious that, though they met quite often, Clare and the grown-ups did not live together in the same way as children in Penny's circle, who were intimately central to the life of the family.

"Had a good day?" Dr Bellamy enquired politely of his daughter as he unrolled his napkin from a silver ring. This making of conversation was different both from the dedicated silence of Cooper meals and the chattering genuine exchanges around the table at homes in the Banjo area. Penny cleared her throat and said:

"I'm not very hungry, Mrs Bellamy. I just had tea."

"Oh dear, of course. We really should have warned the Coopers not to feed you. Well, toy with a morsel dear will you, to keep Clare company."

Keeping Clare company was evidently a useful function. Penny perceived that Clare's position as just one element of her parents' lives, not its central focus, made for an attractive freedom, but also the possibility of a loneliness unknown in the Banjo. It would account for her friend's easy unattachment and have taught the acceptance and the uses of loneliness; making Clare less dependent than Penny was on company. So Penny's arrival might be of mutual benefit

Then again there was her duty to bring Christ into their lives, if He were not already there. Following instructions to be a witness wherever she might find herself, and not to be a trouble to anyone, Penny had said grace at every meal at the Coopers with an ostentatious modesty. The Coopers had not noticed. But her silent mouthing with closed eyes drew attention at the Bellamy table; and the noticeable way she did not quite clasp her hands. Mrs Bellamy paused in serving in the midst of a spoonful and sentence.

"I'm so sorry. Grace, I presume? Might it do afterwards?"

"Yes, of course. We pray at anytime."

"Just this once, then," Dr Bellamy allowed. His wife continued serving. Clare gave her friend and then her father a suspicious stare: she sensed that they were both up to something though something different.

"We don't say grace," said Clare.

"Well if Penny does, we shall in future," said Dr Bellamy. "It's important that she shouldn't be more cut off than necessary from her habitual environment." He included Mrs Bellamy in using longer words. "The effect of uprooting a million of these children may prove psychologically and socially far-reaching." Mrs Bellamy raised her eyebrows. Penny's face caught Clare's suspiciousness; she did not care to consider herself one of 'these children'.

"We might have been killed in London," she protested.

"Yes, indeed. That's why you're here. But we don't want you to be damaged by losing touch with your former traditional behaviour." He munched at toughish meat. "So," he said, laying his knife and fork down, "you must tell us about the customs of your own home, so as not to feel cut off."

So genial an invitation came nearer to cutting her off from her 'habitual environment' than any indifference or cruelty could have accomplished. It implied that behaviour she had assumed universal might be considered rather odd. His extreme kindliness suggested that it might be. She gave him a probing look before answering his questions. She thought of her obligation to teach lost souls the error of their ways and bring them into an understanding of the saving grace of Jesus; but she had never expected to be confronted by lost souls with such attentive, generous expressions.

"Fancy!" Cynthia Bellamy kept exclaiming with rapt surprise.

"I see!" said Dr Bellamy with enthusiastic interest.

It became fairly evident, by the charitable air with which they encouraged her, that they were not on the point of being

Convicted of Sin, nor convinced of the error of their ways. Worse: they seemed genuinely fascinated; as though it were all really very unusual and curious.

They interrupted only to ask her to translate words which had seemed common parlance. They did not know that Self-Denial was a time of year; back-sliders, people who had fallen away from their faith; furlough, a holiday; and dying, being promoted to glory. What had seemed language was revealed as a very small-currency jargon; rather less widely understood than French.

"How very quaint," Mrs Bellamy said.

"Vigorous, though," said the Doctor admiringly. "The habit of so much metaphor and simile as a natural feature of language from earliest childhood, must make Shakespeare, for instance, much more readily accessible."

"Does your Shakespeare have the Sonnets in?" the subject asked, alerted.

"Yes, of course. Don't they all?"

"No, mine doesn't. May I borrow yours please?"

"Naturally. The books are in the study. Help yourself." But he looked a livelier interest and appeared surprised for the first time.

Penny thanked him while the village girl took away their plates. Mrs Bellamy filled the silence in which Penny was trying awkwardly to help.

"We do admire the Salvation Army so," she said, "for their wonderful social work." She even pronounced 'Salvation' wrongly, accenting the second syllable instead of the first.

Penny corrected: "My parents are on the Evangelical side."

"Well, never mind," said Cynthia Bellamy with a radiant gesture. "I'm sure that's splendid, too."

But in the Army it was considered superior to be savers of souls and those who ran hostels were far less likely to reach high rank and positions of influence in Headquarters. It was all very difficult, communicating.

"As the sweet's cold," said Mrs Bellamy helpfully, "this might be a terrifically good moment for your Grace bit Penny." She glanced at the gold watch on her trim wrist.

Penny wanted to demonstrate how different from mumbled slogans her sort of prayers were and waited for the inspiration of the Holy Spirit. It seemed to find the genial atmosphere unconducive. She managed some short gratitude for the Coopers' kindness and a blessing on the Bellamys. Amen.

"Do you always mention people by name?" said Clare. "I mean, wouldn't He *know* who was there without being told? And that you'd got here from the Coopers and everything?"

"Don't be rude, Clare," Dr Bellamy warned.

"No, but . . ."

"All public worship has an element of social communication."

"You mean God like a telephone operator? Putting them through?"

Stifling a smile, "We mustn't make Penny uncomfortable," he said. But she felt more uncomfortable to be treated as though her habits were too peculiar to be even a subject for teasing. To escape their dismaying encouragement, she changed the subject.

"Mr Cooper said you're not a medical doctor. I didn't understand."

"Daddy's a Doctor of Philosophy," Clare announced proudly.

"A philosopher! Like Socrates and people?" Penny was impressed.

Dr Bellamy chuckled shyly. "Not very like. It's just an academic degree. How do you know Socrates, young Penny?"

"He's in my book of Arthur Mee's *Thousand Heroes*."

"Ah. A short entry no doubt? I'll tell you more one day."

"But what are you a doctor *for* then, Dr Bellamy?"

Mrs Bellamy explained: "Julian's a historian, actually."

"I didn't know teachers could be doctors."

"Learners, Penny. I got my doctorate as a research student at Oxford. I've never taught." She was fascinated. Oxford was what lost the Boat Race to Penny and she forgot the import of what she should introduce into their lives in interest in what they could introduce into hers.

But Clare was yawning. "May we leave the table, Mummy?"

"More of this seedy sweet, either of you?"

"No thank you, Mrs Bellamy."

"Oh, Mummy, *obviously* not." Clare displayed an unfinished plate while Penny examined her father shyly.

"Cut along you two," said Dr Bellamy.

"Coffee in the study," said Mrs Bellamy to the maid.

The children lingered; Penny bemused by the odd arrangements, Clare to make a point.

"Mummy: why can't she sleep in my room?"

"Because we've discussed it, darling, and Penny is to sleep in the old nursery."

"Yes, but why? It would be so exciting."

"Quite," said Cynthia Bellamy. "You might not sleep at all." Her look as she said this was extreme but characteristic: an intake of breath and arch of eyebrows made her long, narrow face longer and narrower and her expression more dogmatically disinterested. She had very thin eyebrows drawn on to protuberant brows, which made her eyes seem far away, set deep under a shelf of bone. Yet in those deep caves under the perfunctory commas of pencil high above, her eyes were round, bright blue, and fitted with precise eyelids. Large, and almost painfully tight-fitting, the thin, definite eyelids hooded and unhooded the bright round eyes; noticeable even in the shadow of the brow which sheltered them.

"Just for the first few days," pleaded Clare, twirling on one foot with the back of her dining-chair as a bar, and looking deliberately appealing. Which made her mother sigh.

"Then there'd be a drama at the change. No, darling." But she sounded terribly bored. She had a nose of such remarkable thinness that it seemed all bone, the bridge narrow and notched, the tip curving down slightly, the nostrils invisible from the front, drawn flat on the sides in arches like eyebrows.

"Come on, then," said Clare to Penny, sighing in an imitation of her mother's extreme weariness so accurate that it made her father laugh.

There were a great many new things to learn at the Bellamys and Penny was adept at imitation. On Sundays they wore their oldest, not their best, clothes. Clare was in many ways less protected and allowed to be far less faddy than Penny: you ate up or went hungry and if you lost your gloves you had cold hands. There were far less meticulous tidiness and cleanliness in the house than her mother had insisted upon, and though rooms were larger, they were shabbier too. The Bellamys ate, on the whole, less, but more formally and more often. There were fewer cakes and far less bread. Less fussed over for poor appetite, Penny became less fussy and ate rather more. Nobody asked her about her bowels, but baths were assumed to be a daily, not a weekly, event. The children were left far more to their own devices and you could read as late as you liked without a torch under the bedclothes. They were keener on fresh air and less bothered about dust. Homework was up to you; it bored them. Almost imperceptibly, she adopted the habits of the household.

The big old Rover smelling of petrol and leather soon seemed natural transport, and if she and Clare had to wait outside school for five minutes on a cold wet night, they would scramble into the back seats with indistinguishable cries of agony and complaint. The only sight which disturbed Penny in her new situation was that of Mrs Cooper, lugging a heavy shopping-basket up the hill as she was driven past in comfort. Perhaps because the Coopers formed some specific link with her home, she could not wave but shrank down guiltily. Though the Coopers were in many ways not at all like her parents, they defined some area of treachery otherwise unobtrusive. Dr Bellamy's books made him closer to her father than Mr Cooper had seemed: yet she could not see the Coopers without a pang of disloyalty, shame, and an aching, useless affection. This was so confused that she thought about it as little as possible and was almost annoyed to come upon the Coopers about the village. In the shop, for instance: when Mrs Bellamy called in with the two chattering, bright-cheeked girls in her wake, the queue would tend to make way for her to collect her rations first. Penny's shame-faced silence showed worse against Clare's friendliness.

"Oh hallo, Mrs Cooper! How's your bad back?" The bright indifferent child was thought gracious.

"Much better thank you, Clare m'dear."

The harshly guilty child's sour nod was considered an affront: ungrateful. She knew it; but it takes longer to learn the generosity of the rich to the poor, the strong to the weak; and in this respect Penny failed to acquire the serenely patronising tone of those who —like the Bellamys—are self-accepting. Clare did not understand.

"Come and talk to Cooper," she would say when he came to prune trees in the Bellamy orchard.

"I'd rather not."

"Why? Were they horrid to you?"

"No, of course not."

"I think Cooper's rather nice."

"So do I."

"Then why won't you talk to him?"

Hopeless to try to explain: she could not understand it herself.

"He always asks after you," said Clare critically. "I think you're rather rotten: not to talk."

So did Penny. She felt rotten too. But though her skin reddened all over to hear Clare call him Cooper, she could not talk to him. She thought Mr Cooper ought to mind being called Cooper by a little girl, however kindly. Able to adjust to either world, she could not mix them without embarrassment. She could only avoid confrontation.

Despite the Bellamy parents' encouragement to describe the Salvation Army through many meal times, the well-trained pilgrim did not relent in her hope of converting them until one day when Clare, who was frankly bored and eager to get away from the table to other activities, complained; "They always try to make people feel at home," carelessly; "I don't see why you let them go on so at you; as though you were an African or something. If we had a man from the moon to tea they'd ask him all about it. It is a bit silly of you, to go on playing up to them; when we might be climbing trees or telling stories." This was more shattering; they were humouring her. "*Real* stories," Clare insisted sulkily, "made-up ones that are exciting." So it was plain that in these circumstances a little child should *not* lead them. Rather, their determination not to influence her exerted a strong influence.

She registered also that her real life was dull to Clare, though made-up stories could hold her spellbound night after night.

Despite a modification of her evangelical approach to the Bellamys, Penny retained her stubbornly non-conformist conscience. Its first public manifestation might have disconcerted patrons less confident than the Bellamys. As there was no Army in the neighbourhood, she went to church. Her father said by letter that this was the right thing to do. The Bellamys obligingly accompanied her more often than had been their practice. The Creed acquired an unsuspected drama in the mumbling church from the London child's clear enunciation of those parts of it she did believe and sudden piercing silence at those she did not comprehend. While waiting for guidance from home she lapsed into tight-lipped non-participation on "I believe in the holy catholic church, the communion of saints..." and joined in loudly for "and the life everlasting".

Dr Bellamy had a talk with her about this. It was drawing attention to their pew. He tried to persuade her that catholic did not mean Catholic, and almost certainly included the Salvation Army; but she was so unconvinced by his assurance that saints did not mean Saints and communion had nothing to do with Communion, that he deferred to her request that the matter might wait until an authoritative gloss on the Army's attitude to these matters should arrive from her father.

It was this letter, typed and well-reasoned, which made him begin to talk to her with less exaggerated interest about her background: her father was obviously a man of some mind. It also relieved the village church of its weekly disturbance: Major Carr approved the Creed, in the circumstances, endorsing Dr Bellamy's explanations.

"If your people can ever get away," said Dr Bellamy, "you must tell them we'd be delighted to put them up." Flushed with gratitude, she wrote the letter at once. The Carrs replied that a break was out of the question until Father's furlough in the summer. Still, it was something to look forward to.

For Christmas, Dr Bellamy gave her a copy of the Sonnets in an old and charming binding. This, and the carols and Christmas tree, made her cry. Though the Bellamys found it natural enough that she should feel more homesick at such a time, Clare was puzzled that her friend wept only at nice things. The unexpectedly thoughtful gift, which ought to have pleased her, induced more tears than she had shed in the first desolate days away from home.

"But don't you like it?"

"Yes," she gulped, and was made speechless again by how very kind they were being to her.

Dr Bellamy comforted his own daughter, who did not understand. "But she's very brave about nasty things," Clare protested. "And when she gets sad about her mother and father, she never cries; quarrels sometimes, or thinks of slightly naughty things to do. So why does she cry if she's happy?"

Her father, hugging her, explained: "Some natures are like that. Hardship makes them fierce and strong, but soft things weaken them. Their own pleasure breaks down their defences. Let her cry: it's good for her."

But Clare continued to be disapproving at this apparent contradiction. Eventually: "Perhaps you'd better not open *my* present," she said, pouting; which dried up Penny's tears at once.

That night, with the treasured new book beside her bed, Penny looked out into the dark dry-eyed and remembered Michael who had promised it a year ago. He had walked out of her life so callously; when Mother had actually laid tea with second-best china. She felt braced by hard anger now the undemonstrative Bellamys had shown more thoughtfulness in their reticent way: not words but deeds, Mother often said, show people up in their true light. Not to write a letter or keep in contact even; so that he might be dead or wounded and she would not even know. Some muddle here, for why would she care if she did not care? Still; she put her love for Michael on one side and, if the feelings in the Sonnets recalled to her vividly what she felt for him, she loved Shakespeare more for putting the feelings so well than Michael for evoking and then rejecting the feelings.

And so at first love, then nature, and eventually fear and loneliness and other emotions, became for her subjects rather than experiences. Art, she discovered, supplied a sort of escape. She read more, and more passionately, and she scribbled poems and stories more frequently, not to 'forget', which provided too brief and partial an escape, but to transmute. She would still occasionally 'lose herself' in an adventure story or fantasy remote from real life. But after *The Prisoner of Zenda*, for instance, you had to return to your own circumstances: Ruritania dissolved as you looked up from the last page to discover yourself a long way from home in an alien house in the middle of a war. Whereas other kinds of writing, by putting real-life recognisable feelings into words, drew from them their hurt and unwieldiness. By encompassing they could inoculate overwhelming emotion. If they expressed it really well but in tight and difficult forms, they tamed its power to upset you into a kind of pleasure. You could adapt the general principle to country walks; which she loathed but were an inescapable part of Bellamy life. If you concentrated on rhymes and similes to write poems about what you saw on country walks, you could almost avoid tired legs, scratchy thistles and terrifying ideas of snakes and slugs. Or darkness; death; love and suchlike; which otherwise confounded and made you feel helpless and afraid. Nothing could master you that you could master by 'putting it into words', she discovered.

This discovery had gratifying side-effects. It improved her reading diet remarkably, though leaving her addicted to the romantics. School stories by Angela Brazil about girls' dorms and exotic adventures by Rider Haggard were discarded by her earlier than by most children in her age group. She preferred the Brontës, Keats and Shakespeare because they identified emotion for her in a way which lasted after the book was put down; and so made actual life less real. She also wrote things herself. Imitative, affected, they nevertheless helped her to get over intense homesickness by describing a sunset not too carefully observed. Finding a rhyme for 'westering' got her out of what Clare called her moods more efficiently than any alternative remedy.

Quite incidentally the habit earned bonuses. What started as a device to shelter herself from raw experience gained approval. Teachers beamingly encouraged her. They made her read things aloud in Assembly. She enjoyed the double benefits. The books she read because they helped most turned out to be officially approved as Good Books. The poems she wrote made her praised for unusual sensitivity.

Only Julian Bellamy suspected her 'sensitive' and 'observant' scribblings as a technique for minimising her sensitivity and observation into the confines of her available language; and thus a form of self-robbery. He did not openly express his suspicions as he recognised that she had adopted these methods of dealing with experience in order to survive it. But sometimes from within a concealing cloud of pipe smoke and shaggy clothes he would suggest that, at another time and in another place, she might wish to have retained a capacity to feel and be completely, instead of only in words.

It was Dr Bellamy who first reduced her name to Penn; because she was always scribbling. He made childish jokes from the beginning; gruffly, to be kind. Across the table in the dining-room, he would lob puns at her shyly, as people throw bread-pellets at an animal they wish to make friends with, without any conviction that more personal overtures will be acceptable. They are almost always the ones uneasy creatures will sidle up to: their good intentions are transparent behind their masking gestures. The evacuee was no exception. The kind, mysteriously disappointed man and the out-of-water cockney child struck up a relationship which assuaged in a reticent way some loneliness both felt.

"D'you happen to know what made them call you Penelope?" he asked one day as the girls finished their homework.

They did this in his study as everyone had to save fuel and this

smallish room, easier to keep warm, became more and more the
focus of the house. The loose-covers of its chairs were more
rumpled and washed-out than Mrs Carr would have deemed fit on
a council estate; on the other hand its wall-lining books were more
than Major Carr could dream of.

"I think it was Homer. My father liked a book called the *Odyssey*
and read it to my mother on their honeymoon."

"Have you read it?"

"Not yet."

"You should."

"I'm not much interested in myths and things. Too far-fetched."

"Try it some time. But I was looking you up in the dictionary."

The most astounding of Dr Bellamy's books was the *Oxford
English Dictionary*, which occupied a whole shelf. Penny had never
thought there could be so many words; enough to fill twelve tall
fat volumes.

"In the *dictionary*?" cried Clare disbelievingly. "Why should her
name be in the dictionary? Is mine?"

They scrambled to each side of him, quick with practice; each
girl used one arm of his armchair as a back-rest and sat on the
carpet with outstretched legs. Which of them got the fire-side side
and which the further cooler position depended solely on interest
and agility: the Bellamys were scrupulously fair without fuss.
Cynthia, smoking on the sofa, which was square to the fireplace,
giggled and said they looked like inverted sphinxes flanking his
column. This diverting proposition interrupted them into a search
for illustrations and caused both girls to adopt a new and more
sphinx-like posture: lying on their fronts and resting on their
elbows at the arms of his chair with their bottoms roasting in the
heat from the log fire.

"It's much less comfortable," groaned Clare; propped elegantly
upright from the waist, backwards.

"And there seems more of you to block off the pathetic warmth,"
said Cynthia.

While the girls reverted noisily to their usual position, Julian
gave his wife a loving, grateful look which they were sure to miss.
Sometimes her drinking made her less amusing and kind.

When the girls were resettled in a flurry of limbs, he said: "Clare
is in as a nun: so watch your flighty ways, my darling. But all
the associations with clarity apply." He fondled her pale head at his

86

knee briefly. "But I was looking up Penelope as it happens. Fascinating."

"What?"

"It's in as the web or weaving or time-gaining policy of Penelope. But you'll have to read the *Odyssey* to understand that."

"Oh why?" "Oh please!" "Oh don't be horrid!" they exclaimed. Confident of having induced them perhaps to explore Homer for curiosity's sake, he continued unseduced.

"But its short forms are interesting. Pen means 'a place' in Cornish; which we might have guessed from Penzance and so on. And 'to confine or shut up': which we know from sheep and cows. But also to dam up a river. Fortunately our Pen can or we'd have been flooded at Christmas. But: here's the interesting thing. A writing tool—pen—derives from a feather; wings. Same root as pinion. In late Latin, a writing pen; later, as a verb: to compose or write."

Shifting, petulant, Clare said: "I don't think that's in the least interesting. Do you, Penny?"

Penny was more interested at that moment in the life of words; which she had hardly realised shift and change through time and the use of writers. But:

"Don't you?" said Dr Bellamy mildly. "She has after all migrated to us on her pinions; is weaving time away from the people she loves; and may travel far further and make more complex webs, as a writing tool. If she chooses only strong feathers for her wings. In fact, now I think of her Christmas tears again, she's a perfect fountain pen. Penny for short; Penn with two n's for long."

"Oh, Julian," said Cynthia sighingly, "you do go far too far. All right, darlings, do cut along. There's good chaps."

Cynthia Bellamy was stamped in the mould of the twenties in which she had first escaped, then been recaptured by, her class. She had been a very bright young thing indeed as she flattened her bust and shortened her skirts, scandalising the grim distinguished family of which she was the only daughter, and one of two surviving children. Both her older brothers had died in the war in ways so differently horrible that they might still have been competing as they had at school and home. One was blown up in a trench; the other shot himself through the head in the bathroom a week after his return home unharmed in body but mutilated in

87

mind. The girl Cynthia smoked and sniffed and drank and danced her way through a mood which could not be appropriate without despair; and seemed for a time to escape the depression of the era and the family by being very fast in every sense. In her own car, in other people's aeroplanes, across the Atlantic, through country house parties and innumerable bedrooms, she drove at a pace which combined lassitude with frenzy. Nothing mattered but everything must change rapidly. She succeeded in leaving behind almost totally the square cold house in Kent where elderly survivors nursed their mourning and converted their griefs into grievances. Then came the General Strike; and her stuffy younger brother (who bore the family legacy differently, as though made responsible for the survival of his class by the death of his brothers) left Cambridge to drive a train. Mainly to defy him, Cynthia larkily joined the other side. She found the workers rather adorable and for the miners' sake took to a champion of theirs, the vague unworldly academic Bellamy. In the context, flushed with conviction, principle and active socialism, he appeared excitingly different. By the time the workers had limped back to work and Julian to Oxford, a baby was too far on the way to discard easily. In the drama-ridden early days of conception it had seemed wonderfully consolidating and original to be and to remain pregnant.

The most infuriating thing for Cynthia was that Julian turned out to be so tiresomely suitable. Even the melancholy household of her parents could carp only at his political attitudes. She pouted that if only she had taken one of those delicious miners for her child's father she could have escaped the quiet but fashionable wedding; but with all-day morning sickness, one had to admit to some relief at Julian's comforting size, suitability and temperament. It was not so easy to be so dashing as before. And he was a terrifically decent chap. Though love was not one of her words, being a good chap was then and remained her highest accolade.

But the house was daunting. So was the way of life of a lazy intellectual who had enough income not to have to work as an academic professionally. The Grange had brought her rather down.

"Don't you hate this house?" she once asked Penn with unaccustomed intensity in her voice.

"No, I rather like it."

An intimacy more eccentric than her friendship with Dr Julian and far less reliable crept into Penn's relationship with Clare's mother during that long cold winter. Mrs Bellamy, Penn found, had two distinct personalities. Her off-hand and correct daytime self eluded any touch, wafting in hats just out of reach of even her child's and husband's hands. She was respected in the village as much for her personal remoteness and amiability as for her position. After six, at home, she would sometimes talk with odd intimacy. Penn's status in the house seemed to absolve Cynthia from both her duty to outsiders and to members of the family. She would sometimes call Penn to the drawing-room if she heard her passing through the hall alone to reveal vaguely suspect confidences. ("Call me Cynthia, darling, there's a good chap; it's all too difficult otherwise. And I resolutely refuse to be Aunt to anyone.") At other times she would deny any but the most formal encounter for days at a time. Or abdicate intimacy suddenly, if Julian's voice were heard, calling "Darling?" from the hall in a proprietory yet doubtful tone; or if Clare drifted in to say "Oh there you are", with a bored, indifferent look. Penn needed no explicit instructions, as a habit of doubleness was ingrained. She accepted without tiresome enquiries when Cynthia was Mrs Bellamy or Mrs Bellamy became Cynthia, and did not attempt to impose the rules of one world on the other. Summoned to refill an empty glass with gin, or encourage the fire, she would hesitate until the character of each meeting had been defined by the grown-up. Though her tact was motivated by the self-protective instinct of the outsider and confirmed by recognition that nothing was only or entirely what it seemed, it was nevertheless appreciated: Cynthia Bellamy learned to trust her not to take advantage.

The day when Mrs Bellamy talked about the Grange was in the middle of a bleak patch of late winter weather, when they really did seem cut off from any outside world.

"I suppose it's easier for you not to hate it. I was brought up in a house just like it. When I married this one quite by accident, it seemed to have been waiting with its smug beastly face just to snap me up and shut me in." Cynthia waved bitterly at the big window, blankly blacked-out. "Generation upon generation who started life in one of these Georgian affairs seem bound to fetch up in another, don't you think, however hard they try to run away? D'you suppose there's a network of them all across England? Just the same, square and grey, but positioned outside a different village to deceive the unwary. Inside, exactly the same proportions to the rooms and pattern to the day."

"It sounds like a bad dream," said Penn helpfully.

"Yes, doesn't it. Fainter than nightmares, though. Even the village isn't really different. Would you believe when we first came here, we thought we were quite, quite original? We had unlikely people to stay sometimes. Miners and artists and communists and once some nudists. But it was so far from anywhere, they wouldn't come after a while. And the village accepted our unconventional ways so comfortably that it felt like another convention. I mean, perhaps people in Georgian houses outside villages *have* to have nudists to stay. Perhaps it's all part of the pattern." But she sounded resigned, amused. "The village prevented any excesses, of course. Since they know their place they insist we keep to ours. Julian once tried to organise farm labourers: that was *not* allowed. We had to *import* people to improve. Even then. We tried recidivist criminals but one couldn't keep it up. Anyway they were so terribly bored, I believe word got round. Just like prison really."

Penn considered, surprised but curious. Such houses had appeared from the outside impregnable fortresses of luxury; might they actually imprison those inside? Created and maintained by inescapable privilege to shut in as well as to keep out?

"It seems to me you can do what you want," said Penn.

"Oh quite, darling. Any whim at all. That's what's so damning. Except change anything. Did you know Julian and I met fighting in the class struggle? We were as evangelical as your people, darling; only politically. And now we've only got you. And that was considered just a duty to the traditions we meant not to maintain. You're even clever and clean."

Penn, who had had no idea quite what a weight of disappointed reforming zeal she was required to receive, stared doubtfully.

"You could have taken the bed-wetting ones with lice," she proposed. "Children from bad homes." She looked cross, never intending to be a good cause, only to have one.

"We did sort of mean to. But Clare took a fancy to you and all the horridest children went back to London, so we rather gave up."

Mrs Bellamy, Penn suspected, had given up long before that. Her bouts of lethargy seemed of long-standing: for days at a time she confined herself almost entirely to one room and solitude.

The forbidding frontage of the Grange was indeed secluding, and then she seemed content to be trapped behind its thick walls, able to reproach circumstances for what might otherwise reveal itself as temperament. The girl stood frowning beside the sofa where the thin, exhausted, wayward lady lay.

"Do perch, darling. You're getting too tall to look up to and your socks are coming down which makes a dismal sight of your legs."

"I lost my garters," said Penn, hitching but not perching as bidden.

"Again?"

"Again."

"Nothing seems to attach itself to you for long. As if you really were a sort of bird and constantly in flight." Mrs Bellamy smiled lopsidedly and made the ice chink in her glass deliberately. "Penn. I like your nick-name. Julian had a point, you are after all a fugitive: don't you think?"

Allowed, indeed required, to think, Penn did so.

"Oh and before you settle." Mrs Bellamy waved the glass at her, with deliquescent ice slithering in its emptiness.

"I didn't choose to be here," Penn decided; absorbed, so neither sitting nor refilling.

Mrs Bellamy's glance narrowed: not unfriendly; merely focusing. "Well, nor do fugitives, darling, necessarily. Only to get away from where they were."

Playing for time and consulting with her conscience, Penn poured more gin—it was surely not her responsibility to enforce teetotalism on her benefactors?—and added: "I didn't even choose that."

A slightly mangy fur coat crinkled around Mrs Bellamy's knees against the fickle flames of a fire too small for the drawing-room grate. Her sofa had only one high arm and was flat at the other end. To which she waved the child.

"You're so right: just another victim of circumstance. Tuck under this old musquash, darling, it must be freezing out there."

The fellow victim perched; stroked the squashed fur thoughtfully; stared at Clare's unusual mother. The large room had temporarily lost its good proportions through the effects of the tiny war-time fire. Most of the furniture was either shrouded under sheets or pushed out of its proper position to bring the chaise-longue closer to the fireplace and the drink table closer to the chaise-longue. All was out of order, huddled. So were the tipsy niece of a duke and the researching fugitive from the Banjo. They eyed each other with a camaraderie which seemed to both bizarre but not unwelcome.

"You've got goose-pimples on your knees," observed Cynthia.

"Well, it's cold."

"So tuck them under."

"We'd be too close together. It's not big enough, your coat."

"True. Well, get a dust cover."

"Can I get a cushion instead? From under?"

"Good idea. Those are the downiest." She pointed with her glass. "Is Clare nice?"

"Yes. Very. Fancy asking a thing like that! Don't you know."

"One can't, you see. Being her mother. Really?"

"Yes, really and truly. Most people like her."

"More people than like you?"

"Far more. She's easier to like. Don't you like her?"

"One can't, as I say, tell. Of course, I think she's a frightfully good chap."

"Yes, she is. You'd like her if you got to know her." They giggled. The starving fire faltered out of flame altogether. "Should I poke it?"

Mrs Bellamy shrugged. "Just as you please. It hardly makes a difference. Do you like it here?"

"In a way. Very much in a way. But I would rather be at home."

"Here?"

"No, I didn't mean . . . how funny!"

"You'll be able to choose. Or, of course, not at all. Julian says you're all displaced persons and may feel rootless ever after. But I suspect you're the inheritors and will—" she reached for an extreme gesture, and spilled some gin—"*stalk* across the world. Why can't I talk to Clare like this?"

Penn rearranged the slipping coat over Mrs Bellamy's pointed knees, got up and took upon herself the responsibility for coaxing that day's coal ration into life. Kneeling, blowing into a half-hidden red pocket in the black, she considered the question. With the first sprung yellow flame, she sat back on her heels and turned.

"I expect it's like you said: you not knowing about her and

not letting her know about you. Perhaps it's like that in your sort of family. Not saying such things." Mrs Bellamy put her head on one side and hooded and unhooded the piercingly blue eyes once or twice while she considered the girl.

"Shrewd," she decided appreciatively. "Does it seem cold to you? No, not just the freezing rooms."

"Not cold but different," said Penn guardedly, because it had already been made clear to her that Mrs Bellamy did not appreciate her strain of energetic mysticism and she did not like to be criticised. But:

"You're changing," said Cynthia with a trace of regret. "I do hope we're not undoing your own nature in curbing.... We are very *curbed* you must feel?"

Grateful, Penn exonerated them. "No, it's good for me, I think. Like the Sonnets."

"Now there you've lost me, I confess, darling."

"Just: all the emotion is still there but curbed, if you like, by the rhymes and lines being very strict. But not left out."

Mrs Bellamy still looked quizzical so Penn thought to offer an illustration and began helpfully, "When I first fell in love—"

"When you did what?" Mrs Bellamy sat right up and swivelled her legs on to the floor. "For a moment I thought you said—"

"Fell in love," Penn enunciated more clearly. When she gabbled they could not always understand what she was saying. "With an older boy called Michael. That's how I heard about the Sonnets first, it was him told me."

"He," said Mrs Bellamy faintly.

"Pardon?" said Penn.

"It was he. Grammar."

"Really?" said Penn. "Well anyway. It was he who told me about the Sonnets and when I first read them it was all the feelings about him I recognised, that I had then, but now..."

"Feelings you *had*, darling? Are you sure? I've never felt remotely Shakespearean emotions. Feelings you had *when*?"

"Oh ages ago, more than a year, when I was eleven. And still. Shakespeare puts all the feelings very well I think."

"He *is* said to, darling; yes, he has that reputation."

"Only: now I think the marvellous thing is to keep it all rhyming and scanning as well. Curbed, like you said. That's why you and Dr Julian are so good for me. There was something a bit floppy and squishy about all that emotion. And all the Army religiousness too. The Prayer Book written-down prayers at church get it in, mostly, but in less words than our prayers made up as you go. Though I do miss the band."

Mrs Bellamy stamped once with each foot, fretful or cold, and her old fur coat slithered on to the floor. "Stop changing the subject, darling. We were talking about your falling in love, not about the Army. For once."

Penn glowered. "I wasn't."

"What?"

"Changing the subject. It was curbing. And all the things you and Shakespeare and Dr Julian *curb* are connected. Well they are to me."

"Your God and the band and what's-his-name?"

"Yes," said Penn stubbornly. On the same seat, they had to turn their heads steeply to stare. "Michael: that's his name."

Mrs Bellamy looked away to present her profile again. "This seems to require another drink," she decided.

"I'll do it."

"Thank you, darling."

Watching the girl pour alcohol expertly, Cynthia expressed a twinge of remorse. "Do I drink too much do you think?"

"We think any is too much," Penn explained soothingly; "we never touch a drop." As if that exonerated Mrs Bellamy.

"Thank you." Cynthia accepted the goodwill and the glass. "Now you must tell me all about Michael. All. I insist."

So Penn found an unlikely confidante. Cynthia, alternately shuddering and urging her to go on, displayed a fascination quite different from her polite public interest in the Army and the Banjo. Penn rehearsed and explored the detail often under her probing; until gin and boredom doused it. When Mrs Bellamy slid down into the muffling fur with a sigh, Penn, who was learning their language, knew enough to leave.

Other odd liaisons formed during that huddled winter. Miss Graham, the postmistress and interfering arbiter of village life, caught the naughtiest boy from Dagenham stealing and boxed his ears; standing on tiptoe to reach. His ears were almost as large as her hands. But the boy, whom even the toughest of London teachers dared not punish for fear of reprisals, was soon helping in the shop after school. Once seen together, an unexpected likeness was revealed between the bossy old maid and the bullying boy: both made trouble for boredom's sake. Just as strange was the deep tenderness which developed between Thos Gracey: builder—a man built like an ox—and a wispy little adenoidal girl called Shirley after the film star Temple. The neglected youngest of a large family with several uncles and no father was soon trotting smugly between Mr and Mrs Gracey into church every Sunday, her straggly hair twisted into careful curls, her runny nose perpetually wiped with solicitude by a handkerchief in Mr Gracey's enormous hand. The Coopers made congenial lodging for a plain, bad-tempered geography teacher whose chief weapon of discipline was to make naughty children sit in silence with their hands on their heads and usual method of teaching was to have the whole school shading in blank outline maps of the world with pink, green and yellow crayon according to Empires in 1901. She must have appealed to Mrs Cooper's attachment to official paper. Each of the intimacies, once established, had some evident aptness. Unfelt wants were filled in various lives formerly deprived by the limits of available company.

The lore of two cultures also mingled. If the slum children learned new facts of life—that chickens and sheep in fields, for instance, behaved just like mothers and fathers in bed—the villagers were soon calling 'Fainites!' to drop out of a game and 'Cross my heart and hope to die' when swearing truth, or when telling a lie if the fingers of the other hand were safely crossed behind the back while one hand was stretched over the left breast.

As winter began to open out into spring, the village community found itself to be, though changed, settled. The first winter of war had been full of a nervy claustrophobic tension. In blacked-out houses moping London children had to huddle closer with their unwilling hosts because of smaller fires. A shortage of candles and paraffin for lamps had made the darkness more intense and the long nights were haunted by the quiet crying of children in strange bedrooms under skies of unparalleled blackness which threatened death to their parents. When enemy bombers had failed to materialise out of those skies as expected, many of the children had returned to homely if hazardous London. Those who remained were more at home in the village because of it; and their assimilation was confirmed by the arrival of Czech soldiers at a camp near by. Compared with these total foreigners, the little cockneys seemed positively familiar and part of the community. All those strange uniforms and accents about the place made the villagers wrap the evacuated children more closely into their own families. If London had seemed remote, Prague was improbably exotic. A community which had experienced little outside influence or change in its isolated rural pattern of social life for centuries rang with various accents and accommodated a suddenly wide range of expectations and habits. It held; and absorbed by its superior strength of durable custom and geographical history only what suited it. A few families found foreign dishes tasty and Europeanised their table accordingly; most taught their invaders to conform to their traditions if they sought hospitality.

Though for the most part children had been allocated to homes arbitrarily, they now seemed settled in their adopting families and had, in reply, adopted the ethos and status of their new places. This gave Penn the distinction and faint hauteur of the Bellamy position in the neighbourhood; she and Clare were the acknowledged leaders of junior society. They became a confident double-act in school plays, and were constantly rehearsing or performing scenes from something: often Shakespeare, as the female roles in his comedies might have been written for them, and Penn could talk the elderly English teacher, Mrs James, into anything. *The Taming of the Shrew* launched their top-girl partnership with Penn ranting as the shrew and Clare her docile sister. Portia and Nerissa were obvious follow-ups: they did the trial scene, of course. *As You Like It* was plainly written for them too. Then, for a change, a version of *Pride and Prejudice* offered perfect type-casting of Jane Bennett for Clare and spirited Elizabeth for Penn.

It was accepted that they would take the best parts and that Penn would play the lead. It suited both of them and their styles suited the characters. Penn was taller and had a stronger presence, but Clare was prettier, just like the secondary girl characters. Penn learned by heart easily and lazy Clare preferred the shorter parts and more flattering costumes. So there was no rivalry; and if other girls envied the unquestioned assumption that Penn and Clare should always get the best parts, they would be reminded of what seemed to most a fact of nature: Clare was a *Bellamy*, Dr

Julian Bellamy's daughter; and Penny *lived* at the *Bellamy house.*
So that was manifestly that.

Penn was aware that what had made her eligible for their world
was being 'clever'. Before she met the Bellamys she had read for
pleasure and company and tried to do well at lessons to earn
praise. Now she did these things with a less dilatory fervour. 'Being
clever' proved passport to a more different territory than heaven;
which had always been only just beyond the white ceiling of her
bedroom or the raftered roof of the Hall. If her reading of unexpected books and A's for essays earned her first admittance to
Bellamy privileges, unspoken but evident conditions applied to
her taking up, as it were, residence in their world. One of them
was resigning her citizenship of a handy, extravagant heaven. What
she found in Hamlet, Michael, and her religion—some passionate
otherness through which eternity shafted—was not entirely acceptable. Without harshness or anything resembling ill -will, both
Bellamy parents deplored her tendency to ecstasy.

Eventually she discerned different grounds for disapproval in
their different personalities. To Mrs Bellamy it was in bad taste.
All that Blood of the Lamb intensity and Banjo vigour made her
flinch. A crudity of colour in its language seemed to hurt her eyes.
And among her muted pastels—clothes and decorations—the
garish red, yellow and blue of the Flag Penn remembered did seem
over-bright. "Sorry," she began to say. But: "Don't please apologise, darling; it's just something you'll grow out of." As though on
your fourteenth birthday, say, you paid full-fare on trains and
buses and lost your visionary truculence. In the same category of
light, fastidious exclusion Mrs Bellamy placed romantic music,
poetic drama, love and missionary zeal. When Penn mentioned that
she might convert the heathen when she grew up, Mrs Bellamy
shuddered. "But do they altogether *want* saving?" she wondered.
She would still sometimes encourage confidence about Michael but
Penn became uncomfortable at the mingling of distaste and gloating: Mrs Bellamy wore the face with which she might examine
something fascinating but nasty; like a snake. Mostly, Penn accepted her influence with interest. Mrs Bellamy so much preferred wit
to passion, the Augustans to the Romantics, Mozart to Wagner,
freesias to dahlias, that Penn modified her own 'favourites'. She
did this only partly to oblige; Mrs Bellamy's own style attracted

97

her admiration. Especially as her refinement was not an affectation; and some of Penn's emotionalism was.

Dr Bellamy's reservations were even more cogent. Penn's passions were, he intimated, imprecise. His dislike of her 'poetic' expressions had nothing to do with taste or class but only with accuracy. This was convincing as well as more congenial. He would wrinkle up his nose almost imperceptibly when she came out with some wild phrase and ask her *precisely* what she meant by the careless, euphonious words. Yet he was interested in what she had to say, and was moved to correct her expression of emotions and ideas as much by attraction to them as by concern for language. He would defend her sometimes against his own frivolous, dainty womenfolk's disposition against all extremes; quietly offering her a quieter way of putting it. This particularly appealed to Penn as he proved that the understated was not necessarily unfeeling. He would share with her sometimes the lurid landscape of a storm or the last movement of a symphony which Clare and Mrs Bellamy turned away from. But he refused to go on about it or use extravagant language; which, Penn discovered, might be unnecessary.

Something in him was left over from his marriage and his life of undistinguished scholarship and country gentility which the newcomer revived from dormancy. Though intellectually stringent, he encouraged her to describe activities and to express feelings the others avoided as soppy or crude. He made her try to understand, but not to exclude, the fervour of the Army and the robust excitements of the Banjo. He criticised only shapeless and shabby definitions and descriptions. Most valuably of all, he corrected a tendency in her to pretend to sensibilities dishonestly: she had been in danger of 'putting on' a flimsy poeticism. Clare enjoyed her bed-time stories about little Cavalier girls in crinolines, cut off from their kindred and engaged in thrilling adventures for the King; and teachers praised the pretty similes in her poems. He disdained this sentimental stuff; and something in her recognised that his criticisms were more useful to her than others' praise. She began to seek him out after school.

With the warmer days of early summer, everybody spent more time out of doors as if to compensate for the most shut-in of winters; and she usually found him reading on the lawn between the house and the orchard.

"Hallo."

"Hallo."

"Good day?"

"All right."

When he ignored her, as he sometimes did if he was interested in his book, she would wander not too far on hands and knees catching grasshoppers which she kept in matchboxes. This failing reliably to distract him, she wrote a poem about them; for which he laid his volume across his knee so as not to lose the place. Dr Bellamy nodded slowly with raised eyebrows over the page and confessed he thought it rather good; because, in spite of being poetic, it was not far from accurately observed. Glowing happily into a patch of buttercups, she heard him add that he deplored the matchbox though.

"There is a hole in the lid," she told him.

"Yes. But they can't hop."

"Mrs James gave me an A for the poem."

"Good for Mrs James. But don't you see that if they're called 'grass-hoppers' it's depriving them of identity to prevent them from hopping. You can't do that, Penn."

She chewed a piece of her own hair thoughtfully. "They don't call themselves grasshoppers. You might as well say that all us evacuees lost our identity when they unpinned our labels."

"Did you have labels?"

She could usually win Dr Julian's attention if she told him small true things plainly. For Clare's, she launched a Cavalier; for Mrs James's, a winsome simile from nature. Her only problem was which of them was right; which of her styles was *best*. She was tackling that now. She poked at buttercups and continued, "My label's in Mrs Cooper's dresser drawer now; with the Insurance. If she's taken." Peering surreptitiously through hair, she saw that she had caught him. "Only it says my age not date-of-birth so it's not much good officially now that I'm twelve. When I wanted to start school my mother said it wasn't allowed till I was five and I asked her to alter four to five but she explained how it wasn't written like that. As well as date-of-birth, of course, she said it would be cheating."

"So is preventing grasshoppers from hopping."

"But you just agreed they don't have to because we call them that!"

"No, but I think we call them grasshoppers because they have to hop," said Dr Julian; and retired behind his clouds of smoke beaming.

"Touché," Penn beamed back. "Does that mean I agree you've scored a point?"

"Yes it does. Clever you. Where did you pick that up?"

"Someone called Michael told me. He's the man I love."

"Oh." Dr Julian was typically non-committal.

"He thinks I'm too young even to write to."

"And you don't?"

"Course not. I wish he could meet you and Mrs Bellamy. You don't bother about what's suitable so much."

"That's how it seems is it? Well. What happened to him?"

"He joined the army. The proper army, I mean, not the Salvation one."

Dr Julian gave a sharp glance at this re-arrangement; but said mildly only, "Then he'll be meeting new people too and changing I expect. Poor boy," he added, toeing a matchbox to reprove her.

"Why?" Penn asked suspiciously. But he teased:

"Fancy depriving himself of your poetic letters, for instance." She grunted sulkily; looked briefly sad; then rallied.

"Mrs James gives me A's for all my poems." It was true; and she was proud of it; but hoped he would argue. She liked their arguments.

"Oh dear. How unfortunate," he said with an obliging grimace.

"Why?"

"Do *you* think they're all equal? All excellent? If you write for Mrs James, then, you'll never learn to write any better. Pity. It's not *very* well; and anyway, won't you get bored?"

"But." As long as she made protesting noises he would expound, she hoped.

"She's the arbiter? Then find a more discerning judge. And let those poor creatures out, whatever they're called in the privacy of their own family."

She slid the matchbox lid off and laid the box in the grass; but deliberately, looking at him.

"Would you read my writing?" she said, and began to pick a gnat-bite on her elbow with contorted concentration.

Hop!

Hop! HOP HOP!

He watched the first disconsolate small jump followed by joyful big leaps of freed grasshopper; then turned to her his hair-covered but glinting eyes. He appeared guarded and curious at the same time.

"If you want me to," he said mildly. "I should warn you that I may not like your writing much."

"Never mind." Her manner was inappropriately triumphant.

"What makes you suggest it?" he wondered. Her characteristic stubbornness had ousted her desire for approval, he saw; making him feel that *she* had scored a point.

"Touché?" she teased. Then, seriously: "You said to find a more discerning judge. You, I thought."

"Did you?" He looked at the empty matchbox doubtfully.

"Who else?" she questioned; catching the same or another grasshopper by scooping it up from behind cunningly in a cupped hand. "Who else is there?"

"Well it rather depends what you want," said Dr Julian.

"What you said of course: to write better."

"More than to be praised and flattered?"

"Yes."

"Or to be praised more?"

"Both, of course. As well. How else?" She nodded cheerfully then switched to a wheedling expression. "My father would help, if only I was with him." She looked evacuee-ish but put her grasshopper into the open box; confirming an impression of blackmail openly admitted. The grasshopper sat still though could escape; and rubbed its legs together with a sawing noise. Dr Julian leaned forwards didactically.

"See! Fascinating!"

"Yes, and you can't see so well in grass because it's camouflaged." Under their gaze, it sang then hopped away. "That's why I catch them," said Penn. "And I like letting them go too. It makes them happier after being shut up for a bit. They count their blessings which they don't know until they're taken away. Well, will you?" she finished, looking at him squarely and rubbing her hands together where grass had stained them.

"What? Oh, read? Yes of course."

"Thank you."

"I'd be honoured. But I warn you I may not like them as much as Mrs James or your father."

"Why not? She's a teacher and he may be self-educated but he writes at least as well as you because it gets printed in the *War Cry*."

"No no. I wasn't meaning myself superior; just with different criteria. It's only that my taste is not for the romantic at all."

"Not even Keats?"

"Not even Keats. Well, especially not Keats actually."

"Fancy," said Penn. "Was it you or Mrs Bellamy who decided to like the Augustans first? Virgil and things?" She looked pert on purpose.

"But I don't. Cynthia's the one for eighteenth century satire and the Latin poets."

"And you? What about that poem you were on about, all about Penelope?"

"That's not Roman, you dope. And it's not supposed to be about Penelope. It's about Ulysses and it's Greek not Latin."

"Oh, are they different?" said Penn loudly and happily; because she was getting better and better at making him talk to her and could do without grasshoppers now.

Clare sometimes thought that the way Penn *manipulated* was rather disgraceful. It was not in her nature to be jealous; but she observed Penn testing and finding the nerve to her own, her mother's and her father's attention with some misgiving. Wasn't it rather sly? The good thing about Penn was that you could talk openly to her about such thoughts; or rather, Clare could; but that might be because Clare's own confidently open temperament would not have kept her as a friend if it were not so.

"Isn't it rather sly?" said Clare.

"Sly's a filthy word. You beast."

"Well all right I'll take it back. But you *change* when you're with different people. I notice you doing it." Clare gave judgement enthroned at the head of her bed.

Penn screwed up her nose and nodded with an expression of disgust. "I know. So do I sometimes. Notice myself doing it."

She dropped suddenly, face down as if shot, across the foot of Clare's bed, on which Clare was sitting. She let her head hang over the side and her hair fall down into the fluff she peered at under the bed. "It's a funny thing," said Penn. "I can't seem to help it. But I think sly's a filthy word for it. I thought perhaps it meant I was going to be a great actress." Clare laughed and kicked Penn's bottom with her bare foot. "Or influence people." Each syllable puffed as Clare's foot rocked her to and fro like a bolster at the end of the bed.

"Rubbish," said Clare. "You're just a copy-cat and you imitate people so that they'll like you."

Penn bumped Clare's foot away and sat up with all the blood in her face and fluff in her hair. "It's all very well for you. You just drift through the world absolutely certain that Clare Bellamy is the nicest thing to be and that you're sure who she is."

Clare giggled. "Well it's all I can manage and I don't see the point."

But Penn looked grave. "D'you really think it's sly? It just comes naturally. I don't know what I'm like *naturally*. And lots of heroines do it. Shakespeare's even. His heroines were always dressing up as boys. And Sir Percy Blakeney was never out of disguises. And where would you draw the line? I mean, your father's always correcting my grammar . . . is it pretending if I learn to talk like him and your mother? And *socks* for heaven's sake! Is pulling them up *sly* when people are always on at me to? Trying to make them *like* me for heaven's sake?"

"You're being dopey now. You know perfectly well that's different. Everyone does things to please people—more than you, usually. But they don't *change* like you do. I wonder what you'll be like when your people come?"

So did she. Longing to see them, she worried sometimes if they would still love her; if she had changed too much. 'I want my mother' had been the chorus of these months away from home, the cry of little children, almost a meaningless reflex; how every injury or fright was expressed. Even the older children, who did not so specifically want their mothers, recognised in this atavistic cry a symbol for comfort and safety. Apart from war and separation there had been many small novel fears in the country itself. Accustomed to the dangers of city streets and town gardens, they had all recoiled from the terrors of tall grasses, from which slugs or snails might drop down into your wellingtons; new insects; bigger moths and huge spiders. Penn, moping under the bed again at the problems of change and the approaching reunion with parents who might have changed too, shot up and gathered herself into a ball at the sight of one of these.

"What is it now?" yawned Clare.

"Spider."

"But they can't hurt you." Clare pouted contemptuously at her friend screwed up at the foot of her bed.

"Oh yes they can," claimed Penn.

"How?"

"Frighten."

"More than wasps and gnats?"

"Much."

"That's silly. Wasps and gnats can hurt. Why?"

"They're so soft and furry. They seem frightened too. The way they scurry. Scared and secret along the skirting board."

"Moths too. You make an awful fuss about moths." It was true. When they beat about lamps in a hectic, flopping blindness, she had to leave the room. She tried to justify.

"They hurt themselves. Their wings and legs are liable to tear."

"Why not? I thought you hated them."

"Not hate. No, not hate at all. Just frightened."

Clare stretched in an affected way and got off the bed. "Shall I kill it?" she offered.

"No!"

Clare shrugged.

"You can't *kill* things."

"Speak for yourself," said Clare with a toss of the head, and stamped on the spider.

Though she had to look squeamishly away, Penn admitted a feeling of relief and gratitude. Clare's confident sense was often a good antidote to her sensibility and the traffic of their friendship was two-way; survived best, perhaps, through their differences.

The Carrs were taking their furlough at the end of May and had decided to make the long journey on a borrowed tandem bicycle. Ever since the visit was first mooted, Penn had looked forward to it as the end of a long deprivation. The knowledge that she would see her parents again, and at a given date, had helped her to settle down. Aware of this, the Bellamys often referred to it when she was troubled or upset. It succeeded in making time transitory, to have a definite event located in an exact future.

One of the most distressing elements in the evacuated children's condition was the uncertainty of 'the end of the war'; so that you had no way of measuring your time away from home or even of feeling settled in the village. You could not guess if it was half-way or not. The phrase, 'for the duration', was much used, and its jargonish indefinite air affected everybody's sense of time. The measuring devices of clocks, days and seasons became no longer adequate; they did not tell you what you wanted most to know.

So the Carrs' visit at the end of May had assumed a status in the Bellamy household equal to harvest and superior to the progress of the war as a way of measuring time. Each night ticked off another day 'until your people come'. Eventually it crept so close it changed from being a consolation to slip into sleep by, into an excitement which kept her awake. The date on which they would set out was firmly established for months before; but the exact day and time of arrival must depend on the state of the roads and the rate of their progress on the borrowed bike.

Long before this was likely, Penn began to wander out of the village at every free moment to wait by the hedgerow at the top of the hill on the road they must take. She strained into the distance to spy as soon as possible the longed-for sight. It was a long steep climb up to the High Street and she wanted them so strongly that she hoped to race down to meet the tandem as soon as it appeared on the horizon. Chaining daisies, chewing grasses, she would stare into the distance in a buzz of summer insects voicing her anticipation.

Throughout the last few days of May, waiting became an activity in itself; a state of suspension shared, though for less personal reasons, by all the village. The Dutch had capitulated, the Germans occupied Brussels, an Emergency Powers Act was passed by Parliament, and France was over-run at a rate which shocked, however guardedly the BBC reported it. Dr Bellamy replaced his map quietly at the end of every news and came gravely to the table. When the German Army reached Boulogne a kind of seizure paralysed conversation and all the grown-up people seemed to hold their breath. Young enough to be protected from the adult ominous events, the children sensed some crisis and the atmosphere of waiting, of an approach, seemed mixed up with the imminence of the Carrs' arrival. Others sometimes joined Penn, looking across the long green landscape deep into the dusk. Something, certainly, was to be looked for; getting nearer; might be glimpsed beyond the further hills. Everyone hung about. Only Penn thought she knew what to expect.

Dr and Mrs Bellamy had sent the warmest of invitations to the Carrs to stay at the Grange: "There is plenty of room here." The Carrs had replied politely that they would be bringing a tent and their rations in a side-car: "We do not wish to be any trouble and will enjoy the outdoor life after the confinements of London." So Penn knew that their apparition would be large and unusual enough not to confuse with a hay-cart, a misleading farm-boy's bike or the rare pedestrian or car approaching the village. She gazed until her eyes were sore; resenting occasional company. On the last three evenings, when they really might be expected, she had to be fetched in by a grumpy Clare or a kind but abstracted Dr Julian.

"You know they won't cycle by night," complained Clare. "They said so in their letter."

"Well it's not quite dark yet. They might if they were near."

With a last, longing gaze into the valley filling up with night, she would finally turn towards the Grange and dinner.

"The Belgian Army capitulated," said Dr Julian briefly, carving.

"Oh dear," said Clare. "And Penn's people didn't make it either."

Roaming out during school dinner-break next day to the now-familiar vantage point, Penn dawdled picking grasses to the crest of the hill. So that the sudden sight of them, far nearer than she had intended, half-way up the hill, was a shock.

There they were, heads down over the handle-bars of the tandem, pressing up the steep lane into the village street. Penn saw with telescopic clarity her father's hand-knitted fair-isle sleeveless pull-over shrunk up at the front through much washing to show the buttons of his braces, and the wet patches under her mother's arms. They were zig-zagging; her father always claimed this made steep hills easier on bikes, though longer. Penn felt so embarrassed and tearful suddenly that, without premeditation, she found she had slipped through the gate into the field and stood hidden behind the hedge. The sickly sweet of hawthorn blossom plunged her into nausea as she spied through its thorns at the strangeness of her mother and father. Mother's arms were blotchy red except for a white knot of roughened skin at the point of each elbow and there was a patch of sunburn at the top of her back, around her bun. She had a very short neck and this plump hummock of red flesh like a collar had one crease in it. Her bare pedalling legs were lumpy with varicose veins. Father was quite a good brown colour but the rolled-up sleeves of his shirt were white, not patterned like the outside of the stuff, and his cycle clips showed black office-y shoes and green knitted socks with a brown arrow-design wavering sideways up his ankle.

As they went by, Father panted: "Nearly there now, Cissie." But they *were* there; for she was their arduous destination.

They pedalled on betrayed and glimpsed through a thicket of thorns like those in the crown of the sad man who knocked at a closed door perpetually above the fireplace at home. Home? Where was it now? She had prayed for them and praised them; been homesick; now hid. Horrified, she began to run across the field around whose edge the road curved, to reach the other, the Grange, end of the High Street before them. She found she was sobbing. They must be so tired too. She arrived painfully ahead of them and had to watch it all again. This time they had their heads up and seemed to be looking for her; but did not recognise the taller child in one of Clare's frocks and went past, straining beyond her to find her, their faces furrowed with doubt and hope.

Fortunately Dr Bellamy reached the gate of the Grange drive just as they approached and stepped into their path with a friendly unemphatic smile. "You must be the Carrs," he said, tucking his pipe into his pocket and reaching out a blunt freckled hand to help support the tandem as both riders put one foot on the ground.

"Yes. Dr Bellamy?" Major Carr wiped his hand on his trousers and offered it.

"Now where can Penn have got to?" wondered Dr Julian. He saw her past their shoulders, crumpled against the telephone kiosk with tears streaming down her face. He stared and coughed to register that both parties had somehow awkwardly missed each other. Ducking and shuffling, he looked at a loss. At last Penn came forward and hid her face in her mother's full, appalling bust. From this concealment, she could let out a groan of pardonable tears.

"There there," said Cissie. "Over-excitement I expect," she told Dr Bellamy. The tandem stood toppling. It was not only the child who was disconcerted. Major Carr and Dr Julian exchanged an uneasy look.

"We expected you last evening," said the Doctor helpfully above the bowed heads of Penn and her mother and the tilting frame of the tandem.

"Yes, it was unlucky, we camped only just outside the village. All the signposts are down and we didn't know how near we were."

"You brought a tent then?"

"Yes, and food." Father nodded at the side-car. Penny looked up to recognise how much weight they had laboured to bring so far on their own legs and began to howl afresh.

"Do let's go in," said Dr Bellamy, abashed.

"I'm afraid we are rather travel-stained," said Major Carr, even more downcast. So that Dr Bellamy enlisted the bad war news he had intended to delay; it seemed anything must be a relief to this unmanageable family reunion.

"You won't have heard the news then?" he asked.

"Not for several days."

Father took off his cycle clips and followed with a daunted air up the drive of the Grange.

"We're evacuating France, I'm afraid. It's over in Europe. Our forces are being rescued from Dunkirk. But the casualties are appalling."

The men looked gratefully at each other. "How dreadful," said Major Carr, straightening under this bracing news. "Now we really are on our own." It made them all feel better, more together, to be so endangered.

But Cissie and Penn stumbled along behind, uncomfortably embracing so as not to have to look at each other. It was a hot day and Cynthia Bellamy waited with a welcoming smile at the wide-open door of the deeply forbidding house.

"How lovely," gulped Cissie unhappily, "what a beautiful place, pet."

In such a village, all strangers stand out; it was only imagination which made Penn feel her people more flagrant, out of place. She was grateful for Dunkirk, which took the edge off their advent with its talkable topic. And the sense of imminent invasion and isolation in which all England now folded itself up made a ground for loss and mourning which conveniently obscured the personal loss and estrangement which neither Penn, nor her parents, nor the Bellamys who felt responsible, knew how to deal with. They put the strain of the week of the visit down to the pressure of world events; and waved goodbye with suitable tears.

When the tandem had wobbled out of reach down the hill, Penn began to run after it. They did not see her or turn back, and she did not really want to catch them. But she ran on for a while to try to escape the feeling that their departure was a shameful relief and that relief made it a bereavement which was, in some indefinable way, permanent.

That night, Dr Julian scratched at the door of her room. "All right?" he asked, sitting on her bed without turning the light on. She was crying quietly and did not answer. "You miss them, I expect? Your parents?"

"Yes," she said, "but. . ."

"You miss what you remembered before they came?" The bed creaked in the thick warm dark of country quiet. A train far off wailed through black England. "That's gone for good. The past is always lost. While you cry for it, the present is joining it. Learn to live *now*."

She twisted and sat up at the unusual emphasis in his manner. The white of a handkerchief became visible to his accustoming eyes. She said, "But nothing is ever only now. Things are more real to me when I think them over afterwards. Or before."

"Spoken like a true writer," he said, encouragingly; relieved to see the white flag of her hanky mopping up.

"No, but don't you see," she argued: "it means while they were here they spoiled what I remembered and missed before. They knew it too, that's what's so awful. I feel so sorry for them."

He went to the window and drew back curtains on to a blacker dark. "My Aunt Dolly used to say that compassion was self-pity extrapolated on to others. She wouldn't allow those big muddly concepts in the house." A muffled laugh, half sob, reached him.

"But now when I feel homesick, what do I feel sick *for*? It's a terrible position to be in."

"Rubbish. Self-pity. Don't indulge it, it's the least attractive vice. Be at home everywhere. Use your wry advantages."

"I can't, I don't feel it."

"Well try. Be a brave girl. They've had to let you go; the least you can do is learn to be able to go back, for their sake. You'll only be able to do that if you become yourself." His tone was unusually firm. She slid down into the bed. He turned towards her darkness, drawing the curtains closed behind him. He coughed, and said gruffly: "I don't know what Aunt Dolly would have said, I'm sure; but I feel damned sorry for you all too. Goodnight, Penn. Feel at home here as long as you can."

When he had gone, Penn got up and stared into the night, thinking of her little mother sleeping tiredly on hard ground; prisoners of war, perhaps Michael, cut off beyond the sea in stranger countries; all not at home any more. Thinking over what Dr Julian had said, she wondered if he were tempted to self-pity himself. He seemed unable to go anywhere, when perhaps he would prefer it. And Mrs Bellamy, who complained of being too much at home in a house she could not escape from. Perhaps he was right: perhaps she was lucky in a way.

During that summer, other parents who dared the journey found themselves more lost than their vaguely-embarrassed offspring. Such casualties weighed light against the fall of France. They neither expected nor were given much sympathy but took the train home trying to be glad that the children had settled down so well. Few made a second visit: to feel outsiders and also grateful and helpless was demoralising.

Their children felt the same, and doubly deprived. Homesickness became a chronic and confusing condition for which there could be no treatment: one of those ailments which have been proved to have no cause or cure, but make their sufferers hurt all the same. Time eased the split emotions which confused anguish; and even restored a capacity for straightforward fear when the Blitz began. When London parents were being killed in horrifying numbers, in nightly raids reported by the BBC, the children could miss them again. Their adopting families could at the same time express more affectionate sympathy from their increased security. No likelihood of their evacuee being snatched back to London at short notice now.

Now they were all stuck, and would make the best of it; as isolated as England. There was a kind of bitter relief in it; the kind Cynthia expressed, trapped in the inevitability of the Grange.

PART THREE

THE AMERICAN SUMMER—as the village would remember it—was unprecedentedly summery. Whether or not it was actually hotter or longer than other summers was a matter of opinion; it was something about the atmosphere.

Children reared in London, even those with gardens and a green-fingered mother like Mrs Carr, were surprised for the third year running by the extravagance of country gardens; so profusely planted that there was no earth at all visible among the flimsy pastels of sweet peas, the densely-packed buds of roses and the violent scarlets of geraniums.

Various nationalities had briefly occupied the nearby camp, arriving and departing as secretly as their mysterious training and the missions which snatched them back to oblivion. Their transitoriness, and their foreign accents in the formerly isolated community, made the London children seem more and more settled residents. The Americans at least spoke a similar language, like the children, but more familiar from films; and they penetrated more deeply into village life. Their affluence and cheerfulness, combined with warm weather, made 1942 a more spreading, outdoor, crowded summer. The High Street was always full of people. They perched on the churchyard wall, leaned on trees, gathered around the pond or strolled up and down; and even the local people talked to each other more.

The climax of the hot expansive months was an August Thursday, the day of the Fête. This was a combination of school breaking-up (they ordered these things differently where help with harvesting was a factor) and the departure of the unit. Also, there seemed some subtler need for an occasion. The lull in the war and the lassitude of the weather made people more relaxed but uneasy. They felt weakened from the resolve which hardship and danger after Dunkirk had forced upon them, but knew it was not over yet. The idea of a party gave everybody a purpose. The Americans were to contribute a bounty of food in short supply and a dance band; the village would provide flags, side-shows, a combined choir and a school play.

The collaborators seemed more like rivals when they filled the village hall with frantic confusion on the actual morning. Mrs Hayle, the new English teacher, was rehearsing the play on the platform while village ladies laid tables and a dazed-looking GI strummed loudly on the out-of-tune piano. In another corner a massed choir of school, church and Women's Institute was practising 'The Stars and Stripes for Ever'. The rest of the hall was filled with people decorating as if to compete with the gardens outside. Already as little of the earth-coloured wood of walls and ceiling was visible as soil in gardens.

"Children!" called Mrs Hayle in a shout as tiny as her fluttering hands and miniature madonna face with dark hair drawn back severely. "Pay attention, please!" She glared up at them—for all the big girls were taller than she was—in pale but impressive fury. Since she rarely raised her voice, she communicated an extraordinary despair by this minute extravagance, and they tore their eyes from the distractions to struggle on with their lines.

Mr Cooper, adept at ladders from his experience of lopping trees, was climbing slowly in a necklace of bunting to the very peak of the pitched roof. He waved recklessly when he reached the top and the long ladder undulated from its foothold in the centre of the floor. Mr Gracey the builder rested one foot on its lowest rung and held it firmly in his big used hands, red as beef and chipped by his trade. Mr Cooper was carrying a hammer between his teeth, the way Spanish dancers are pictured biting on a flower-stem. It gave him a rakish look and stretched his usually inexpressive face into a fierce grin. Holding on with one hand, he reached into his pocket with the other for tacks and began to nail a tape of pennants to the arch of rafters.

"Hail to the chief," sang the sopranos, and 'hey bob a re bob' went the piano.

Dr Bellamy and the baker were setting up trestle tables along the sides of the hall. While they wrestled with hinged props to support the long boards, eager ladies stood by with white cloths unfolded in their hands, as poised and impatient as matadors. As soon as one table was safely balanced, they flung a cape of snowy linen over it and shook out the next.

Big wicker baskets and tea-chests stood open in the middle of the hall disgorging bright stuffs and tinsel, Christmas tree baubles, Chinese lanterns, the long, coloured ribbons of the Maypole, and masses of Union Jacks in various sizes. The trappings of all celebrations—May Day, the Silver Jubilee, Christmas, several Coronations—were to decorate this desperate festival. Its purpose of farewell rumbled like thunder just beyond the horizon of its gaiety.

Mrs Hayle cried "Stop!" as if in pain. She had a habit of pressing the fingers of both hands to her forehead as though their voices made her head ache, even without the addition of such hammerings and music, such a constant banging of the door as more women arrived with Harvest tea-pots and home-cooked contributions.

"I'd meant us to have a dress rehearsal this afternoon but it's obviously out of the question with all this distraction." She cast a grieved look over the hall, now fluttering with flags of the allied nations in dyed cheese-cloth. Mr Cooper gave an extra loud blow to a nail and some of the ladies shuffled cutlery with a clatter. Anna Hayle was no more popular in the village than with her pupils. She had come to share the home of a married sister after her officer-husband had been killed and people were prepared to be sorry for her. But she rejected any expression of sympathy with quivering narrow nostrils and an air of distaste which seemed critical. The school authorities had been glad to get her but everyone else was less enthusiastic. This pinched, pained woman might be, as they said admiringly, a university graduate of rare academic distinction, but she had none of the attributes of a successful teacher and exuded a tight, unspoken misery which evoked hostility rather than pity in colleagues and neighbours.

In person, she was extremely small, almost to the point of deformity. Her tiny feet, little face and frail hands made people feel clumsy; and they liked her less for that.

She succeeded Mrs James and taught English; so Penn had more cause than most to resent her. Mrs Hayle gave nobody 'A' for anything, as she said that nothing they could write was likely to have the excellence 'A' implied. Penn got lower marks in her best subject and had to try to explain in letters home that her work was not suddenly falling off. This was an embarrassing thing to have to do; it smacked of excuses, unconvincing. Dr Bellamy involved himself by endorsing Penn's explanations to her father. He also pointed out to Penn—who though hurt was impressed by Mrs Hayle's argument—that it was inappropriate for teachers to grade children's work by reference to the greats of English Literature. As he gently put it to Mrs Hayle herself, such a policy might lead to curious results: if Shakespeare, say, deserved an A for *Hamlet* he might warrant only a B-plus for *Two Gentlemen of Verona*; bringing Keats, for instance, to at best B-minus and Swinburne a pathetic average of C. So that when one reached Penn's latest and best poem one would be bound to travel further down the alphabet than was generally acceptable. About H-minus-minus perhaps? Mrs Hayle flushed at this but continued to offer B-plus as her highest mark.

The Bellamys quite often invited Mrs Hayle to drinks or tea, and she came as close to relaxing in their company as was possible to her nature. However, she was so determined to show no favouritism that Clare and Penn in class on succeeding days seemed rather to be punished than rewarded for the liberty of having approached her in a human context.

Clare detested her; but Penn was fascinated. She followed Mrs Hayle with a wary expression and enlisted for all her extra lessons, because the territory she led to was of such interest. Mrs Hayle shuddered at Penn's crude excitement over her introduction to new poets but could not altogether withhold her most beloved authors. There were, after all, few in the village who wanted to know anything she had to communicate to them. They made an odd couple: the gawky fourteen-year-old stooping with clumsy eagerness and faint belligerence over the tiny, bitter woman who looked up with cross absorption. There was a queer compound of hostility and attraction between them and they often treated each other nastily.

The casting of the play for the American party had been an occasion for Mrs Hayle to be particularly cruel to her unfriendly disciple. The girls had been saving up *As You Like It*; it was another play Shakespeare seemed to have designed especially for them. Penn was plainly Rosalind with absent parents, a desire to dress up as a boy and the largest part; Clare was made for the more feminine Celia—cousin and confidante at whose home the disinherited girl lived. They really were very keen on this one and knew it would go well in the village if they 'brought out the meaning'. Mrs Hayle agreed to the text adapted by Penn with a few quibbles (Penn had been cutting out the dull bits for years now; even after Arthur Mee's emendations were abandoned, she took him as a precedent for more swingeing editing) and announced auditions. Auditions? "It's unnecessary," said Clare; but Penn nudged her into acceptance. Though unexpected, auditions would surely prove a formality, and Penn had already learned most of the scene.

Mrs Hayle heard the London accents with a displeasure which verged on anguish. The local country children appalled her ear almost as horribly; her sister's long residence in the village prevented them from being unfamiliar or quaint. Only Clare's vowels permitted her a respite from wincing, and Clare was cast as Rosalind.

All baulked; including Clare. Even other girls who had been envious felt outraged at so careless and insulting a break with tradition. "We don't do it that way," they informed her firmly. Anna Hayle flushed but, facing unanimous sullen disapproval, expressed her sour decision that she could not endure to hear Shakespeare so massacred and the production must be abandoned.

After a few mutinous days, the headmistress—who though only an LRAM to Mrs Hayle's first class MA from Oxford, had a grasp of the psychology of the community and was not averse to the local conviction that the more letters you had after your name the better —proposed *The Bishop's Candlesticks* instead. Mrs Hayle closed her eyes briefly as if in pain and agreed. A sulky truce reigned over rehearsals. She insisted on Clare for the Bishop who was on stage throughout. Penn might act the Convict.

Penn had never considered that how she talked was other than proper English. She was less mortified than grimly interested. She began to listen and practise vowels privately, while continuing to play the Convict's part in cockney.

"Well, I suppose it is in character," sighed Mrs Hayle. She lost a good deal of Penn's respect by failing to discern that the cockney accent was actually becoming exaggerated as Penn had to put it on to conceal her increasingly Bellamy pronunciations. Penn was not one to revenge such a slight un-noticed. She made her plans. The change in her accent was gradual and uninteresting enough for the Bellamys not to register it, and at school she slid about among her available ways of speech unheeded. They all shouted in the playground in quite different voices from those they used in class anyway and there was everywhere a mingling of country, London and American intonations and vocabulary that summer.

"*I'm a beast now and they made me what I am*," the Convict insisted in penetrating soprano cockney above the boogie-woogie beat in a lull of choir practice.

"*They chained me up like a wild animal, they lashed me like a hound*." Mrs Hayle's poised hand and expression suggested that she was preparing to abandon the rehearsal; but Penn with an aggrieved look ignored the signs. She was, she suggested, on Mrs Hayle's side against the obtrusive activity of the hall, and she might as well appreciate it; and even if she did not Penn was not going to stop now as she especially relished the next bit.

"*I fed on filth, I was covered with vermin, I slept on boards and I complained. Then they lashed me again. For ten years, ten years. Oh God!*"

"That will do," said Mrs Hayle with a note of shrillness.

"*Oh God!*" groaned Penn again, taking advantage of the possibility that she had not heard, and of the text.

"Quite hopeless to continue in these circumstances," insisted Mrs Hayle, quelling Penn with her brimmingly brown eyes. "You know your parts and moves and I expect you to be dressed and ready to perform at this end of the hall by seven. So."

Her shrug was wasted: most of her cast turned away at once. "Clare Bellamy and Penelope Carr stay behind if you please." Penn was in fact paying attention, but Clare sighed ostentatiously and slumped her whole body in a sighing gesture.

Mrs Hayle eyed her severely. "Yours are the major roles, and the Bishop, Clare, demands rather more dignity than you are apparently prepared to muster. It's the longest part and you really must try." Yet she seemed faintly beseeching; as though wanting to win over her strongest enemy in spite of having no manner but sternness to employ. Penn and Clare both resented this discrimination though for opposite reasons. Through Mrs Hayle they had begun also to resent each other. All three glowered.

In her precise little voice with its prim vowels, Mrs Hayle continued, "Your robe may help: you'll remember to collect it from the Vicar?"

"Of course," said Clare contemptuously.

Her failure with the Bellamy girl drove Mrs Hayle to unpredictable alternations between charmless coaxing and anger. She did not attempt to make anyone else like her. Inevitably Clare despised her most for this attitude to herself. She sighed again noisily. Penn would have welcomed as much attention; which was no doubt why she was denied it.

"Just something rather shabby, Penelope, for the Convict."

"Well, I thought perhaps . . ."

"Don't overdo it," pleaded Mrs Hayle with pained narrowing of nostrils. She turned away. "It's a shoddy little playlet," she told nobody in particular. "I hardly suppose it matters what you do with it."

The girls almost exchanged a look; then, remembering that they were not talking, peeled away to opposite sides of the hall, leaving the white withered bud of a woman alone.

Men on ladders were still draping loops of pennants strung on white tape from rafter to rafter. The American sergeant and Mr Cooper were in charge here; and would call to the curate and the grocer, propped against opposite walls, to take up a bit of slack or let out some more flags until all strings drooped at the same level. Dr Bellamy was now helping the blacksmith to do something rather clumsy at the windows with Christmas paper-chains. These refused to hang straight and, as Dr Bellamy had a particularly bad eye for symmetry, none of the big paper bells meant to be central was quite in the middle. Jim Perkins the blacksmith had trouble handling such fragile things with his big hands and paper kept tearing. Sergeant Bickmeyer, inspecting, told them off roundly. It had been a bad piece of casting and Bellamy and Perkins gave way to Farmer Gantry's two lads willingly. The sergeant set the discards to the more suitable task of lifting and carrying, as they were both strong men.

The white cloths on the trestle tables were now submerged beneath platefuls of bright food. They looked like snowy flower-beds filled with blooms. Mrs Bellamy had been in earlier to deliver scores of small cakes in frilled cases of impartially patriotic red, white and blue collected from outlying cottage cooks. Now Miss Graham the postmistress was busy rearranging Cynthia's placing of them. She was bossily set upon a completely symmetrical arrangement: if there was a large bowl of trifle at one end of a long table there should be one at the other. A subtler pattern was introduced with buns and biscuits, and jellies towered like sand-castles towards the back. Miss Graham's flower garden was un-equalled for its meticulous edging of blue and white lobelia and the perfect order of contrasting colours behind. The tables now began to look like her herbacious border. When the Vicar's wife set down a dish of strawberries carelessly, Miss Graham tutted loudly and removed it quickly. Mrs Fawcett apologised and was sent back to the Vicarage for another bowl.

"To balance," said Miss Graham sternly.

"Yes, of course," said Mrs Fawcett, blushing.

Miss Graham kept glancing in a calculating way at one par-ticular table which was only half laid because at one end a mixed party of school teachers, farmers' wives and servicemen was still buttering bread and cutting Spam for sandwiches. This presented a problem as Miss Graham must arrange the other end with an eye on ultimate symmetry. Her impatience grew until the headmistress dared to tick her off; saying that if they had made sandwiches any earlier they would be too dry to eat by tea-time. Miss Graham retired looking cross.

She employed her bad temper and recovered her dominant status by complaining loudly that it was difficult enough to have to step over the decorating litter strewn everywhere without having the schoolchildren all over it as well. Miss Hull stood up with dignity, waved a buttery knife in one hand and a slice of bread in the other, and called in her loudest Assembly voice for the children's atten-tion. "Clear the Hall," she ordered, "go home for your dinners, and behave nicely at the Fête. Be off with you then," she finished, with a last eloquent flourish of the knife, and sat down again with the air of a person in authority, glaring at Miss Graham. The town and country children picked their way through paper chains and tinsel, jumping over tea-chests and hampers, skirting the laden tables with deliberately risky closeness, quick to catch and exploit divided authority. Miss Graham trembled but nothing was actually upset and she satisfied herself with a deft arrangement of indivi-dual trifles frilled with stretched crepe paper in red, white or blue and the placing of additional stars in cut-out cardboard to emphasise the American aspect of the colour-theme.

Julian Bellamy caught Penn in conversation with Mr Perkins—Clare had already left—and suggested they walk home to lunch together as Cynthia was using the car to ferry further bounty from outer farmhouses. Penn looked stealthy and agreed with a dark look at the blacksmith to impose secrecy.

The interior of the hall was by now so gaudy that outside did not present so strong a contrast. Bright flower-beds around its drab brown weather-boarding appeared rather an extension of the colour inside. But after the stuffiness of the hall Penn sniffed the astonishing smells deeply, puckering her mouth to make her nose wide to sensation. Dr Julian was wearing the tweed jacket which exactly matched his gingery greying hair. He looked particularly like himself as he paused to light his pipe beside Miss Graham's pillar box. Penn lagged to a standstill and gazed at vivid flower-beds and square green lawns intently.

"I often think," said Dr Julian between puffs at his reluctant pipe, "that Miss Graham's garden is more like gardens were meant to be than any other garden I know. A sort of archetypal, absolute garden. Real, almost."

Penn looked from the garden to his face. "That's what I was just thinking. Sort of."

Drawing on his pipe, he launched them into walking again. "About Miss Graham's garden?"

"About everything. It seems more real at some times. How d'you mean, *almost*? More. As if you recognised something you knew already but only sometimes see like it should be."

Dr Julian stabbed a sideways look from under his concealing fringe of thick thatch-like hair; with tattered thatch of a cottage roof behind him. "Pure Platonism," he said. But for once she did not rise to his bait and ask him about the word. He saw her mind grasshopper. "What are you thinking?"

"I was thinking . . ." she paused, frowning. "Lighting your pipe, you reminded me of Michael. The day I met him he lit a cigarette just like that. Well, not exactly, because it was autumn and in a wood; and his flame was the colour and shape of leaves, somehow. Whereas your flame was squatter because of sucking through your pipe and more orange because of summer, so more like Miss Graham's wallflower petals. And it all went click in a bit of my mind, as if the moments were the same. Leaf-flames and petal-flames, your match and Michael's. Funny."

"Very," Dr Julian agreed gruffly; "but not unprecedented. He really did make an impression, Michael, didn't he? How long ago? Years and years." He mocked with a mild glance.

"Well. But at least he writes to me now."

"Of thoughts like this? Of love?"

"Of course not, it wouldn't be suitable. I'm still only fourteen after all."

"I see. You agree now what's suitable?" he teased. "Let's hope the rest of us conform."

"You and Mrs Bellamy taught me," she complained.

"But what might you have taught us?"

Michael's first letter had arrived in early spring, re-addressed from London. Yawning to the breakfast table, Penn had stopped dead at the sight of it beside her plate. "Michael," she had gulped in a voice mounting so suddenly from drowsiness to ecstasy that both Julian and Cynthia Bellamy looked up from their own correspondence.

"Really, darling? How can you tell?" Cynthia had asked, with rare interest, watching the way the girl held the envelope as though it were communication enough for the time being; as though touching it should be fully savoured.

Julian had murmured deprecatingly, "She's unlikely to know hordes of soldiers with Field Post-office addresses."

"Why not?" Cynthia had too sharply argued. "Lots of boys from her Banjo and the Band must have been called up by now. Don't you want to open it and find out, darling?" She pushed her plate away and lit a cigarette.

"In a minute."

Penn missed the inappropriately quarrelsome air of the Bellamy exchange in euphoric wonderment. "Michael," she said in awe. The handwriting, plump but angular, went with art training; and though she had never seen it before she was determined to recognise Michael's hand in it. As well as the hand of destiny in her instant recognition. Eventually she opened the letter with religious carefulness.

Its manner was entirely familiar and immediately counteracted her devout significance. He wrote that there seemed to be this paper about and, as you did not have to pay for stamps, it seemed extravagant not to take advantage. As she had once measured her increased height against him, now she discovered she must have grown up because she recognised youthful uncertainty beneath the defensively jocular tone: he had seemed so extremely old and sophisticated when they first met and he was seventeen. He wrote from an unspecified war-front:

'And I should like to think the censor will have a problem if I tell you that I look well in my desert boots; as they have become a kind of unofficial uniform among some troops who are not necessarily fighting in the desert.' He name-dropped some authors she had heard of and some she had not. She would add them to her library list later.

'Are you still an Ovalteeny? I am still mad about Turner, especially after falling through skies—and what will the censor make of that I wonder.'

She paused to wonder too. "He must be a paratrooper," she triumphantly deduced.

"Highly probable, with an Airborne Division as address," said Dr Julian crisply; but his curtness was directed more at the avid expression in Cynthia's eyes behind her smoke-screen. At the end of his letter, Michael said he presumed she was used to doing real joined-up writing now; and added in a flare of brackets that this was his way of hoping she would reply.

She did, of course. The correspondence took a large place in her life despite all the things they did not say. Both postured, showing how clever they were rather than anything they felt. Through lines of deadly battles they exchanged her poetic descriptions of nature for his recognisable imitations of Hemingway's curt style. Sometimes he quoted French at her affectedly and made her wrestle with the dictionary. As a side-effect, this improved her position in the French class. Her excess and his dearth of adjectives told them little about each other of any importance; except that they were still in contact and at loggerheads.

The arrival of Michael's letters beside her breakfast plate, and the preening mysteriousness of her writing back (sometimes checking spelling, metaphor, or a curious French word with Dr Julian) made Michael an equivocal presence in the Bellamy household. Preoccupied with her own part, and trying to keep things like grasshoppers and *The Bishop's Candlesticks* out of her letters as perhaps childish, Penn hardly registered the effect on Mrs Bellamy and Dr Julian.

As she walked beside the doctor on the day of the Fête, she was surprised to hear him ask with uncharacteristic peevishness: "This

Michael of yours: is he real, d'you think? Or another figment of your over-fertile imagination?"

They walked on a step or two through clear glittering scented sunlight while she looked reproachful but considered the question. "It's something he stands for. What he made me feel is real and the letters prove it somehow. Though not in what they say."

Dr Julian's eyes dropped before her obstinate gaze. "Quite," he said.

"Your whatnot again? Like Miss Graham's garden? Only, love?" Though love had not been a Bellamy notion, Cynthia's curiosity had encouraged Penn to flaunt the thin manila envelopes. Dr Julian grunted. They crossed the road into the sudden shade of an ancient elm tree over the stile into fields. He changed the subject abruptly. "And what extravagance are you hatching with Perkins?"

"It's to do with the play. I'm the convict."

"Yes, I know."

"I want to be dirty."

"Oh?" said Dr Julian, carefully noncommittal.

"Can I borrow some old trousers of yours? That it doesn't matter getting dirty?"

"Certainly," he said. "What were you supposed to do?"

"Mrs Hayle said slacks. But I'd rather."

"Yes, of course. No problem. Clare's the Bishop isn't she?"

"Yes. In a lovely purple thing from the church. I thought—" She stopped. Aware that she might be caught out in some ulterior motive, she hesitated; but preferred after all to be understood. "I thought I, well *it* would be better if I was more of a contrast than just slacks and a jumper as Mrs Hayle said."

Dr Julian puffed and walked in attentive silence.

"So if I could wear very old real trousers and a cap I'm borrowing from Mr Cooper and dirty it all and my face with oily soot from Mr Perkins' forge . . . it would be more, well, realistic."

"And your face?"

His interest without alarm encouraged further confidences.

"Actually I thought I'd do my hair funnily as well; part it the other way so that it hangs down unevenly, and put dirt on it," she confided. He discerned that any initial malice in her plan was now submerged in sheer enthusiasm.

"Is Mrs Hayle expecting this?" he queried mildly.

"We never got round to a dress rehearsal," she evaded.

He stopped to knock his pipe out on the last tree trunk before the open meadow. Penn watched him, forced to recall her plan's genesis in pique that Clare had the more glamorous part and Mrs Hayle liked her better.

"It'll certainly upstage the Bishop," he said at last, smiling with a trace of ruefulness. "You'll steal the show; which was the idea I expect? Incidentally, burnt cork is better than soot."

Coming out into full sunlight again, she was forced to blink. Buttercups formed a crust of creamy gold on the sweet curve of pale green; made the horizon blurred yellow.

"Not only," she protested. "It will make the play better too. Me so poor and desperate will make the Bishop kinder."

"Less kind, surely?"

"Well, it's in the story, in the words too. How he had to steal with his wife starving. It will be more *dramatic*."

"Yes it will certainly be that. Does Clare know?"

"Nobody knows."

"She'll see when you get dressed up though, won't she?"

"I suppose so."

"So why not tell her about it this afternoon? She could help with the dirt. And you two 'not talking' makes meals awkward—passing things and so on. And so much duller."

"Yes, all right," said Penn. Clare was not really to blame for queening about as the Bishop. It was Mrs Hayle's fault.

Larks rose in the bright air, their clear notes fountained.

"Poor Mrs Hayle," said Dr Julian. "She may be somewhat surprised."

"So what?" said Penn. "She's rotten at producing and nasty to children. Especially me."

"What sort of nasty?"

"Sarcastic."

"Yes, that's the worst," he agreed.

They had been looking down at their feet moving through tall stalks over matted grass. Now Dr Julian looked up and Penn heard him catch his breath. She followed his eyes' direction. Across the horizon at the top of a gentle hill two people were outlined against lucid blue sky in silhouette.

"Isn't that Mrs Bellamy?" Penn exclaimed, staring.

Dr Julian grabbed her elbow to turn her at a right-angle to

their former course and hurried her towards the hedge. "But I recognise the dress she's wearing," the girl protested as her elbow was pulled ahead of the rest of her. She twisted herself free to turn back. She saw that the two figures on the horizon were joined by a loop of silhouette black. One ahead of the other, they were linked by a thread of arms tied in a knot of hands. It was Penn's turn to gasp.

"Actually," she said, "a lot of people in the village have dresses like that," and hurried on obediently at Dr Julian's side, away from the couple holding hands on the hillside.

The village had been welcoming when the Americans arrived. After so much experience of invasion it had developed a grudging, unflappable resignation towards the incursion of strangers. The Americans' eagerness to join in local life, and what they offered in return, led to the adoption of one of them by most families who already had an evacuee. But the child was made to feel actually more one of the family. The prosperous newcomers repaid hospitality with nylons and Spam; which cost them less than the raw need of the displaced children and bought them a less intimate acceptance. So they were popular with the Londoners as well as with the locals. Most evacuees discovered that 'our American' improved their diet and made them feel even more at home.

No so Penn. Chris Lester, a shy, scholarly ex-university teacher from Philadelphia, put her nose out of joint. The Bellamys were as interested in his experience as they had been in hers. Worse: he himself was an anthropologist and further damaged her sense of being special by treating her unusual background as no more curious than the agricultural system in which he now found himself—almost untouched by the Industrial Revolution!—and considerably less than the tribal systems in East Africa he planned to investigate after the war. Otherwise he treated her as just a kid.

In the early days, Penn was particularly jealous of Dr Bellamy's stolen attention; and it seemed a just retribution when Chris began to occupy Mrs Bellamy's time more. This not only restored the companionship of Dr Julian, who seemed to seek her out more than before, but introduced a new element into her habit of suspect intimacy with Cynthia. "No, come in, darling, it's all right," Cynthia would call if Penn retreated on finding her alone with Chris in the drawing-room. She was curiously eager to take Penn with them on walks and to keep her with them while they talked and drank in the lengthening light evenings.

Because Penn could not follow their conversation—its ostensible subject-matter was often beyond her—she was perhaps more alert to tones of voice, movements of ice or air, sudden flares of argument and resonant silences. She decided some time before they did that they were falling in love. After all, she was the expert in romantic passion; which Mrs Bellamy had so often decried. Certainly at first Mrs Bellamy's determination to keep her with them seemed an attempt to ward off the emotion itself. Later, Penn was sometimes not wanted but still required often to be around. Her position as neither an outsider nor a member of the family made her the ideal chaperone and it perhaps eased the extreme loneliness of Cynthia's situation to have the conniving girl as sympathetic witness.

Penn and Dr Julian walked on towards the house with eyes down in uncomfortable silence. Both must have known; it was the other's knowing which embarrassed them. The cut-out image of Chris and Cynthia, with its blob of clasped hands, moving along the rim of gold at the edge of the curved earth, had a drama which made it linger on the retina. It was like when you stared at a light, thought Penn, and then when you shut your eyes you saw the lamp-shape black in your eye. This black picture had turned too bright once they looked away from it.

Her enjoyment of a conspiratorial role in an intense adult emotion had gradually lost its charm and now died altogether. At first it had satisfied her to see Cynthia's brightened feverish eyes: that cool lady's excitement seemed to endorse, even to justify, Penn's own inclinations. Soon a snapping tension had taken its place; as uncomfortable as an elastic hat-band under the chin. Her convert to love's extremes regarded her sometimes as an ally, but sometimes seemed irked and irritable. And she was definitely not happy, as she had been at first.

Only that morning, before rehearsals, Cynthia had delayed her by talking in her new indecorous way over breakfast.

"Don't you find the world a very puzzling and ridiculous place?"

"I ought to be getting off to the hall, Mrs Bellamy."

"Can you remember—I keep remembering—when you first

came here? I didn't appreciate how out-of-water you must have felt. Yet you seem to accept all those idiotic conventions we imposed on you now. But still—" Mrs Bellamy waved toast and spoke wildly—"you might allow madness as a condition too." The big girl shuffled protestingly at the side of the table.

"Well, I'm used to it from Hamlet and the woman next door was queer. Mrs Parker," she added helpfully.

"But you don't succumb to it? Didn't feel, when everythting you knew changed, that you could or might?"

"What, go mad? No. I think I'm too young for it."

Cynthia grinned bleakly. "You are comical sometimes." But she seemed to regret, even to resent, that the truculent visionary extremes of her awkward guest had been abdicated; though at her insistence. Pushing her cup away with inappropriate emphasis, she complained, "You go along with our standards and things so easily. As if the flags and trifles and party mattered, or what Miss Graham thinks. I find it intolerable. My brother couldn't face our sort of life after the trenches. I didn't understand then. That it might become difficult to go on conforming. Brave face, all that."

"I can see how it might," said Penn. "Sometimes." But was reserved. Since she had been taught to keep anguish, terror and ecstasy within bounds, how should her mentor now require her sympathy in these deplored extremes? At breakfast, even, and on the day of the Fête? She narrowed her nostrils in unconscious imitation of Cynthia's former expression.

For she did feel critical. To fall in love and talk carelessly of madness was not Mrs Bellamy's style; and she had set so much store by style. It occurred to Penn that it might be dangerous to tame life so early and so adamantly as Mrs Bellamy had appeared to do. If something were to break the pen which shut up emotions, you would be more staggered than if you had taken them for granted. You might be overthrown by them. You might have no-where to go back to. Or see no way of getting back there. You would also surprise and upset those who were used to you as you were before, in an unfair way.

"Have you got a wine cork I could borrow," Penn asked Dr Julian with solicitude.

"I think we can rustle one up," he said gratefully.

In falling off from her own standards, Mrs Bellamy had at last taught Penn that there was some point in them.

"I hope you like the play."

"I'm sure I shall."

You couldn't go sloshing your own emotions all over the place, Penn thought disapprovingly; it wasn't fair to other people.

Lunch, always rather a scrappy meal at the Grange, was more than usually perfunctory on the day of the Fête. The sociable tea which was to follow the afternoon's side-shows would be of such dimensions that eating beforehand, Cynthia defended over a meagre salad, might ruin the family reputation for joining in. "One mightn't be able to do one's duty by everybody's beastly cakes," she explained nervily, dropping ash into mayonnaise and then apologising for her clumsiness.

Dr Julian passed an ashtray, saying, "The family reputation must be guarded jealously." He smiled to prove it was only a joke but then looked away.

The day was blazingly bright. Half-closed shutters protected the dining-room from its havoc of light. But deliberate twilight seemed to expose more revealingly. Cynthia's face looked whiter than the walls, her hooded eyes piercingly blue and her un-made-up mouth too naked. Pale, thin, vulnerable lips looked wounded. She excused herself and left the table.

"Have you told Clare about the play?" asked Dr Julian with a keen openness which seemed momentarily betraying to Penn. Then her reproachful look foundered on his distracted, cheerful expression.

"No, but I will, I will right away," she said; too ardently understanding his change of subject. "Come on, Clare."

The girls went out into the day. Hot and blatant, its weather was too perfect for the celebrations; invited calamity. Both felt uneasy and forgot their slight estrangement. Penn's small subterfuge, confessed, was slightly diverting but no longer important.

They lay on their backs in long grass and looked up at the sky through leaves and were silent. Sky had no longer its former charm since news of bombing had become familiar and even here the occasional aeroplane missed its path to the aerodrome and droned over the orchard like a heavy bee with acquaintances from the camp presumably in its belly. Sky's blue had been what Michael occasionally appeared out of, its stars had chimed with the notions of old poets. It had also been the location of Heaven,

129

to which people looked piously in the open air meeting when addressing God. Now it had become the source of death and would never look the same again.

"That boy at Miss Graham's said more than six thousand people were killed and another six thousand injured in one month in the Blitz," said Penn.

"Still; there hasn't been a raid on London for ages."

"I know. I wonder how much longer. Are they dropped, do you think, by parachute when they go on these raids?"

"The Americans? That's the rumour. Not supposed to know, though." They stared at a lace of dark green leaves with blue between like a doiley Mrs Carr put under cakes and sighed.

Penn said, "I read somewhere that the Spanish name for a parachute is rose of death. It's frightening but poetic."

"Oh you and your poetic."

"Sorry. It helps not to think about it."

The sky rained blue silence on them as they lay at the orchard's edge in companionable anxiety.

"Are you still worried about your mother and father?" asked Clare.

"Not *especially*."

"Actually I'm a bit worried about mine," said Clare. She had her mother's reticence and distaste for intimate confidences, so Penn had learned to respect her by not being intense.

"Your parents?" she said, looking the other way.

"Yes."

They sucked the sweet white stems of coarse grasses unsheathed; both shy now that it was out in the open.

"Do you like Chris Lester?" Penn asked casually.

"He's all right, I suppose," said Clare. "Do you?"

"In himself. I don't mind him in himself."

"That's what I meant."

"But I'm not sorry he's going away."

"Quite," said Clare.

They shifted to another side and subject.

"I wish Mrs Hayle would go away," said Clare.

"I know what you mean."

"But you hang round her so."

"She knows interesting things."

"Still. I can't see why you hang round her so."

Penn plucked another grass. "She likes you," she said.

"Well it's not mutual. I think she's got a pash on Daddy."

"No! Really?"

"She goes that disgusting pink whenever he speaks to her. I can't think why he encourages her. It's disgusting."

"Do you really think?" They spluttered into giggles, rolled over and buried their faces; sneezed in the long grass.

"Oh there you are," said Dr Julian. "Ready for the Fête?"

"Not yet," said Clare, sitting up irritably. "The sideshows are going to be pathetic. Perhaps for tea."

"Penn?" He appeared importunate though off-hand. She stood up, remembering the vision on the hill-top guiltily. Her mother's brisk sour cliché that she was sorry not for wrong-doing but for being found out proved true; but reasonable. There actually was not so much harm in things not discovered.

"Coming," she said. Hurting people was what was bad: if only he hadn't seen them holding hands she would not feel so ashamed of the collusion which now appeared betrayal.

"Anyway," said Clare grumpily, "I've got to get my surplice." Her response to the situation was a general resentment against both parents. She avoided them both to avoid worry, and blamed them for involving her in an uneasy atmosphere rather than for anything they might get up to among themselves.

"Thank you," said Dr Julian to Penn as they set off. "I'm not yearning for the side-shows, I confess. Let's go the long way."

They walked in silence, making for higher ground as though the slight effort of uphill climbing suited their mood. Penitential and soothing, the rough going made Penn struggle in the hot afternoon; but she felt better to punish herself in the circumstances.

"Don't tire yourself out," said Dr Julian as she panted up ahead of him unnecessarily fast. Then, since her pace did not slacken; "Or me," he begged, stopping. "Anyone would think you had a train to catch!" She stopped and turned. "Well perhaps you have. There's something valedictory about today."

"What's valedictory mean?"

"Saying goodbye. Just and exactly that."

"Thanks." She mouthed the word to remember, noticed the wry smile with which he watched her, and felt a sudden wave of affection and concern for him.

"You have taught me such a lot," said Penn; but shuffled;

because one of the things they had taught her was to avoid outright emotional expressions of feeling between people.

"Have we? Good. If it was good for you to learn."

"Isn't everything?"

"Some would say not. Some would say one can know too much."

"I wouldn't."

"No. You wouldn't. You have taught us a lot too."

Surprise broke her reserve and she cried, "*Have* I?" in her old voice, raucously. "What?"

He touched her elbow with smiling reproof; then his face fell again and he sighed. "You've no idea, Penn, how fixed we were in our expectations of people with different social backgrounds."

"But you were very nice about it."

"Yes, wasn't that awful?"

"Yes, that was a bit awful," she agreed; "that was the one thing which made me nervous."

He chuckled and scuffed tufts of uneven meadow grass with the sides of his shoes, losing his balance as if deliberately, as he began to walk uphill again ahead of her.

"That was the thing enlightened radicals of my class and principles were particularly determined on. You would be just the same as we were if you hadn't been deprived of our advantages. So what we had to do was admit you to our advantages to change society. Meanwhile we didn't want you to feel too awkward about your lacks and differences."

"So? How was I a problem to that?"

"You actually *were* just like us, in the way you approached us. You were polite about our strange ways and just as smug as we were about your own. We were offering you access to our way of life—which we'd always assumed a tremendous advantage—while you tried to introduce us to yours; just as sure yours was special. There you'd sit, being syringa-significant *and* practical about dustbins—easier to keep clean if they were painted or something—in between trying to convert us. Dustbins were washed in Jeyes fluid, as I recall, and souls in the Blood of the Lamb."

"How did you know we had a syringa bush by the dustbin?"

"You told us. You told us everything remorselessly as though it must be interesting."

"Well you asked. Was it a bore?"

"Of course we asked: that was polite. No it wasn't a bore:

which was surprising for a start. Your sacramental view of the world was unfamiliar to us in everyday life. We'd read some of the mystics, of course; but were unprepared to find this sacramental attitude in an evacuee from Dagenham."

She noticed his deliberate use of an unfamiliar word to tempt her to demand enlightenment: he enjoyed teaching her words. One of the charms of their reticent intimacy was a lack of altruism in the way they manipulated each other, each respecting the other's technique.

"What do you mean, sacramental?" she asked obligingly. But sternly; after all, the Army was against what the Church called sacraments because communion wine was alcoholic and so an unfair temptation to drunkards who had just signed the pledge.

"Actually," he said, "you have a sacramental view of the universe with a strongly self-centred bias." He nibbled the white end of a piece of grass as she had taught him and waited for her to rise to insults in her usual fashion.

"Go on." She was too busy to be offended, remembering a similar criticism from Michael and trying to think of the word. "Egotistical?" she tried.

"That's far too unkind. Ego-centric, perhaps. Not the same."

"Let's get back to sacramental," she proposed firmly.

"May I combine them?"

"Please do. You say I do anyway."

"Quite." They grinned warmly at each other. "You apparently consider that everything in the world, absolutely everything, points beyond itself to some eternity or other; and, in the opposite direction, straight at Penelope Carr."

"But of course," she said. "You mean God out there and me down here and everything in between related? Well naturally. Like a letter or a book to read, explaining."

"There you go again. Your personal branch of Platonism."

"Not *just* me. Anyone who sees it that way." She looked at the sensible yellow air and the undulating lie of the green land outlined by blue limits of sky. How could it not have a meaning, waiting to be transcribed? She said rather grumpily, "You keep hinting at this platowhatnot."

"Hint is what you do," he said, touching her arm to prove she need not take offence. "You keep hinting; I merely mention occasionally. Prompted by your hints."

133

"Well: explain."

"You claimed to know Socrates intimately the night you came."

"The philosopher? One of Arthur Mee's *smaller* thousand heroes?" He saw she was being deliberately provocative.

"Is nothing sacred?" he cried in mock anguish.

She nailed him to the rising ground by stopping suddenly. "Yes: everything," she said decidedly. "Touché? That's what you say I'm meaning isn't it?"

He tottered to a halt a step ahead of her and leaned against the horizon. Surrounded by such a depth of blue and with the light behind him, he presented a fudged, typical outline.

"So go on then tell me." She squinted into dazzle. He responded by sitting down where he stood to leave her staring belligerently at the sun. So she sat down too; said "Ouch" at gorse; resettled herself at his feet.

"Go on then," said Penn. "Stop just teasing."

Dr Julian nodded and began carefully. "Platonism maintains that there is an absolute to everything we see or experience in this life . . . elsewhere. It says, for instance, that we call all green things green because of an ideal of absolute greenness in our minds which we're born with. We even know that some are more and some less green; which we only could if there were a perfect green we were referring them to. According to Platonism, men recognise these absolute standards outside of our experience all the time. We judge things to be green—or good, which is more difficult—according to how closely they reflect that perfect and absolute green. Or good. Or garden, like Miss Graham's this morning. We saw it as very garden-like, remember? As if we knew what a garden should be, and decided hers came nearer than usual to its ideal."

"Just like St Paul," said Penn, dabbing spit on a scratch.

"I beg your pardon?"

" '*Now I see through a glass, darkly, but then face to face. Now I know in part, but then shall I know even as also I am known.*' "

"Goodness," said Dr Julian. "St Paul you say? Are you sure?"

"I can prove it if we get a Bible," said Penn indignantly. "It's all about love actually, only some translations call it charity." He looked both glum and suspicious. "Honest," she said.

"Love, eh? Is it. What was that bit again?"

She repeated it patiently. He brightened. "Great Scott," he said enthusiastically, "it's the Platonic cave idea."

"Pardon?" said Penn.

"That we see only shadows of the real as we crouch in the cave of the senses and look at what we think is the world. Shadows thrown by the fire on the wall of the cave which we mistake for reality, though that is in fact somewhere else."

"Heaven," Penn suggested, nodding cheerfully.

"Well so you seemed to think. Most heavens repelled us. Yours shone through hopscotch and your mother's washing-day buckets of blue. We'd expected that slum-clearance housing estates like yours would be ruled by the meanest struggle for existence. The Banjo sounded rich and jolly as well as good feeding-ground for mysticism. We meant to rescue you from the drab life of poverty. You didn't seem to need saving; planned, rather, to save us from the drab life we led."

"Not me: Jesus." Just to keep the record straight.

"Well, frankly, he presented no threat. We'd dismissed Jesus some time before except as a prophet of social reform. No, it was you. And then there was this 'love' thing of yours; which you insist on introducing into sensible discussions still. Attached to some lad called Michael you'd met twice."

"Three times," said Penn.

"As though that too were a feature of this practical other-worldliness of yours."

"Well I think it is."

"Quite. Most unsettling. And then Chris Lester came along."

"Oh." Did he mean that Mrs Bellamy had somehow caught love from her as if it were measles? Both looked shifty. A breeze at the top of the rise blew their hair and smudged their faces into dangerous smiles. Dr Julian rescued them from the brink of impropriety and embarrassment. He said, "As an anthropologist." Coughed. "Chris told us that tribal Africans had their own, perhaps superior, systems of social organisation, ritual and law."

"Like the Banjo?"

"Very. Same general principle anyway. It seemed less and less feasible to believe that sharing ours was any sort of cause. Not that we ever planned any missionary or imperialist extension. But we did suppose England might be improved by spreading our advantages more fairly. Until you, then he . . ."

Penn considered this puzzling problem, which was far from clear. "Hang on a mo," she said. "Couldn't you swop? Like *we* did, if you really mean I gave you something in exchange? You could get interesting things from these Africans and in return you could teach them good manners and ideas like whatnot. Honestly, it might work. People in the Banjo don't know about all that and I don't suppose black people do either."

He laughed and shook his head. "Just like you to pick on those advantages. Most reformers think it's our worldly goods we should distribute more equably."

"Well those too," she said agreeably. "I knew hardly anyone at school in London who had a piano. And ours is an upright."

His laughter made her frown, but when it faded he sighed so deeply that she would rather be ridiculous than see him so sad. "It's not so clear a cause as it seemed to us before," he tried to explain. "Cynthia and I met as you know through shared ideals about political and social reform. And they remained something we could share. I'm a bit of a dilettante otherwise and our life here is a bit dull for her. It gave us a vague sort of purpose. Until recently."

He shook his thatched head suddenly, embarrassed, and hauled himself to his feet. "Goodness, Penn, however did I get on to all this? You've taught me to talk about too many things."

But he had taught her to talk about less, and they walked on down to the village hall with only a loud buzzing of insects between them.

By the time the play was due to begin, enough dusk had turned the decorated windows blue to focus attention on the platform when the lights went on. Make-shift, perfunctory, the tilted lamps rigged up by Mr Howell fixed that end of the hall dramatically enough to allow the play to begin in silence. They quite dazzled the performers who had never been exposed in rehearsals to a wall of brightness beyond which you could not see, only feel people. The rustle and stir of silence settling upon the audience made it unlike rehearsals. This so unnerved the small-part players who began the scene that attention had begun to waver by the time Clare made her entrance. Blinking into the unrehearsed brilliance with her yellow hair curling angelically into the collar of her bor-rowed purple, Clare walked tentatively downstage. Even her faltering first lines fitted the characterisation; whispering hushed again to listen to the soft, unworldly Bishop, chided by his bossy sister for giving all his goods away to the needy of the parish.

Penn, waiting in the wings, frowned to hear herself forestalled in that particular trick, and rubbed her filthy fingers over her face again. She registered without having time to explore the fact that all the different, over-fed, excited, bored or fearful people in the hall became united as an audience only now and then. Peeping, she could see them singly becoming themselves again; as the dialogue between the Bishop and his sister dragged on, they slackened into yawns or flirting. Annoyance ousted her nervousness.

'*Enter the Convict stealthily, he has a long knife and seizes the Bishop from behind.*'

She managed to surprise even Clare; entering so stealthily, and from a rather different angle than when they had rehearsed, that a gasp united all the stage and hall of people. But Penn had a further shock for Mrs Hayle.

"*If you call out, you are a dead man!*" she enunciated in a careful, elocuted voice. Not being cockney was the secret she had guarded for weeks: Mrs Hayle should never mock her accent again. Unfortunately, the meticulous vowels in her girlish soprano accorded so oddly with her excessively naturalistic appearance as the Convict, that only politeness stifled mockery there and then in the hall. She sensed the audience shifting to escape and made a quite unintended lunge at the Bishop with her knife where the stage direction read only '*(drinks)*' before gulping. This gathered some back into her web but left the fringes fraying. The Convict unexpectedly flung the empty wine-bottle over his shoulder with a growl. It narrowly missed an alarmed prompter; but succeeded in drawing scattered people into an audience again.

One of the attractions of the part of the Convict, almost compensating for not being heroically noble or dressed in a becoming purple surplice, was that he used bad language a good deal. Penn enjoyed the opportunity to swear with impunity.

'*Damn me*,' said the Convict with relish and an upper-class accent. But something was wrong. She rolled her mud-caked eyes at them to quell a rustle in the third row. It worked. It was heady, that attention; it made her thirsty. She decided that it meant more to her than her new posh voice. Her big speech was happening while another part of her mind thought about this.

Convict: "*It's so long ago I forgot but I had a little cottage, there were vines growing on it (dreamily) they looked pretty with the evening sun on them and, and—*" Penn saw imaginary vines in evening sun . . . in France, of course, lost and never-known France . . . with shutters like the Grange, green-painted. "*—and there was a woman,*" said the Convict wonderingly, slipping into cockney, "*she was (thinking hard)—she must have been my wife— yes (suddenly and very rapidly), yes, I remember! She was ill, we had no food. . . .*"

It all came back to them, Penn and the Convict: Jeannette was dying. . . . Of course! Why had she never thought of it in rehearsal? —Netta at the end of Netta's Mission lay just so white and starving. . . . Jeannette and Netta lay in her mind's eye, identified.

"*The night I was sentenced the gaoler told me—told me Jeannette was dead (sobs, with fury). Ah, damn them, damn them. God curse them all*" (*he sinks on the table sobbing*).

When the Convict looked up, real tears had made runnels down Penn's muddy cheeks. The Convict blinked to remember where he was—in the Bishop's house—and scrubbed his fists roughly into his weeping eyes. Penn blinked out at the hall, bewildered to remember where *she* was, and felt the tears on her eyelashes glitter in Mr Howell's lamps. The audience had become an intensely silent, single thing. A white hand touched her arm gently and Clare/Bishop said quietly, with a break of emotion in her voice,

"*Now tell me about the prison ship, about Hell.*"

They held their audience until the end. The Bishop gave his candlesticks to the Convict after he had tried to steal them: The Convict asked (*hanging his head very shamefacedly*) for his blessing. Mrs Cooper in the front row had her handkerchief out, it glimmered; further back a big man—Mr Perkins?—gulped audibly. The Bishop and the Convict opened the door into the night and a safe path (or the wall of unlit planks at the back of the village hall) and knew it was almost over.

"*A thanks, thanks, Monseigneur. I—I (he sobs) I'm a fool, a child to cry, but somehow you have made me feel that—that it is just as if something had come into me—as if I were a man again and not a wild beast.*

Bishop (putting his hand on his shoulder): Always remember, my son that this poor body is the Temple of the Living God.

Convict (with great awe): The Temple of the Living God. I'll remember. (Exit L.C.)

(The Bishop closes the door and goes quietly to the Prie Dieu in the window R., he sinks on his knees and bows his head in prayer.)"

SLOW CURTAIN.'

After a pause the clapping started. Both girls sipped at it, tentative, bemused. They came forward and the sound of clapping swelled. It fed some undiscovered appetite. Clare improvised an extra blessing, Penn fell on her knees and bowed her head, the hall echoed to cheers. They drank it in, becoming themselves again, and greedy. The minor players grouped round them bowing. Too soon, Mr Howell turned on the rest of the lights and it was over. But, as nobody told them not to, the performers could mingle in costume, glittering with praise.

"Gee," said the Staff Sergeant, "when he gave up trying to talk like the Bishop . . . that was a helluva good moment. Remembering back, he'd go back to his own dialect. How did you think of that?"

Penn thanked demurely, with a weather eye on Dr Bellamy's twinkle of kind amusement and on Mrs Hayle beside him. She stood so compactly against a tinselled wall that it was impossible to tell if she was amazed or angry.

Dr Bellamy turned to her, saying, "Congratulations to the producer, don't you think, Sergeant?"

Though enjoying triumphant progress round the hall, Penn and Clare looked closely for her approval. She did indeed turn pink at Dr Julian's words, in a blotched unbeautiful way, like a doll whose painted cheeks have run in the rain.

"I can take no—" she hesitated—"*credit* for what transpired this evening." Anna Hayle shuddered slightly. Dr Julian saw the girls' radiance nipped at her frost. He looked regretful and grave.

"It was great," said the Sergeant aggressively. "Dramatic.'

Clare begged, "Was it all right, really, Daddy? Did *you* think so?"

"It was remarkable certainly. How did you feel about it?"

"Marvellous. But it was a bit frightening."

"I can imagine. That slight hysteria of performance."

Penn said, "I didn't think it was frightening at all." She glowered at Mrs Hayle. "It was very exciting as though you were two things at once and one bit of you had to control the other bit which worked on its own, in a different way."

Dr Julian nodded with a serious face. "I should have foreseen that."

Penn felt blamed. "What's wrong about it?" Tear-streaked, muddy, hair awry, she looked ready to burst out crying if he were critical as well as Mrs Hayle.

"Nothing's wrong about it. I meant just that I should have foreseen that the particular duplicity of acting would be likely to appeal to your nature."

Duplicity? Wasn't that the same as lying? Tears welled.

"We'll talk about it later," he said with compunction. "Be off, both of you, and enjoy the admiration you deserve."

But it was somehow spoiled. Clare glowed around the hall, accepting tributes gracefully; but Penn sought out only those who had been actually moved. She collected signs of real tears with a touchy, morbid greed.

Some reaction was inevitable; and she had felt the Convict so closely, however dubious the identification, that his dirt and exile and rejection still hung about her mind, inextricably mixed with her own distance from home, the war, and reservations of Dr Bellamy and Mrs Hayle.

The wooden interior of the hall was not actually bare wood, but painted carefully to look like wood, with knots and grain skilfully imitated in fawn on brown. Yet underneath this imitation was, indeed, real wood. Might she too act what was also true? And was this deceit or art? Poems and paintings were not what they evoked; but true.

Fractious and confused, she wandered soon outside.

The stars appeared nearer than in London and tonight unusually close. They were not, though, so sharp as the far, pointed stars in a winter night-sky, but quivered in soft blobs in the thick blue above her head. It was not quite dark; and the horizon westwards still showed a stain as bright as geraniums or blood. This lurid colour over-dramatised the view. If Dr Julian was right about Miss Graham's garden and an ideal garden, this was not nearly so absolute a night-sky as the one when she met Michael. That black air had been ethereal; this summer dark was dense and flossy in comparison. Smells thickened it. A green, moist twilight dew made grass and plants give off too rich a sweetness. This was laced with the dry scent of a haystack and a deeper pungency of hens and dunged soil. The warm air was like a blanket and oppressive.

Why had Dr Julian and Mrs Hayle spoiled it all? Their reservations had made the praise and admiration afterwards cloying and distasteful. They had even robbed of its thrill—or revealed as too thrilling—the silence of the audience when she felt it in her power. It seemed in retrospect too easy, warm and affectionate; like slobbering dogs whose lick first comforts and then disgusts. Afterwards you felt dirty.

She was, of course, dirty. She scooped her hair back towards its proper parting but a handkerchief was no match for the amount of mixed messes she had spread over her face and hands. She longed suddenly for her mother; who made her scrub her nails until they were like little pearls. But now even that felt suspect. 'Crying for her mother' was like a piece of stage-direction, suddenly. Was everything she did 'acting'? But also, what was acting? For something quite unlike pretending had taken place in the experience on the stage The vines she had imagined had made her cry. But then she had tilted her face to catch the light upon the genuine tears; and could move other people only by combining an abdication of one kind of thought with an observant and unscrupulous exploitation of both other people and her own experience.

Kicking at gravel so that it spluttered like distant machine-guns against the side of the hall, she worried this thought.

Though now, in this way of putting it to herself, it appeared odious, she would not forget the exhilaration of its actuality. It was more acutely alive and aware than anything else she had experienced except being in love. Or like writing: sometimes a word or rhyme or image came like that. Such arrivals must not be striven after but one must coax them by making circumstances propitious to them. Writing, in fact, was more exact for this occasional splendour and did not leave an aftertaste of degradation. She thought perhaps she would revert to being an author when she grew up rather than an actress after all.

The dark, which had been creeping and now possessed all the landscape, was split suddenly by a flash of flame. It was near by, and the smell of sulphur from a match struck her nostrils as piercingly as the light her eyes. When you have thought yourself alone it is startling to be revealed as seen. Penn turned quickly away but was halted by a tone as doubtful and shaken as she felt: obviously she had interrupted as well as been interrupted.

"It that Penn by any chance?" called Cynthia's voice from the middle of dark. She sounded husky and tense. Penn discovered a red comet of cigarette-tip waving at her from the gate at the side of the village hall which led into the field with the haystack.

"Is that you Mrs Bellamy?" She took an uneasy step towards the waving point of red, star-sized.

"Call me Cynthia, darling, don't you think ... at a time like this?"

Some silent shift of the dark towards the back door of the hall drew Penn's eyes. Cynthia called: "Look where you're going, darling, or you'll fall into the ditch!" in a tone too peremptory; but the girl had guessed Chris without sight.

"Come and sit on this idyllic five-barred whatnot with me," called Cynthia in the light but thick voice which meant she had been drinking. The smoke-smell of her cigarette guided Penn and also made the white gate faintly visible; focusing one sense through another. "You were a terrific success then," said Cynthia with an effort.

"Yes," said Penn carelessly. The play had made her forget everything else which she now remembered, ashamed. She hitched herself on to the now definite gate and looked towards Mrs Bellamy's dark outline against the sky which had become lighter.

"Do you remember when you first told me about falling in love? When you were ludicrously young?" Cynthia said.

"Yes. You were pretty scathing about it."

"Was I? It seemed such a grotesque idea then. It's all your fault in a way." But she did not sound critical; only vaguely surprised. Penn saw the whiteness of Mrs Bellamy's face turned towards her with the red of her cigarette tip glowing brighter as she sucked it. "Was it hell?" she said, waving the small burning signal away from her face. "I think probably it must always be hell." And turned away.

Penn thought. "Well, but it was marvellous too. More awful and more marvellous than everyday life," she offered.

Cynthia said tiredly: "How clever of you, darling. Yes of course. So that makes it all right does it?" Aloof, her vague voice drifted with smoke. Then she suddenly and quietly began to cry. The

142

shocking silence had the same weight as a stage pause when the audience must hold its breath.

What to do was a problem. Penn relieved Cynthia's hand of the cigarette and dropped it on the road, then said awkwardly, "Will they come back after they leave tomorrow do you think?"

"No," said Cynthia. Penn fell carefully backwards, gripping the gate under her knees like a Banjo rail so that Cynthia should not be shaken. She felt it might be easier upside down. Her muddy hair trailed against the trodden meadow grass.

"No, because he couldn't come back here and it be the same? Or not at all?"

"Both," said Cynthia. Her two words had been projected out of silent weeping, explosions of held breath. Now from upside down Penn heard her control the crying. Words came into her head from the Bible bit Dr Julian had found interesting earlier. '*Love beareth all things, believeth all things, hopeth all things, endureth all things . . .*' It seemed appropriate.

"Do you have to do recitations at me, darling?" interrupted Cynthia brutally. "This mission is likely to kill a lot of them, rumour has it."

"Sorry," said Penn.

"I do actually have rather more than enough quotations and sensitive understanding from Julian."

"Yes," said Penn.

"And you're such a bloody good little cuckoo that I really don't need *proof*, darling, of how clever you are."

"No," said Penn. "Sorry."

She cautiously righted herself and gazed stonily at the soft and cruel sky as Cynthia unhitched herself from the gate.

"Cuckoo is really rather good, though I meant parrot," said Cynthia, lighting another cigarette where she stood in the road. "Wrong nest; baby bird growing too big for her boots. Or I suppose that's a mixed metaphor and birds don't have boots. Oh God," said Cynthia, suddenly very quietly. "I do apologise."

"That's all right," said Penn.

"I didn't mean to be beastly."

"That's all right," said Penn.

Another silence held them captured beside the gate. One stood elegant and taut, pirouetting on high heels to rob the encounter of significance but close to despair; the other—shorter and younger—

nevertheless towered by perching still on the top rung of the gate against a barrage of stars. Both looked away, against their impropriety, and could find nothing to look at but an offensively indifferent summer night sky or the blacked-out hall from which raucous sounds of merriment assaulted them.

"It must be awful," said Penn awkwardly. "I'm sorry I can't help." She balanced in hurt and estrangement insecurely on the gate which wobbled since she was left to pin it down alone. Cynthia unexpectedly began to sob again, bending her head to Penn's knees which were still encased in a pair of Dr Julian's old trousers. Since all her words were wrong and she did not dare touch, Penn simply kept still while Mrs Bellamy cried her heart out. A sliver of nervous light showed to Penn but not her cruel patient the opening of the back door of the village hall; but an increase in the sound-level of jollity jerked Mrs Bellamy's head away. Blind with both tears and night, she recognised Chris and stumbled away towards him.

At first Penn did not watch, and then watched, with the same intense attention. She had to see what she could see. It was only two shadows becoming one in a silence and darkness that screamed against the merriment of the Farewell Fête.

The celebrations in the hall when Penn went in again seemed at first shockingly irrelevant and then lethally apt; now that she knew. Even the silliest giggling hug between an American GI and a village girl showed some sign of human love when you knew that it must be prelude to separation and probably death. The war had rarely been as real to her; and the times when it had seemed connected with this time. There was the night when Hitler's invasion of Czechoslovakia had made news to listen to with Michael and their families. And that day when mother said war was inevitable and she had changed the newts' water and Michael said goodbye. Then evacuation itself; leaving home and friends. And Dunkirk, but only as mother and father cycled off into threatened London. Lost battles, occupied countries, devastated cities did not reach beyond words and facts unless some human love and loss brought it home to you.

"You were great," said an isolated American, rolling off a perch on the platform as she passed by. She looked at him blankly, forgetting the fictional Convict who had been briefly real there so recently. 'Ego-centric' was that the word? Where else could you be but in the middle of yourself?

"Oh thanks," she said to the American. "I say: are you all right?" Her intensity sobered him.

"Fine," he said, straightening. "How about you?"

"No, but I mean," she gazed into his soft, threatened face; "I mean . . . you all leaving tomorrow . . . the war . . . you know." The soldier looked with scared and angry eyes back into hers. Then he turned his head away and straightened his uniform.

"Shut your mouth, kid," he said.

It was proving very difficult this evening to be kind to people without offending them, Penn decided. But could not abdicate entirely. It really would be frightful if Mrs Bellamy and Chris were discovered, even disturbed.

"Have you seen Dr Bellamy anywhere?" she asked the cross soldier who was gripping her wrist in a loose but locked fist.

"Sure. By the door, see?"

"Oh yes. Gosh. I must go. Sorry I couldn't say the right thing."

"Nobody asked you, kid," said the soldier, letting her go.

Dodging through people with trifle, or dancing, or unhooking decorations, or making last-minute friends, she reached the door only just before Dr Julian was through it and grabbed his arm.

"You can't go now," she panted; out of breath and still caked with mud from her part in the play.

"Why not?" he said, recoiling visibly from her grime and importunity. She was going to have to offend someone else. Scrubbing at her face ineffectually, she racked her brain for some good reason to delay him. The soldier's attitude provided the only clue; though it was hardly likely to make her popular. But he continued to lean towards stumbling over his wife and her lover; so Penn hurled herself on as eagerly as she had made herself look so extremely ugly in the play because she could not look pretty.

"We'll never see any of them again, I only just realised."

He removed his hand from the door and looked at her; critically. "Most of us have known that for some time." His eyes flicked warningly to left and right, coldly emphasising that her piercing egotistical shout was announcing their danger to scores of men trying to forget it.

"Well I didn't," she yelled above the music. "Please don't go."

He turned as she had hoped away from the door altogether; but his look was uncommonly disapproving.

"Penn, dear; I realise it's been an exciting day for you but please try to exercise a little self-control." Self-control was what her father had continuously and pessimistically exhorted her to practise. She was aware that she did most reprehensibly lack it—being ostentatiously terrified of swimming-baths and bicycles. Her father's loving but regretful face took form in her imagination as Netta's death had done. She saw him haul her screaming from the shallow end, or wheel her bike home while she trailed sobbing and refused to remount after a tumble. Her father: who might at this very moment be being smashed to smithereens in London by a German bomb. Part of a smithereen would be labelled by an identity bracelet. She began to cry.

Dr Julian edged her away from the cheerful desperate throng and put an arm round her shoulder. She thought: Oh good, he won't find them for the time being; and Daddy might easily be cycling back from International Headquarters when a bomb hit the City and his hand that I held is in a gutter bleeding. She sobbed. Dr Julian's concern became less perfunctory when she gulped, "Daddy kept on about self-control but might be killed now."

"Why now, Penn? What is it, whatever is it?" He squeezed her shoulder awkwardly. "You were so brave during the Blitz."

That gave her the next cue; though the question of timing was a delicate one as she could not possibly explain why *now*? So she would have to transpose. She registered in passing that it was apparently a good idea not to cry or suchlike so often that people stopped taking you seriously. Time, fears and themes were now a fragile web in her mind, through which she must weave her way.

"A boy said that there are hundreds of thousands of cardboard coffins in London because so many people get killed they can't make proper funerals, even."

"And that upset you?"

She nodded. It had upset her, it was true. But it had been ages ago. Then, she had kept the ugly gossip to herself. She had prayed all night for weeks at the open window of a cold room to keep herself awake, in the hope that God would hardly dare to massacre her parents while she was actually on her knees. At the time, she had refused to explain her bleached exhaustion and loss of atten-

146

tion, feeling that it would be not only vulgar but somehow risky to expose her private vigils to sympathy: neither Mrs Bellamy nor God would approve if she made a thing about it. Perhaps this gave her a kind of credit note now. Something had to keep Dr Julian safely in the hall. With all those men who were going to be killed in action. While Daddy's hand might be blown off by an odd bomb. She mined the anguish which had been solitary, added the more recent memory of Mrs Bellamy uncharacteristically weeping on her knees, glanced at the squalid gaiety around them which meant torn red paper-chains might be bracelets of blood tomorrow, and sobbed convincingly.

"Poor Penn," said Dr Julian, fully attentive at last.

She felt a bit of a fraud but that the truth might owe her this usage in a good cause. Even pompous old Wordsworth justified emotion recollected in tranquillity; and acting worked only if you recollected and used emotion not in tranquillity at all but on the spur of the moment. This was part acting, part writing, wholly life; or the only way she could find to work it at the moment. She conjured wilfully—but the images were vivid and almost more real than sight itself—her father's hand bleeding in a gutter and the dark shadows of Chris and Cynthia conjoining as if otherwise mutilated. Slight shame made her cry more.

Sighing, responsible but distracted, Dr Julian led her to a quieter corner. Now that the pub was open and cases of beer had been brought from the camp, the hall where the pretend-bishop had blessed the pretend-convict was becoming far from blessed and it was difficult to find an area where nobody was making love or being sick. They trod in trifle.

"This is hardly the time and the place," said Dr Julian, looking away in some confusion.

"Well, we have to be here and now, you told me," said Penn; "there isn't anything else." He grinned with sudden warmth at her smeared but bossy face.

"Oh Penn," he said; "outside would be far pleasanter."

"No it wouldn't," said Penn. "Go on."

"Well," said Dr Julian. "It's very natural that you're distressed at the idea of death. It hits most people at about your age. And this mission brought it home suddenly to you. Tell me: do you still believe in Heaven?"

At least he was now gratifyingly pinned to a safe place by an idea. She beamed through tear-ploughed mud at him and wiped her nose on the back of her hand in the convict's gesture with inappropriate cheerfulness.

"Not the angels-with-harps one, where everyone is just the same and meets again and lives in mansions," she helped.

"That's what I thought. And that's largely my fault. So you must let me tell you more about what I was saying this morning; but you were too busy to listen through calculating how to get as filthy as you are. But it could make a better kind of sense to you and give back some credible consolation against the fact of human death. Still, as I said, not now." He seemed about to go away; out.

"Oh please now," she said. "I know there is more to it all than this life," she hurriedly insisted. "But it can't be the same as this, can it?"

"N-no," he acknowledged, doubtfully bullied among baubles.

"I do believe my father's spirit would go on. But it's his body I love too. I mean, he couldn't smell things and I couldn't touch him. All people dying will lose this particular kind of being; the feeling, touching, smelling kind. And that's dreadful. Whatever comes after, though it may be very interesting."

All the stench and bravado of the fag-end of the Fête came at them, hot as the summer night and with the same pervading tension which must split when it was drawn tight enough; as lowering weather must break in lightning. "I forget," said Dr Julian, "how passionately you're attached to physical reality too. We never had that much, Cynthia and I. It's one of the things you brought in your little bundle from the East End. With the blanket. But I still think my friend Plato and you should be introduced."

She tilted in sudden surprise. "Oh. Is it a person? I thought it was just an idea."

He began to laugh.

"You kept saying platonism," she justified: "I thought it was a thing like anthropology or history. But a person! How do you spell him?"

"P." "Obviously."

"L." (Someone shouted against a burst of gramophone.)

"A?" she wondered.

"T," he nodded. A couple dancing tripped over them. ("Sorry.")

"O. (That's all right.)" But a sad bewildered laughter filled Dr Julian's eyes.

"Plato," said Penn. "Got that."

Clare arrived at them out of the crowd with a look of complaining relief. "Oh, there you are. It's boring now, isn't it. Can we go home?"

"Not just now, darling. I'm talking to Penn." But he contradicted his excluding words by reaching an arm to tuck her into his armpit, and sipped at the whisky held in its hand, thus closing the embrace. Clare smiled out of his woolly arm which she was now wearing like a fox-fur round her shoulders. His hand with an amber glass in it fitted at the point of her chin where fox-furs usually fastened with a paw.

"I'll join in then," said Clare; having done so. "Why are you hugging me?"

"Don't I often?"

"Hardly ever."

"No you don't touch much in your family," said Penn.

"Hmm," said Dr Julian. "Have you ever thought," he said, punching Clare's face gently in his direction, "how suitable to our Penn that motto of hers? Blood and Fire?"

"Oh *that*."

Clare undid her father's arm and wandered away, comforted but bored. Dr Julian looked after her, perhaps inclined to escape. So Penn prompted eagerly.

"Why's the Salvation Army motto suitable? Please?"

"I see the Blood part as physical; flesh."

"It's the Blood of Jesus," she explained, "shed for our—"

"Well quite," said Dr Julian. "God made flesh. Body, anyway."

From where she was standing, Penn saw Mrs Bellamy entering the hall from the darkish door at the back of the platform.

"And Fire," said Dr Julian, "is as I understand it not body but mind. The insubstantial part."

"Well actually the Holy Spirit," said Penn hurriedly, "which sanctifies our souls after they're saved by—"

"Quite," said Dr Julian, oblivious to all but his thesis. "Same thing, from my point of view. Blood for flesh and Fire for mind. You might be what your parents would call an 'illustration' of it. You're such an intricate little bundle of thought and sensation, spirit and earthy physical reality. And I do mean earthy." He touched her grubby face, smiling. "God knows how you'll manage

149

when you grow up. You practically have mental passions and physical thoughts." His eyes were fogged by Mr Howell's whisky and the smoky room. "Hell for the men in your life," he said, teasing but affectionate. Then he seemed to register Penn's unconvincing attention and turned away from her to discover what she was so carefully not looking at beyond his shoulder. Cynthia's stumbling progress through a shambles of tipsy couples hugged close to an excuse of music had the nervy probing whiteness of a searchlight. She picked her way steadily towards them, ignoring deterrents, with a blank, pale face above her dark dress.

"Hallo, cuckoo," said Cynthia as soon as she arrived. She looked at Julian, though; with the tenacity of someone drowning, her eyes clung to his. "Wasn't that funny, darling, when I called Penny cuckoo by mistake?"

"When was that?" Dr Julian looked grave, and his voice became level, even curt.

"Earlier. Before." Cynthia's eyebrows shrugged slightly.

"Not a bit funny," he said.

"No? No. Sorry Penn. Can't think of any good jokes any more."

Dr Julian said, "I think we'd better go home now," and reached to take her arm. She twitched it away.

"Home?" she said in her light, breathy voice. She seemed sincerely puzzled for a moment; then blinked and turned to look around the room. Her face assumed an expression of the most aloof displeasure; then, instead of holding it, screwed up tighter into a grimace, the lips slowly opening as if drawn back. She screamed. Some wailing saxophones half-hid the sound, and Dr Julian and Penn muffled her from either side. After the one raw cry, Mrs Bellamy pulled herself together and pulled her arms away. She said: "I do apologise," with bleak politeness, looking from one to the other of them as though they were people in a bus queue who had pushed in front. She began to walk away towards the door, but stumbled and accepted Penn's support, turning from her husband's offered arm. "One can't, you must see," she murmured to him. He fell back and followed them towards the door.

Because of slumped or leaning people and tilted tables and chairs the journey took some minutes. Mrs Bellamy smiled fixedly at Penn against some few who peered. "Was I always beastly?" she asked with dead eyes above this social smile. Penn shook her head. "Try and smile, darling, one looks too odd otherwise. You and Clare were quite marvellous in the play, you know, and I expect it will all be perfectly all right in a little while. I truly didn't mean to be beastly but it is all rather ghastly at the moment. Say something, darling, for God's sake, or Miss Graham will think something's wrong." Then she began to giggle. Penn said loudly: "You'll feel better outside Mrs Bellamy, it's the heat." But the quivering of suppressed laughter shook Cynthia until they had got through the door. Then, the sudden dark doused all sound and Penn found her arm released.

She heard from a small distance: "Poor Penn, poor Penn," in Mrs Bellamy's voice.

Dr Julian said: "She was only trying to save you."

"Yes I know," said Cynthia. "Poor Penn."

Something woke Penn with a start and at first she did not know where or who she was. She lay watching the world reassemble after the swarming sea of sleep into the comparative stability of consciousness. First, she placed a bedroom at the Grange; secondly, a quality in the darkness which revealed that night was almost worn out; and thirdly, that she was in a body. Putting her self together would take longer but human eyes were what she looked out of at the creak of first daylight under the door. She moved the object's toes and a stir of bedclothes mountained, grey on grey, to prove she was in it and in control. Or was she?

Now suddenly not slowly she grabbed those remote feet up to crowd the thing into the tightest possible unit. She also closed her eyes tight shut because what had woken her was some escape from this knot of flesh. Something was leaking out. She checked its apertures. She was not crying; had not been sick; had not wet the bed. Though that was nearer. Her hands were braceleted round her ankles and her forehead touched her knees: she had rolled up like wood-lice. A small swell inside her and a trickle of something warm on to her wrists shocked her outright awake.

She scrambled out of bed, clutching the gathered stuff of her nightdress between her legs with one hand and fumbling for matches to light her candle with the other. Her first thought had been to protect her inner self, her second, the bed; it was the intermediate body which was up to something on its own which threatened both. As soon as the match flared and touched the familiar wick so that she could see, she shut her eyes again out of fear of seeing. She felt once more a welling warmth inside spill out and chill against her thighs and fingers.

It was an alarming feeling; but she felt better as soon as she remembered the word. This must be menstruating; though the sensation was so much stronger and more alarming than the word. She re-opened her eyes with interest and some gratification. She and Clare, leaders in everything else, had been lagging members of this mystery: some of the younger girls were already missing Games with a shy but smug air. The curiosity with which she drew the curtains to inspect the situation reeled at the actual sight. She was quite brightly bleeding. Imagination had failed to connect the fascinating unknown of this distinctive moment with the known and fearful scarlet of injury. Banjo victims who cut their heads open and even the wounds of soldiers could be no more red. She felt sudden gratitude to all the grown-up women who had overcome embarrassment to save her from total ignorance or playground innuendo. Mother had told her about *being unwell* during the Dunkirk visit; Miss Hull had mentioned *Monthly Periods* in a blushing lecture about babies; and Mrs Bellamy had been characteristically airy about the practicalities. "When the curse strikes, darlings, you know where to find things? Lots of san-towels in my bottom bathroom drawer if I'm not in or you prefer not to mention. You know all about it I assume?" And yes, they had known, and appreciated her casual reticence. "With all the shortages and so on Miss Graham advised to lay in a tiny stock. Belts too. Be prepared, she said: doesn't run the scouts for nothing, our Miss Graham."

So Penn knew where to go and what to do, and felt excited as well as amazed. At least she had beaten Clare to becoming a woman. But; no wonder they had all been a bit embarrassed about it. It did seem guilty, if only because it made such a mess; and private, if only because it happened in such a private region of your body. Penn's first instinct was to cover her tracks; she cleaned the stained sheet.

Labouring with a chilly flannel in the equivocal dim light of earliest dawn and candle flame, her mind was invaded by memories of the previous evening. Unbidden, like over-confident mice, they peered, crept out and over-ran her. Showing off in the play; Mrs Bellamy crying by the gate; what she had stared to see in the darkness where Chris Lester met her; Dr Julian deceived into talking of Plato in the gaudy hall while ... this moment could not be accidental. All the explanations about its naturalness could not explain why at one time rather than another, why that particular night, her body had broken out of its usual container and made such a mess. She had been so full of herself after the performance and all the scenes when it was over that her body had been perhaps *distended* by self-importance until some of it leaked out. She had been smug in a particularly nasty way on the walk back to the Grange. She had lagged behind tactfully but not too far to hear.

"They'll be killed, won't they?" Cynthia had said.

"Shush. Some of them may be."

"Must be."

"Must be, then."

"Some of them must be."

Plodding behind them, Penn had seen Mrs Bellamy stumble and Dr Julian's arm politely available; not intimate.

"Why can't he die quietly if he has to, instead of noisily and publicly. He'll hate that."

"Try not to think."

"Not think? That's pretty funny, from you."

"Not to talk, at least."

"Gosh. I thought you always wanted me to talk more."

"I meant: it is supposed to be vital that this raid is secret. Losses would be even heavier if ..."

"Gosh. D'you think there might be spies in the field? Or Penn perhaps is in the pay of the Nazi hordes?"

"Do control yourself, Cynthia, please."

"Why? What for? I always agreed so, that careless talk costs lives, long before the war. You were the careless talker, darling. Such lots and lots of pretty words and high ideals. Not me."

"Then keep it up."

Silence and a stagger, then a giggle and inevitable reprisal.

"You sound like a government slogan. I've been 'keeping it up' all my life and I don't want to any more."

"Try, damn you."

Penn had eavesdropped, fascinated by their complete change of tone, as Mrs Bellamy loped lightly over the hill, calling ringingly her too revealing words as though it did not matter any more. And Penn knew why. She knew more than Dr Julian did about Mrs Bellamy and Chris Lester; and she knew more about Dr Julian's principles than his wife and daughter did. And while Clare had gone off bored to the Grange, she was avidly catching every word of their private row and observing how it changed their voices and movements. Dr Julian's usually fuzzy, soft speech had an edge which matched a new, hard walk; and Mrs Bellamy's light, usually percussive voice was loud and slurred.

Penn had felt self-important, to know more than the others, to be in on all their secrets. And now look what had happened. It might be natural; but wickedness was natural too.

When she had cleaned her bed, plugged herself with a handkerchief and covered her nightdress with a dressing-gown, she set off for Mrs Bellamy's bathroom. Daylight in the hall indicated that someone else was awake, to have drawn the black-out curtain. But it was only just past dawn and the early sun turned mist to opal and the passage quivered with soft uncertain light. It matched the mixture of pride and panic that she felt. She wanted comfort and admiration: it was an equivocal event.

More memories returned and dwarfed her own drama. They were to land at dawn, she remembered from careless talk last night. So at this very moment Chris and the other Americans must be facing death and blood more unnatural than hers. And today Mrs Bellamy would somehow—how?—have to know that and face ordinary life: breakfast, shopping at Miss Graham's, flowers for the drawing-room. Penn stopped dead and forgot her private errand at so impossible an understanding. For how could Cynthia take up again this thin normality? And if she could, with her rigorous training, overcome her own feelings, how could she face the knowing world? Dr Julian knew; half the village must guess, had anyway witnessed her drunkenness, heard her scream. She who depended upon not being known, who hid in the prison of her fine house all her private moods, could probably endure anything except this loss of face. Her pride was stronger for being of such small scope: she prided herself only on being a good chap, not making a fuss and doing the decent thing towards other people. For all her eccentricities, she had kept this basic code.

Until last night. Poor Mrs Bellamy would have more to think about than Penn's little crisis. And poor Dr Julian, whose dignified loneliness and disappointment were now exposed. Penn turned the corner quietly, taking in this difficult dawn and forgetting for the moment anything except the most practical part of her personal errand.

This was a part of the house the children rarely visited; the parents' bedroom and adjacent bathroom were down a short passage, in a small wing. One of the earliest lessons Clare had taught was that this area was private. It would need the singular event of starting the curse in the night to make either of the girls approach Mrs Bellamy's bathroom, and Penn hesitated before opening the door. Still; the singular event had occurred and justified intrusion.

Her first reaction was embarrassment, to come upon Mrs Bellamy in the bath. Halted in the doorway, she stared for a long instant at the first grown-up body she had seen naked; and it brought to mind those photographs Michael had hidden. The white breasts were bare, and the pale torso—there was only a shallow, war-time level of water at the bottom of the bath. She suddenly realised that love and nakedness were connected. In a shock of shyness, she imagined Mrs Bellamy and Chris Lester touching and knew why Michael had blushed when she spied at his pictures.

At first it seemed a displacement of that blush and the shamed mess her own body was making when she thought she noticed that the water around Mrs Bellamy's legs was red. She shut her eyes and opened them again; for the impression was like looking at the sun through the red of your own eyelids. The white tiles shone in the dim dawn light with a ripple of reflections running upwards in faint waves of pink. She pulled her dressing-gown closer against the guilty feeling which was making her imagine blood.

"Penn! What are you doing here?"

Turning into the passage, she saw Dr Julian and his face glimmered whiter than the tiles. This too must be an effect of the new shyness having a woman's body had taught her. As she moved towards him he pushed past her and shut the bathroom door and stood against it with his arms stretched out.

"I'm sorry," said Penn, "but I needed something that's kept in there. It's all right."

Something odd in his attitude, spread-eagled against the door, struck her.

"No, Penn, I'm afraid it's not all right." He took one step towards her and controlled his voice. "Go back to your room,

155

Penn, and stay there. Listen carefully for Clare waking, then go to her room and keep her there. Something very terrible has happened. I've just telephoned and the doctor is on his way. You must keep away and keep Clare away. I'll come as soon as I can. Do you understand?"

"Yes," said Penn. She gave him a long look and then did what he had told her.

Later that morning the village learned that Mrs Bellamy had committed suicide by cutting her wrists in the bath in what Anna Hayle described as the ancient Roman fashion. The violence of gesture seemed so unlike her customary discretion that 'the balance of her mind' must, in the official expression, have been 'disturbed'. Some of the villagers were less charitable than the coroner, especially after news that more than half its brief inhabitants had been killed in the commando raid. Chris Lester was among them. "At such a time," people said disapprovingly; "when so many are forced to die in a good cause, she *chose*."

As far as she could think about it at all, Penn felt she understood Cynthia's necessity and respected her decisive choice. But she and all the household were in the chaos of shock: grief had no space yet to affect them.

Dr Julian's first plans were to get both girls away from the house and the village before the funeral. This was no appropriate death to learn mourning by and he meant to protect them from the gossipy atmosphere which could only be harmful. He appeared white, calm and angry. An aunt arrived to take Clare off in her car. As the bombing of London was in abeyance at that stage of the war, it was thought best for Penn to go back to her parents. It was all arranged very quickly.

On her way to the station in the taxi, Penn stared at the village hall, bewildered by the elasticity of time. It was only three days since they had been decorating it for the Fête but it seemed a lifetime ago. And was indeed at least two lives times past. It looked most strange in its familiar morning quiet, with sweet peas nodding, a black cat washing, and three crouching boys playing five-stones.

"Could you stop for a minute, please," she asked the driver.

"Not unless you want to miss that train I can't."

"No. All right. Better keep going then," said Penn.

156

PART FOUR

THE VERY AIR seemed more authentic and Penn lagged at the end of the Banjo sniffing it up. Country air had a different texture as well as different odours. She had been deprived of this potent mixture for three long years.

"Come along," called her father, and coughed uneasily, standing with her two cases in his hands half-way along the narrower handle-end before broaching the circle at the top and their house. He had seen the twitch of lace curtain and knew Cissie at the window, eager, expectant and perhaps less sensitive than he was to possible difficulty in Penny's return. Cissie had confidently resurrected real eggs from their cold pail of isinglass, and a starched tablecloth of hand-woven lace stored 'for the duration' from tissue paper. "And I've been saving the last tin of loganberries. They were always her favourite."

But he suspected Penny's tastes might have changed. She might not appreciate the high tea so prodigally prepared in honour of her home-coming; might even be less sure than her mother that this was still her home. He did not want to see either of them hurt; but feared it might prove inevitable. His doubts had increased since he met the train. The long-legged girl of fourteen, though tired, rumpled and with familiar eyes, had responded shyly to his shy conversation in an accent and with an air entirely unfamiliar. Now the girl lagged, breathing. Her reactions were unreadable but her gawping attitude triggered an unequivocal paternal response. Her remembered loitering reminded him and he called, "Hurry up, your mother's waiting!" restored to his role by her characteristic stance.

"I'm just coming," she called ahead as she always had, with the old complaining cockney whine in her new voice; and he marched on, reassured, ploughing a straight furrow to their own front door.

The railings at the road-end of the Banjo had gone, she saw. Concrete posts stood with rust-stained holes in them around the greens with nothing between to make the trodden grass seem private. The present Banjo children had been deprived of the singular opportunity of the railings for daring or contemplation. Presumably nobody ever again would cut their heads open in ambitious acrobatics or hang dreaming upside down with their hair brushing the grass. Any more than Cynthia would ever again confide mumblingly over the tinkle of ice in a glass of gin or Penn would not bleed monthly. Time was a ruthless mystery.

But father had disappeared beyond their own path and the pavement still had hopscotch numbers scrawled in chalk and mother was waiting and time was not. So Penn walked slowly up the Banjo, frowningly unaware of curtains twitching, but with an increasing sense of anticipation, a rush of the senses' response to remembered sights and smells. This was the actual opposite of homesickness: not joy, but recognition; and not so much of a place but of connection with former selves: inducing the same faint nausea and giddiness as the longing at a distance rightly called sickness. She passed the Locks' gate, wondering what had happened to Connie and Grace and remembering the dying grandfather in his smell of sick and flowers. She hopped from the 4 to the 5 on the paving stones—a tricky, inviting transition in hopscotch—but toppled and trod on a line. She reached her own gate and walked up the path turning her head slightly to the left to look as if at gardens away from the embarrassingly close window of Mrs Parker's kitchen, as they always did. There once she had seen father praying on his knees on the floor in front of the gas stove. The tact of not staring was a reflex her body had stored for walking this path. Such physical remembrances were making her tingle. She saw that her own front door was open, that the lamp in the hall was lit though night had not yet begun to cast even its shadow, and knew that she was home.

Richard Carr (now promoted to the rank of Brigadier) observed his stranger child and intimate wife exclaim in admiration of the loaded table. Penny pointed at the tinned loganberries in a cut-glass bowl and Cissie nodded with complacent pleasure. It was just as she had intended and expected; and if it was a surprise to him—how pleased and natural his daughter seemed to be back at home—it was also a relief. Watching them under the gas-light he thought ruefully of other occasions when he had felt betrayed, though mercifully, by his daughter's being less different than he had hoped or feared and by his wife's firm, unimaginative grasp which held some simple bond correctly tight. The tall, well-spoken girl was transformed under his pleased but puzzled smile into the child he recollected and his wife took for granted. Tinned loganberries were still a favourite; especially with condensed milk.

Penn was indeed glad to be home. Her father's fears proved unnecessary because she saw no conflict yet between old and acquired expectations. She had missed her mother and her mother's lavish teas and gleaming cleanliness; she had missed the Banjo and spent half that night hanging out of her bedroom window to relish the different darkness of a peopled town, the different atmosphere of the air and sky between close houses. But she presumed to recover what she had lost and at the same time to keep what she had found. It was, after all, her self which had been fed on changes; and that muddled entity enjoyed restored delights with unconsidering confidence. At that first meal, her father discovered that the small new assumptions she brought home with her unconsciously were additions not rejections; and again, his practical wife accepted them with placid ease.

"May I have coffee rather than tea? D'you mind? Let me get it."

"No I'll do it. I think I've got a bottle of Camp tucked away at the back of the larder."

Father, more sensitive, had to face more disturbing new expectations.

"May I see your *Times* Daddy? I'm dying to get to the theatre."

The Brigadier shook his head at this first token of trouble. "We don't take *The Times*, pet. And the Army doesn't allow theatres and cinemas. Surely you remember?"

"Well, of course. I didn't mean Music Halls. Shakespeare or something. They can't mind Shakespeare, surely, darlings? He's for School Certificate."

This was the only indigestible element in the high tea or sign of problem in the family reunion. She had been away from the influence of the Army during formative years, he realised, and perhaps the most ominous thing was that she seemed unaware of spiritual danger. Her tone had been airy, not defiant. When they knelt for a word of prayer after their meal, her mother offered to God nothing but gratitude for safe return; her father agreed that their bodies' preservation was cause for rejoicing but hinted that souls were more important. Even the young, even unknowingly, might become backsliders. Penn had forgotten this odd uncomfortable word for those who fell away from the Army. Chewing it over and easing her knees, she missed his implication.

There were five days to go before Sunday and the first Meeting. Mrs Carr happily looked forward to showing off her proud restored possession and Penn, too, was enthusiastic. She had so missed the Band. "And churches pitch hymns too high—I always hated that thin straining sound the singing made in church." Only the Brigadier felt misgivings and he kept them to himself and his private prayers.

Meanwhile Penn had all the rest of her former world to explore and rediscover. Alice had stayed in the Banjo at first, but left with the new grammar school on the second wave of evacuation when the Blitz began. Alice's parents, the engine-driver's mate and his wife, welcomed Penn's morning visit but seemed a little distracted.

She found them in the garden. They had three smaller children at home and Mrs Jackson sniffed reproachfully about Alice's staying away when she could do with her help. Apparently her eldest girl was boarded with two old ladies, retired school teachers, who had seduced her into book-learning. The old ladies had been quite nasty when the parents wanted to take her away from school at the proper leaving-age of fourteen: Penn gathered there was some sort of allowance resentfully accepted. Alice's Mum turned drying nappies top to bottom on the line with pegs in her mouth and the sun in her fading red hair and Alice's Dad coughed over a flowerbed. He was thinner and grey-faced: night duty on the trains through the bombing had drained him of his old mateyness. They promised to let her have Alice's address, but later; the baby was crying and the little boy had knocked the dustbin over on his sister. Such a flap and din throughout their garden made Alice's father seem more quiet, shadowy and sad as he weeded slowly with a cigarette smoking up into his eyes, and Penn left to revisit the Locks.

The twins had left school and helped, but in a lazy, superior

way, in their father's shop. It shared the prosperity which shortages had brought to small shopkeepers and Mr Lock was now one
of the kings of the High Street. Neighbourhood whispers of black-
market profits were tolerant: he 'looked after' friends in the Banjo
loyally and had a useful arrangement about offal with the butcher's
shop next door to his own. An under-the-counter piece of rare
liver quietened any criticism. Their house was glossy with bright
new furniture and the twins now shared a bedroom very like one
of the windows of Harrison Gibson's they all used to gaze into
longingly. Connie and Grace were at first reserved and suspicious.
Parrot-voiced Penn quickly dropped her lah-di-dah accent and
enthused sincerely over their pink satin bed-covers. They wore
smart square-shouldered suits and lipstick: Penn was impressed.
But so were they by the tales she had to tell, especially the fatal
love story of Cynthia Bellamy. Connie and Grace were very keen
on fatal love and had seen *Gone with the Wind* four times. By
the end of the week they were all embroidering their adventures
sprawled companionably on rumpled satin beds and knitting themselves lacy-patterned jumpers. Mr Lock had a little something
going with the lady at the wool shop too; and Penn was fixed up
with number twelve needles, a pattern, and seven ounces of pale
blue wool. The open-work shell-shapes required concentration and
dexterity, especially when decreasing, and the exciting parts of
stories sometimes had to be shushed as one of the girls turned a
critical corner or reached an armhole. Knit one purl three loop one
knit one pass slipped stitch over ... Once when Penn was lingering dramatically over the deep and tender glances which passed
between Mrs Bellamy and Lieutenant Lester, Connie missed out
a whole shell, right in the front, and had to unpick rows and rows,
moaning.

Apart from love, and films they had seen, and where you could
get *Knight's Castile* for your soap ration if you went early on a
Tuesday, they told Penn about the Blitz. How twice all the windows had been blown out and once Mr Lock had seen a strange
man in their garden from the doorway of the shelter and thought
him a German who had parachuted down. But he was only a chap
taken short on the way to the bus who dodged behind their hedge
to relieve himself. That had been a lark. At the height of the
bombing the Locks had abandoned their Anderson shelter at the end
of the garden and gone up West in the van to sleep in the

underground. That had been a lark too. Connie, the prettier one, had met a nice boy and had her first kiss by the escalators when she crept through bundled bodies away from her family group on the platform. Grace, the plainer one, hinted that this was nothing, compared ... An older man in the party sleeping next to theirs had done something mysterious but apparently rather nice to her under the blanket. Penn's letters from Michael were mentioned successfully; it made her somehow more like them to be in love, especially at a distance, separated. They sighed over their knitting and compared it all with *Dangerous Moonlight*, which was ever such a sad and lovely film. They had a record of the Warsaw Concerto and played it on their gramophone.

It got darker sooner in the city; and anyway the year had reached that late-August moment when dusk falls more steeply each evening. The girls sat on, their knitting lying limply in their laps, as greying daylight and romantic music fitted their thoughts and creeping chill hinted at the end of summer. Penn had not experienced an air raid, German bombers might return with the longer nights of winter.

"Weren't you frightened?" she wondered as Grace with a sigh got up to fix the black-out curtains and turn on the light.

"What? When he touched me, you mean?"

"No, I mean the Blitz."

"Oh that. Not a bit. Well perhaps at the beginning."

Connie said: "Come off it, you know you were scared stiff at the beginning."

Grace said: "What about you then?" To Penn: "She wet herself every time the siren went."

They both giggled. "But only in the beginning," said Connie.

"You get used to it," said Grace.

There had been no raids on London for more than a year but Mrs Carr kept the shelter at the end of the garden prepared. She cleaned it regularly like another room, carrying her dusters and brooms down the garden path through the trellis arch a-bob with rambler roses. She had got Father to lay lino on the earth floor, there was a rug beside the big mattress which took up most of the floor-space, neatly folded blankets and a calendar with a text for every day hanging in a wobbly way on the wavy corrugated-iron walls. Father had built a little shelf beside the bed and a few books smelled damp on it, 'from the condensation', mother explained, laying them out on the lawn to get the benefit of the drying sun. Apparently the cold metal walls sweated with your breath and no doubt sweat, when you had to spend every night there with a blanket nailed across the door-hole so that the Germans couldn't see the candle-light. The books were mostly devotional—prayers and Bible readings—but among them were a German dictionary and a new yellow-covered *Teach Yourself German* manual.

To Penn's curious look, Mrs Carr said, "You know your father," giving both the books a flick with her duster; "he was trying to teach me, even. Said if a pilot dropped into the garden on a parachute it would be useful to be able to talk to him. He's always been one for study; that's where you get it from you know."

Penn nodded, leafing through *The Imitation of Christ* in a red cover mottled with the human wetness of the shelter.

"Were you afraid?"

"Me? No. Our lives are in the Lord's hands." Mrs Carr had climbed down into the dark cave and turned to poke her round rosy face out into the sun. "Mind you, I'd not like to be badly injured. That was what worried me: to be a burden and have to be looked after."

By the time Sunday came, Mother was making tea later as Penny wasn't hungry for it at their usual time and serving her coffee at the end of the meal instead of tea with it, and Father had rigged up a battery lamp for her room so that she could read in bed. In return, Penn was learning German from her father, washing up and dusting while Mother went off on welfare work, and accustoming her knees to polished lino again in frequent prayers. Mrs Carr sang about the house, her true clear contralto proclaimed her happiness in choruses. Father too discovered pleasure in conversations with his daughter after the nine o'clock news. They disagreed about Russia, and Mother called it arguing, but it was stimulating to teach her. How, despite the wonderful courage of Soviet resistance to the German advance, and our natural allied hope that Stalingrad would stand, Russia had not changed her ideology and Communism remained as great a threat as Nazism to Christian believers everywhere. Penn advanced arguments learned from Dr Julian, Father countered that though a great deal about their doctrine was in accordance with the Gospels and certainly he agreed with the need for more social equality, nothing could make the Communists' avowed enmity to God other than wicked and dangerous. Penn was quiet because she did not know as much about it as he did. But on one point they were glad to agree: the hypocrisy of the change in people's attitudes. Either the Russians were, or were not, of common cause with us.

"I hate hypocrisy most," said Penn. All through the thirties, father told her, propaganda had been against Russia; then overnight the government told us they were our allies and friends, the *Daily Worker* was published again and the BBC played the Internationale. But military necessity did not alter principles.

"The ideological position hasn't changed; it's just expediency," father asserted.

"Expediency?" she responded as if to Dr Julian. They looked it up, and suddenly, over the dictionary, exchanged their first shy sudden hug. Mother beamed. And tomorrow was Sunday, too.

Penny's old singing company uniform was far too small. Naturally; though Mrs Carr had kept it carefully and seemed momentarily disappointed to find her daughter had so drastically outgrown the crimson silk blouse. She was not yet entitled to the Uniform (you could not be sworn in as a Senior Soldier until sixteen) so, even if one of Mrs Carr's plump tunics could have been made to fit, it would have been improper and Penny had to go to the meeting in 'private'. Her clothes were drably discreet—the Bellamys had not introduced her wardrobe to Lock worldliness, and that was a mercy—so Mrs Carr was satisfied as they set off.

The war had changed the neighbourhood attitude to the Army. Nobody now called contemptuous 'Barmy' at them. Forces sons had reported better tea at Red Shield Canteens than the Naafi and the Uniform was always early on the scene after a raid. Mrs Carr in her bonnet had swept up glass, scrubbed floors, comforted bereaved, nursed injured, and taken those made homeless to hostels throughout the worst days after the worst nights of bombing. There was a new affectionate respect in people's greetings on the way to the bus stop which cheered Penn. Being mocked was the worst chronic memory of childhood.

So she arrived at the Hall hopefully, looking forward to it all. It had shrunk in her absence and she was amazed by the smallness of the room with a raised place at one end above the Penitent Form and a partition at the other shutting off the Officers' Room. This was where those conducting meetings prepared themselves before progress to the platform. She had never been allowed inside before, not at their own corps, but Mrs Carr took her firmly to be introduced to the corps officers on such an important occasion. Penn saw that preparation included tea: there was a gas-stove in the corner beside the poor table piled with Bibles and Song Books. The officers were two youngish women—not unusual for so small a corps even before the war—and new, of course. It was Army policy to move corps officers annually, usually to a different division, to prevent the danger of their putting down roots outside of Heaven and the Army, or getting too intimate with soldiers. The Farewell meeting and the Welcome meeting in May, when marching orders were issued, were exciting occasions each year. Now Penn thought for the first time how hard it must be for people to be sent to unknown towns to be inspected by the local congregation and to own nothing—for all Quarters were furnished and personal possessions discouraged—not even a sense of belonging in one place or local friendships.

Cups of tea steamed as they knelt in prayer. Mrs Carr withdrew saying, "After the meeting, then," without mortification. Father's job in International Headquarters gave the Carrs glamour as well as a permanent home in London. Mrs Carr respected her own higher rank. She led the way serenely down the centre aisle between wooden benches to their usual place exactly half-way. Once seated, the Carrs knelt. Penny joined them, missing the comfort of hassocks. You asked a blessing on the meeting and then sat up and looked around. Mrs Carr's bonnet nodded in all directions in silent greetings, tilting to indicate Penn with a proud beam and a nudge to make Penn turn too and smile at some forgotten Soldier.

The hall smelled of stove and babies and sweaty serge. It was all much shabbier than she remembered but also doubtless actually shabbier through war's shortages. The Flag, draped in its usual place above the stove, was worn and faded. Wall showed through the thinned red stuff for the Blood of the Lamb and the yellow centre star of the Holy Spirit had space between the weave of coarse threads. The blue edge was frayed and there was a neat but noticeable darn at its proudest tip. The Singing Company was ranged beside the stove—such little children. "I must pass your uniform on," whispered Mrs Carr, pointing her bonnet at a fair-haired little girl in the front row. "You remember Shirley? You recited at her Dedication." But Penn did not. The Band came up the aisle with their instruments. Their ranks were diminished by war-service to old men and young boys and a girl or two with an incongruous-looking cornet. Their brave scarlet uniforms had darkened and dulled and did not fit well. Their progress past the benches left a lingering smell of Brylcreem, metallic saliva and old uncleaned tunics.

It was both poignant and irksome, to meet so much so well-remembered so changed, either in fact, or through her view of it. Mother's running commentary was both helpful and discordant—people did not chat in church. "She's not a good preacher but she does have a lovely way with Testimonies," Mrs Carr reported as the young girl Lieutenant rose at the end of the first song and came forward to lead them all into this now unfamiliar piece of worship.

Dreaming, distracted by confused sensation, Penn was shaken into horrid alertness by the sound of her own name. She was being called upon to speak and every head in the hall was turned expectantly in her direction. She stood up in a flurry of nervousness with mind blank. Rising from her bench like that, placing one hand on the back-rail of the bench in front, prompted memory of the old language. At first tentatively, then in clearer tones, she heard herself running through familiar clichés about being gathered together, and by Divine Grace, and where two or three...

During these automatic preliminaries her mind was scurrying through its stores like a hard-up housewife opening cupboards to find unprepared hospitality. All that presented itself as appropriate from the memories she touched, disturbed, rejected, was the play. *The Bishop's Candlesticks* had a religious message and they might not know the story. With a deftness which seemed to have improved in spite of lack of public practice, she turned her platitudes towards a Personal Experience. "And I remember how this was borne out when in a strange village among strange people we children from this district..." When she got to the bit about the Temple of the Living God, her voice was not only firm but had returned to its posh accent. Though the procedure was inverted from the performance in the village hall, this too was a performance and the effect was similar. Sitting down, Penn felt the hush of genuine emotion. The young Lieutenant had her handkerchief out and Mother was openly weeping. Penn bowed her head. '*The Temple of the Living God: I'll remember.*' The Convict's last line. She had remembered to 'turn' it into an illustration, ending in a lower voice, "May we all remember that always: I know I always will."

It had been true as she sat down. It was still, in a way, true. But something was false. She looked up suddenly from the hiding, devotional posture and caught Father's eye. It was full of an unexpectedly keen light under the softness of affection. It shone warningly, though quite without irony. She dropped her face again and stared at the stained floor between her knees. Performance, that pleasurable sickening thing: was that all anything was? Meetings, anyway?

This one proceeded after a chorus into prayer. Various people referred to the beautiful Message from the Young Lamb returned to the Fold. She was gratified; but could not help remembering something Clare had said about people praying spontaneously: they addressed each other rather than God, treating Him like a telephone operator on an enormous exchange to put them through.

After the meeting, Brigadier Carr succeeded in cutting short his wife's boastful display of their trophy. He did this with firmness, convinced of Cissie's sin in such pride; but humbly, knowing his wife closer in many ways to the Lord of the Army teaching. Works were recommended rather than mysticism or contemplation. And it was Cissie who laboured untiringly to do good in practical ways, as well as continuing to run their home with customary zeal under all difficulties. Sometimes he was almost outraged at the store she set by dusted window sills—"Those bombs!" she'd complain, "make such a mess." But he was also soothed by her patient narrow-sightedness. It reduced total war to an inconvenience; which she tackled methodically.

'Methodical' was one of her favourite words. Penny and Dick were not, but she could manage, tutting, to maintain order in spite of their temperament and the world's turmoil. Cleaning at the Grange had been haphazard. Here, cleanliness was not only next to Godliness, it seemed almost a manifestation of it. Mrs Carr's routines had in them the elements of ritual. Monday was washing day whatever the weather or the news. You lit the copper before breakfast (a fire made with paper, wood and coal was the only way to heat water for the boiler) and prayed that it would draw. Later you brought in the mangle from the garden shed and the big zinc bath to be filled with Reckitt's Blue—the Holy

Ghost's colour—for a last rinse to make the whites shine like
sanctified souls. Waiting for the copper to come to the boil was
a weekly suspense, and a weekly climax came when bubbles
began to break on the surface and multiply until sheets and under-
wear seethed in an eruption almost volcanic. The boil was always
celebrated with a hearty stir with the pounding wooden copper-
stick, a cup of tea, and a word of prayer.

Tuesday was ironing day. Starched linen crackled, was damped
and rolled. Two flat-irons took their turn, one on the stove, one
in the hand smoothing deftly into corners. If the iron sizzled
when you spat on its smooth surface, it was hot enough.

Wednesdays bedrooms. If the day was dry, you started by
throwing all rugs out of the window, hung them over the washing-
line and lashed them with a carpet-beater made of cane twirled
into epaulette shapes. Bedroom-cleaning finished, hours later, when
the rugs were replaced on lino now polished on hands and knees
to a deep shine. On Thursdays you did all the downstairs rooms
and Friday's baking imbued the house with a smell which identified the weekend's opening.

Such regiments of days marshalled Penn into the consoling
disciplines of home sooner than anyone except Mrs Carr would
have expected. When the new term started, she went to a muddled
school composed of children who had stayed behind or returned
from evacuation, whatever their 'proper' school. It was defined by
area only, not sex or having passed the scholarship, and this made
it easier to be anything; or various things in turn. She took up
shorthand and typing for a bit, joining the girls from the tech-
nical college. Then swapped to Latin, late, because a young
teacher pining for her husband fighting in the desert told her
about a college called King's in London. Penn liked Mrs Conran
so decided to go to King's; and that meant she had to matricu-
late in Latin. She learned this accidentally while deliberately
learning a lot of history because that was Mrs Conran's subject
and with ingenuity you could get her to talk about love and
college as well as Walpole sometimes.

She learned to be good at French through a pash on the French
master. The teachers had been scrambled as arbitrarily as the
pupils. Mr Howard had taught at the best boys' school in the
district. He played the piano at Assembly, wore a gown and
occasionally sang Schumann songs in a light true tenor which was

deeply moving. In German. Penn improved her French mark from fourteen per cent to seventy-five per cent in a term and dropped anonymous poems into his pigeon-hole in the office.

In spite of these daunting missives, he took an interest in her sudden success in his subject and introduced her to Rachmaninov (his Piano Concerto was almost better than the Warsaw one), T. S. Eliot and the name of a man who made peculiar sculptures and drawings of people sleeping in the underground. Henry Moore's drawings reminded her of Grace Lock's fascinating experience on Bond Street platform. So everything remained mixed up for her and no experience imposed alternatives upon her disposition. Modern Art and the Lock twins linked quite naturally; Mr Howard's handsome profile and classical music knitted as neatly as a slipped stitch passed over; and if Mrs Conran was especially sparkling about Metternich in a morning History period it meant of course that she had had a letter from the front and her husband was still alive and loved her.

The school was a new one which had had no chance to establish traditions before its population was swept away by war and had become the local melting-pot for pupils who came and went and perhaps returned according to the waves of danger and respite from the air. A well-meaning headmistress had intended to create the standards of older schools and tried valiantly to maintain them in impossible circumstances. You were supposed to wear uniform. But as at least a dozen schools were represented you could always claim that what you were wearing *was* your 'proper' school's uniform if stopped in a corridor.

In practice it established a tradition of unusual flexibility. Later classical scholars took up woodwork and some later wood-workers learned a little Greek. Threading the maze of sand-bag walls in the corridor, a person could find instruction in making pastry from the Domestic Science teacher left behind from the Council School, an ex-apprentice of Henry Moore's in the Art Room insisting that the stupidest boy in the school was a genius and demanding larger sheets of drawing paper despite the shortage, or a distinguished elderly physicist from a Public School explaining Einstein. It was ideal from Penn's point of view. Even the playing fields were unusable due to pits dug to prevent an invading army occupying the red-brick building by tank attack. The upturned earth beside the troughs made excellent cover for pupils investigating the opposite sex. Penn did not enlist in this subject, but tripped over them without embarrassment.

What was embarrassing was the Salvation Army. She accompanied her parents every Sunday but she did not like it any more. After that first return, Mother in her pride and pleasure at the testimony had beamed over gravy-making: "Just think: only just over a year and you can be sworn in as a Senior Soldier." A steaming silence from Penn and her father had prompted Mrs Carr to turn, still stirring, and reassure: "Don't worry about the coupons, I can alter one of my uniforms. And the bonnet will suit you, it's always lovely with fair hair." But silence still encompassed the kitchen. Then Father said in his level voice, quietly, so that Cissie knew it was important: "She's been away from the Army for a long time. I don't think we should even discuss it at this stage, Mummy." Mummy (what did they call each other while she was away?) had looked annoyance but accepted his verdict as she always did with a mixture of pride and gratified pique: men ought to make decisions just as women should complain at the decisions they made. The bonnet was tried on and did indeed suit Penn. But the Brigadier was adamant, especially at such frivolous coaxing. "It's a solemn step. Let's read the Articles of War together after tea."

"Of course my ribbons all tie," said Mrs Carr. "I don't hold with the ready-made bow done up with a press-stud. She does look bonny in it."

"We'll read it together," said Brigadier Carr. After that, Mother kept quiet. She had forgotten quite how solemn a renunciation of the world and all its works was called for and how total a commitment to the Salvation War; because *she* made both so completely.

Father agreed with Mother that Penny should join the Songsters as they were seriously depleted now that women were called up. Songster Practice interfered with homework, listening to the wireless, and knitting another open-work jumper—this time in turquoise—with the Lock twins.

The war turned. Church bells rang out in an unpractised euphoria of muddled bells to celebrate the victory at El Alamein. The brave if sinister Communists began to drive the Nazi hordes back out of Russia. The study of German grammar languished as the likelihood of conversation-classes in the garden declined; and anyway Penn didn't need another modern language for School Certificate now that she was doing so well at French.

When raids on London began again in January, her baptism of fire and danger was most remarked by the discussion with Father about whether murder could be moral even in war. This raid was a reprisal for our bombing of Berlin. Though no advance in German grammar was made, she learned that Father was right in saying that it was much less frightening if you could see what was happening. They stood on the lawn in the dark ("*Do be careful not to tread on the crocuses*," Mother called crossly from the dug-out shelter) watching the searchlights sweep across dark sky as gracefully as dancers, separate and probing, until their converging seemed beautiful rather than ominous. As they all met on an enemy aircraft like a wild, earth-bound star which had found its centre, Brigadier Carr and his daughter gave a frail, absent-minded cheer. Anti-aircraft guns banged round them like bonfire-night parties. When the dot of plane with a man in it, even if German, eluded the bright fingers and noisy fireworks, they had to cheer again. Later, drinking Mother's thermos of hot cocoa in the shelter, they discussed several critical matters. "There is a danger of watching as a spectacle and forgetting the sanctity of life," Father said.

"Yes. But I wouldn't have minded them getting him as long as he wasn't killed."

"People are. He was, is, one of God's children, unique as we. The women and children in Berlin were just like us except they speak and think German."

"I'm still a pacifist, too, I think," said Penn. "But being in it is exciting when you know it's history."

"And a spiritual problem for pacifists is the certain evil of Hitler's cause," Father confided. "I've found it difficult."

Penn nodded fondly. "There must be other spiritual problems for you. Heaven can't be up there because now we can see it isn't."

"Shush," said Mrs Carr. "Drink up your cocoa, the all-clear will be sounding in a minute. Don't be blasphemous."

Father drank up his cocoa obediently and said: "Heaven doesn't need to be up there. It's just a way of putting it."

"Do you know about Plato?" said Penn.

"Of course. Some of his ideas anticipated Our Lord in a remarkable way."

"Well apart from that."

"There it goes," said Mrs Carr as the siren climbed to its single high note. "Let's get to bed, for goodness' sake." And for goodness' sake they abandoned debate and carried back the cocoa and had a word of prayer, gratefully. But the Brigadier and his daughter eyed each other lovingly and as antagonists.

After that, she began to cut Songster Practice occasionally.

"But I've got exams," she tried to justify; "and anyway I can't sing."

"That's not the point," said her mother. "It's a witness." But she could not be a witness any more; having seen.

The war was a sub-plot: Penn recognised its position in their lives from all those Shakespeare plays from which she had cut sub-plots to prepare the acting version. While 1943 ran towards the victory people had always presumed with an actual improvement in the allied position, the foreground battle in the Carr household was over Penny's soul. There was nothing unusual about the Carr priorities. The Locks were more concerned over Grace's precocious interest in men (especially as Connie had been the pretty one) than any setback in Tunisia; and the Jacksons by the fact that Alice's father was off work more often than not with what the doctor called chronic bronchitis. He smoked and coughed in a chair outside their front door as the evenings drew out and make-shift hoops and skipping ropes reappeared. His health, and whether it was rash to let girls have lengths of old clothes-line to skip with, occupied most occupants of the Banjo more than the international situation.

Some of the sixth-form boys at school once brought up this small-minded parochialism in an open discussion period. Mr Howard and Mrs Conran approved their seriousness but suggested that this attitude in England had been an element in the gallant but illogical stand after Dunkirk. "We had quite clearly lost the war at that point," said Mr Howard; "only everybody refused to notice. And if we win now, it will be that apparently stupid optimism which will have saved the world for democracy."

"Yes," said Mrs Conran; "and private concerns will always outweigh public events in the lives of individual people. That's

174

partly—to preserve that very freedom—what the war is about. And certainly art. Think of Tolstoy's *War and Peace* for example, which sets very small and family matters in the foreground."

Few of them were capable of thinking of Tolstoy's vast novel; but Penn bumped into two senior boys on her way out of the library that evening with the only copy.

So in February the German sixth army surrendered at Stalingrad and Penn finished *War and Peace* and the turquoise jumper; some older boys started a Communist cell at school and hopscotch scrawled the paving stones which had stayed bare through winter's rain. In March the Locks thought Grace might be pregnant (though Grace privately sneered, "Rubbish: I was standing up") and the girls all knitted Balaclava helmets during this crisis partly for the brave cold Russians and partly as a rest from thin-needled intricate patterns. When the emergency was over ("I told you so," said Grace) they abandoned head-wear for the Russian army but it continued to advance and Penn got her friends to mourn the death of Rachmaninov largely for Stalin's sake: they still thought Richard Adinsell's Piano Concerto from *Dangerous Moonlight* was better than the Russian's.

At this time, too, just before Easter, Penn had to help her Mother collect for Self Denial—the Army's practical version of Lent. Members of the Army went without even more than war and rationing proscribed to donate the savings to the Salvation war. They were also required to make a more painful sacrifice by risking snubs on cold evenings going from door to door to collect donations. Penny took alternate gates in a richer district with Mother, slinking through sodden, sooty laurel bushes to cringe on the doorsteps. Whether people were mean, generous or outright rude, you had to say "God Bless You" on the way out. This seemed like hypocrisy when she was burning with embarrassment anyway and anger if they treated her condescendingly; after all, the Bellamys were far more posh than these smug suburbanites. Mother was sympathetic but insistent: she said it was heaping coals of fire on their heads and later they might feel convicted if they had sent you away empty-handed. The metaphor helped. Penn called "God Bless You" with a smile fierce with fiery hatred when she was turned back snubbingly, and was sometimes gratified by the flicker of doubt on their faces at her posh voice.

In April the Eighth Army met up with American forces in North Africa and Penn thought that Mrs Conran's husband might have met Christopher Lester, if he had not been killed. This prompted a rare letter to the Bellamys. For a few weeks after her return to London she and Clare had exchanged importunate correspondence ('Write *at once*') and then dwindled into silence. Dr Julian began and continued to write occasionally and in May, when he had to be in London, came to tea. Penn found it surprising, even slightly insulting, that the village was going on though she had left it. Mrs Cooper was coming in to clean and cook at the Grange and Clare seemed fond of her; as she was of Mrs Hayle.

"But we hated her," protested Penn.

"Did you?" said Dr Julian mildly. "She's settled down better now I believe."

"Clare or Mrs Hayle?"

"Both."

Dr Julian seemed older and more lined but also less haunted now that Cynthia was actually dead.

"How about Plato, then?" he asked as he left.

"Yes indeed." She shifted feet obligingly. "Daddy and I discuss it sometimes."

His hair was now a shock of white, as thick, but bleached to flax. He looked amused at her politely dismissive tone and set off down their path with slightly offended jauntiness. Later she remembered how much he had taught her with perfunctory regret.

She didn't make the Lock twins mourn the death of Arthur Mee as she had not forgiven him for leaving out the Sonnets and giving Socrates a small entry among his Heroes.

In July, skipping was in full swing in the Banjo, the allies invaded Sicily and Mrs Carr made Penn try on the bonnet again. It was particularly becoming now that she was pinning the front of her hair up into a plump upstanding roll which filled the brim. It was tempting to give in but temptation was what it seemed. "It wouldn't be right," Penn said, gazing into the looking-glass with some longing.

"What's that supposed to mean?" Mrs Carr demanded crossly. She put the bonnet back in its box, protectively folding the ribbons into the crown. What, indeed, was that supposed to mean, Penn wondered. "It would be hypocritical," she tried. Mrs Carr sniffed.

This hypocrisy was hydra-headed. It was true, as Penn protested, that the Army doctrine was unformulated on various matters which occupied her intellect. It was more compellingly true that she found Songster Practice a bore and the ladies with babies at the Home League smelly. A well-trained sense of sin convicted her of snobbery and worldly pride. Taking it to the Lord in prayer, the Army's disapproval of theological questioning soon tinged her guilt with doubt. She did not believe her questions wrong—her father had, perhaps perilously, always encouraged the probing mind she had inherited from him. But reason was so tangled with emotion; quest for truth with self-interest; intellectual doubt with distaste for many unattractive though saved people, that she had to mistrust her own motives. But then again: the charm of clapping in unison, especially off-beat, to the choruses and the devoutly pretty effect of her new hairstyle under the brim of the bonnet were appealing in a way equally suspect.

Spirals of uncertainty made her tired. The doctor's diagnosis of anaemia was timely. It got her out of Corps Cadets as well as Songster Practice and the Sunday evening meeting. Also, her mother found a cache of Virol in an old chemist's shop and dipped into the tin of gas-bill money on the mantelpiece to buy it up. 'Growing girls need it' said the tin placards outside Liverpool Street Station; though so did expectant mothers and toddlers.

The Man with the Lantern continued to look gravely down from above the mantelpiece, knocking at the door of her heart, just beyond the rifled gas-bill-money tin. The taste of Virol, though delicious, was tainted with self-condemnation. So were such thoughts, she had learned from the Bellamys. 'Feeling convicted', which was what the Carrs called such thoughts approvingly, would be considered 'wallowing' by the Bellamys. The selfishness of sucking the Virol spoon and being cossetted would only be compounded, according to Bellamy standards, by moping about it. Such self-absorption was self-indulgent and she imagined Cynthia drawling: "What does your tiny little soul matter, darling? Don't be such a bore about it."

Remembering Mrs Bellamy, Penn noticed critically as well as guiltily a certain gloating in her mother's concern for the state of her soul and body. Cissie fed Virol and a sense of sin with the same spoon.

So, after declining for a month or two, Penn got sick of her self and recovered in time for the school play. Even the doctor diagnosed a physical improvement. She felt a fraud but put in for the main part and got it and cheered up.

Rehearsals kept her away from evening activities at the Hall. Father and Mother kept praying pointedly about a sense of values but now she shuffled her knees protestingly: they seemed to prefer her ill and self-centred so that they could minister to her and call it a spiritual crisis.

Monday, washing; Tuesday, ironing; Wednesday, bedrooms: it was all now irksomely familiar and shaming at the same time. They were so good. But the reproachfulness in their virtue smacked of Bellamy bad form; especially when Mother actually polished round the book she was learning her part from on the dining-room table with such pained elbow-grease.

During August a valuable convoy crossed the Atlantic undamaged. A large pack of U-boats was driven off; and the anniversary of Mrs Bellamy's suicide brought heightened reminiscence of her tone of voice and mind. Penn had been home for a whole year, so the crisis of becoming a Soldier or a Back-slider was becoming acute. The Russians continued to recapture places and the expanding school-Communist group met during the holidays in an out-building among unused cricket-bats. The Carrs allowed Penny to accompany the Locks to the cinema to see *For Whom the Bell Tolls* after research indicated that Hemingway was an important writer and the title came from a seventeenth-century sermon. Father told Mother that a person in their daughter's position could not sincerely renounce the world and all its works without cautious permission to investigate them. Some of the dialogue reminded her of Michael. She walked back from the Picture Palace with the twins through gutters filled with bright marbles. "Yah, get off," shouted little intent children as the big girls kicked brilliant blue-fires carelessly out-of-place, in deep discussion about what transpired in the sleeping-bag.

In September Italy gave in and so did Alice's Dad. He took to his bed as the sun declined on his place in the front garden and sent, via Penn, for Brigadier Carr. Father came back sadly preoccupied by the ethics of death-bed conversion. It turned out that 'chronic bronchitis' masked a growth too malignant to be named aloud; and that the engine-driver had long nursed a sneaking regard for the uniformed Carrs who walked so regularly down their garden path on Sunday being a witness and used to send his little girl back home with nails like little pearls.

"There you are, you see," said Mother, "it proves it is a witness and Alice brought God into their lives. Lo," said Mother, "a little child shall lead them," beaming at Penn. Father, after private prayer and official consultation, enrolled Mr Jackson as a soldier of the Salvation Army in the front bedroom. The Colour-Sergeant brought the Flag and it drooped above the mock-oak bed-head from Harrison Gibson's and the waif-thin man who had stoked engine-fires and been matey to his daughter's friend. The Brigadier, at home with cocoa after this ordeal, consoled himself with the impression that Mrs Jackson had been 'influenced' and might bring the littler Jackson children to the Hall where they too might be saved. Penn was impressed; especially when the Band came to play in the Banjo outside the dying man's window. 'Nearer my God to Thee'. The tender richness of the sound and its brassy certainty offered a consolation almost tangible; perhaps the only possible comfort to fears of death by illness which had come now so near home. Violent death had seemed less shocking. She longed to succumb to what was as warm if as woolly as an old blanket.

But despite her gauche, ungrateful distance with Dr Julian at their re-meeting, what he had told her about the meaning of her name often came back to Penn's mind. The obligation to fly far and possibly high on her nominal pinions had more influence at this time than he might have approved. Whenever she was almost persuaded to settle, the recollection of his casual semantics sent her flying off at a tangent. The Bellamys had given her wider perspectives; but it was the Army itself which had bred her commitment to working out her own salvation. Now the appeal of the Army was in conflict with its own ineradicable influence to set high value on an individual destiny in the all-seeing eyes of the Lord. She dare not cheat. It would have been easy enough to give in and pay convenient lip-service by Bellamy standards; but by those of her earliest training it was impossible. To join the Army would be, paradoxically, to betray it. If she could only be a completely Bellamy sort of person, she could have looked pretty in the bonnet, indulged in brass band rhapsodies and pleased her mother without bothering whether she truly meant all it implied. "Does it matter so very much?" a Bellamy person might have asked. But because her parents had taught her that personal conscience was all-important, not outward forms, they had to be denied polite pretence. She could not explain how much their influence prevented her agreeing to be sworn-in as a Soldier. She fluttered on her dedicated wings; but could not quite settle for the salvation of the Army or the safety of home's old nest.

And in the same September Michael's return from the battle-field into this tiny war in P. Carr's soul reinforced her resistance. Their letters had continued, though spasmodic on his part. The thin fawn envelopes addressed to her in fat spider writing had aroused surprise and alarm in the household; not completely allayed by Penn's letting her parents read them. Though there was nothing specifically wicked—he still wrote unrevealing banter, serious only about authors, artists and ideas—Brigadier and Mrs Carr felt themselves faced with an insidious enemy; both in the very idea of that Michael and in his influence. A more direct challenge—the sort of problem poor Mrs Lock had with Grace for instance—would have been more susceptible to prayer and penitence. They could have dealt with that. The Brigadier advised against interference or criticism, as Penny's openness showed a good spirit and her extra-curricular visits to the library to look up his references were, in a way, educative. But both knew that the correspondence made their young soldier more elusive to the claims of full-time service; and uneasiness hung over the breakfast table whenever a letter from Michael appeared.

One did, that September, after a silence of some weeks. It announced in his off-hand way that he had been on leave in England and if she'd care to hazard a meeting she could see him off that evening at Liverpool Street station. He would be in the buffet an hour before the troop train left. Mrs Carr made so much ado about the rudeness and carelessness—"On the actual day, even!"—and Penn defended him so automatically, that her own pique was soon worn out and only anticipation and nervousness accompanied her on the train from Seven Kings. 'I think you're making yourself cheap to go at all in the circumstances," Mrs Carr had sniffed as she left home. "Growing girls need it," said the Virol posters as the carriage twitched across the many points and short sooty tunnels which heralded the terminus.

Michael was not in the buffet but waiting at the end of the platform. She recognised him at once, but, though he must have researched probable train-arrivals to be there looking for her, he seemed surprised and rather annoyed when she greeted him.

"Hallo," said Penn boldly because she felt shy.

"God," said Michael: "you've grown up."

"Inevitable, wouldn't you think, in four years," said Penn coldly.

"What a pity. You were such a nice plain child. You've got almost pretty." He used the word as though it were the worst complaining insult.

"Frightfully sorry to disappoint you," said Penn furiously.

People with cases or kitbags bustled and jostled them. Their voices were raised; pitched and clipped to carry across the sounds of the station and the more confounding obstacle of their being actually together like this, in the flesh. They stood tilted like rifles at each other's heads until he slumped and grinned suddenly.

"We seem to be having a row," he said amiably, taking her elbow.

"Again," she agreed, relieved to find shyness lost.

He led her a little stumblingly into the people and activity from which they had held back. The dark red beret tucked flat in his belt bashed against her side thinly covered by a summer dress.

"You're much taller," he charged her sternly as they stepped together into the buffet, to mask the faint trembling in his finger-tips and her elbow which threatened to abash them.

"Well, I'd have been a midget if I hadn't grown a bit," she protested with the same motive; "I'm nearly sixteen."

They relinquished contact with relief, glancing curiously into each other's faces, then away at crowded tables and bright chromium urns.

"And cake?" said Michael.

"Yes, cake," she said.

While he waited at the counter she had time to check the parting in her hair, bite her lips to redden them and smooth and darken her eyebrows with the licked forefinger which used to ward off fever. It was what the twins recommended, as make-up was forbidden by the Carrs.

He caught her at it as he turned and she blushed and said busily, "So you're a Sergeant," as she accepted a slopped cup of tea.

"That's true," he said, amused. "Very true. And what rank do you hold now? Or have you been demobbed from your army?" He stirred his tea vigorously then looked up for an answer with the teasing but somehow tender expression she recognised from a long-ago dinner table.

She shook her head. "It's a bit of a problem at home." He examined the inside of his roll. It revealed a scrape of margarine on one side only and a thin slice of ham dried to a grim maroon-colour and cardboard-texture. "Remind you of anything?" he asked, showing it to her. "That terrible picture over your mantel-piece with Jesus looking soppy." She stared down into her held cup to find a tea-coloured reflection of a window and the pattern of her dress.

"It's easy for you to be rude," she said.

"Yes, I've never found it too difficult," he said. "You can't seriously swallow all that sloppy thinking and cheap emotion now you're a big girl, can you?"

She put her cup down with a clatter and approached the block of yellow sponge with pink icing. "Now there's a better colour scheme," Michael pointed. "Almost as jolly as the flag. Nice contrasts." It seemed almost an apology.

The cake suddenly broke into sawdust at a clumsy touch and sprinkled them both as well as the table. Michael stared surprised at crumbs all over his khaki, lodging in the tabs of a lot of pockets. She stared too. The wide spread of one smallish square of sponge impressed rather than embarrassed at first sight.

"Christ," said Michael admiringly, brushing all ten fingers loosely down his front without much conviction of dislodging so very many crumbs. "There you were, being sensitive in your old way but talking in your pretty new voice; and all of a sudden you hurl cake further than is humanly possible." She gazed down at her plate at this ambiguous approval. The icing lay limply in a pink curl entirely deprived of cake. "That new voice by the way: I rather miss the cockney. You'd obviously write posh but I thought you'd still speak cockney. Where did you leave that?"

She tossed a cluster of pale crumbs out of her hair. "On a stage in a village hall. Where I was evacuated. But I can still do cockney too."

"Like newts," said Michael. He seemed relieved by her clumsiness with the cake from having to be aggressive to her. "You haven't forgotten your newts phase? Amphibious. Like you. Slithering between cockney and lah-di-dah, the Banjo and—the Grange, wasn't it? Sounds rather grand."

She nodded, moved to be remembered for the newts which had seemed part only of her private memories of him.

"Well surely they taught you to mistrust evangelism and pictures of sentimental chaps begging at back doors?"

"Yes, of course. And love. And poetry of the romantic movement. And extreme effects in nature. And you," she finished.

"Oh good," he said, spooning more sugar. "Not that I see quite how I come in. Still, mistrust is good, in a general way."

"Not exactly you. Well, me I mean, only . . ." Embarrassed suddenly, she ate a bit of the squishy pink icing. But he accepted without comment her implication that they were related in a secret way. "Mrs Bellamy killed herself. And I'm still not sure that we, well I, didn't have something to do with it. Influence works both ways, Dr Julian said." She broke off another sliver of tacky icing, un-nerved.

"Cigarette?" offered Michael. She shook her head. "Pity." He bent to the match in his cupped hands.

"Why?" But she stared, remembering flames shaped like wallflower petals. These connections: was it her Army training which made her see connections everywhere? Or were they *really* as Dr Julian and his friend Plato said? It could hardly be the Holy Ghost; not with smoking as a link. Well; not the Army's Holy Ghost anyway.

"Why?" she prompted. Michael looked curiously at her past his waving match.

"Smoking might do something for that wholesome look of yours."

She scowled. "No, I am not an Ovalteeny; before you ask *again*."

"Do I repeat myself?" He seemed put out.

"Often," she told him firmly. But his downcast air reprieved him.

"Actually, I know what you mean about my face. Bonny, my mother calls it." She gave him Banjo shorthand for being sick— a retching noise and boss-eyed gape—then recomposed herself. She picked daintily at the remnants of icing on her plate. She asked, "It that why you didn't get in touch until the last day of your leave?" And rashly looked up to flinch.

"Partly," said Michael. "You scare me stiff." He threw ash towards the ashtray; then shrugged. "Anyway. Might've had to spend hours watching you throw cake all over the place and contemplating Holman-Hunt-reproduction-ham-rolls. How old did you say you were? Fifteen?"

"Nearly sixteen," she corrected. But the brutal relish with which he always reminded her how impossible they were was always perversely encouraging. He agreed *they were*; if impossible. So she dared a faintly flirting comment.

"Mummy thought you'd have married a WAAF by now," she said.

"No." He narrowed his eyes at her, not recognising and plainly not much liking the influence of the Lock twins. "No. There's a girl called Toto in Cairo who's rather gorgeous." She suddenly remember sneezing when his sister had tempted her to powder. "But she's not a WAAF." He blew a long spume of smoke upwards and then stubbed out his cigarette. She tried to hide her face, which must show the pang of her jealousy and the shame of presuming too much from this meeting.

He said, "I'll send you a box of Abdullas; for after prayer-meetings." But might just be showing off. "Turkish. Oval. Black, perhaps," he added carelessly, confirming the boasting impression.

"Black!" she dared to tease. "To leave dark red lipstick on, no doubt. Me." So that both had to grin. He clapped a whole blunt hand across his mouth to end or hide the smile's tendency to spread into delirious beaming between them, and turned away from the glow with which self-mockery had lit her face. Stained tables, old cakes and waitresses only made more piquant and ridiculous the image of a bonny girl with a black cigarette. She blew imaginary smoke languidly through a pursed mouth; then her smile died. "Actually, Cynthia used to smoke them sometimes."

"Who? Oh the suicide lady. Well you see where black fags can lead."

Though too much beaming disconcerted, he was disappointed that he could not make her smile now. "Why did she do it?" he asked.

"She was in love," the girl mumbled, gazing.

"So? It's not necessarily fatal." But the flinching boldness with which they held each other's eyes became too difficult and he made a deliberate turn to look around the crowded drab room. "We ought to be making a move," he said. "Look: let's stop trying to do a repeat performance of when you were eleven and trying out being in love with me. And don't be a precocious twenty either because it doesn't suit you. Be yourself. And drink up because my train's almost due."

He stood up, pulling his beret out of his belt and looking away from her through steamy windows on to the world outside. When he put his beret on he looked quite different, like a soldier, like a man she did not know. Scoffing her cold dregs of tea, she was suddenly daunted and followed him nervously.

Outside, there were so many men who looked just like him in their uniforms that he seemed to have disappeared already. "I'll write," she almost shouted; though he was beside her, he felt already distant.

"Yes, do. I'll send you the Sonnets for Christmas," he called distantly.

"You said that before. But didn't. Don't bother, I've got them."

He gave her a short bitter stare. "You see the danger of this self-parody then." His face had become the texture of khaki as well as its colour; harsh and masking. Buffeted by other people —the gap he kept between them was inconvenient to the crowd squeezing on to the platform—she yelled: "I'm not criticising, honestly. I think the repetitions are significant, not a conversational gaffe."

A shudder and stir riffled through the khaki platform to herald the imminent train. Swaying in this breeze, he closed the gap between them. "That's my old transcendental Ha'penny," he said, grabbing her arm with his old warm contempt. But she was as stiff as a coarse stalk; would not bend; though might break like a return ticket. Hers was safe in her pocket, she touched it with her free hand to reassure that the Army and the twins and the Banjo were still there for her to get back to.

"I think I'll go," she said.

She had already turned away when she felt his hand grip her upper arm to pull her back towards him. Before she could anticipate it, their faces bumped into each other. So that her first kiss was a muddled meeting of lips and teeth in the shadow of the train. Chuff-chuff-chuff . . . whoo, it sighed to a standstill as she thought, 'Gosh, he's kissing me'. But felt only surprise, pain and silliness at this inexpert and awkward moment of contact. The longed-for union of souls became a blunder of mouths. He pushed her away as abruptly as if he read her reactions. Neither looked again. He turned at once to the train and she hurried away along the platform, tasting blood on her lip.

After that, Michael wrote more often but mentioned their encounter only obliquely, with a teasing triumph and dismay; so Penn could still let her parents read his letters though she was more secretive about her replies. Brigadier and Mrs Carr felt that the correspondence as well as school and the books both made her read were taking her further away from them and the Army than outright sin. The winter drifted on uncertain tides. *Be good sweet maid and let who will be clever*. Mrs Carr thought it often and Michael quoted it in the letter which arrived on the day of the French Oral exam in June.

'I begin to see what they meant when they kept quoting it in your autograph album,' he wrote. 'It's difficult to get to know you through all your fancy talk. Green ink's a symptom. Your latest bit of Shelley I just don't care for—could you try John Donne? Could you change your ink? Could you ever be *bad*, sweet maid, and let who will be clever?'

Penn concealed this letter from her parents in the flurrying hurry to school and the exam. She changed her pen; but could not forget all through the day.

And all through the day aircraft droned overhead and military lorries rumbled past the examination room far more than was usual.

"Voici une jeune fille." The outside examiner showed Penn a picture and pitched her voice above the noise of heavy transport and some interfering atmosphere of excitement seeping into the room from the sand-bagged corridors.

"Donnez-moi une description." Penn scrutinised the thumbed illustration of a French girl with fair hair not unlike her own. She replied with sudden inspiration: "Il est une fille aux cheveux de lin." Michael's voice 'spoke' to her as clearly as the Holy Spirit's, and she pursued her description with verve.

As she left the room she remembered she had got the gender wrong; but was swept into growing speculation that all this traffic must mean the invasion of Europe was imminent. By the time school broke up for the afternoon the Second Front was assumed with more certainty. The bus was abuzz with it in the wake of convoys. New and cryptic signposts had been unveiled beside bus-stops and the conductor was telling people on the upper deck how all day the route had been altered and his run delayed. Throughout the evening the Carrs kept popping outside to stand on the lawn and listen to planes in wave after wave driving steadily towards France. Penn did wish she had not said 'il' instead of 'elle' as she stared up into the dark towards the invisible drama. Some of the men up there would be killed; perhaps many; and would the allies hold the beach-head and advance and win the war? And would an unexpected metaphor from Debussy make up for wrong genders and a muddle with tenses? And what did Michael mean about her being bad, and green ink?

"I'm going out front," she said eventually, restless.

Grown-ups in the Banjo went out front more than before the war but the public pavement and greens were still usually left to children. Mother and Father stayed in the back garden while Penn faltered into the murmuring speculation outside. Above the pulse of excitement about invasion, another whisper ran through the Banjo. Mr Jackson was dying; was dead; the doctor was there now; see, that was his car at the end.

Penn went to see and the rumour about the doctor's car was true. While she considered its ominous black sides and the blacked-out windows of Alice's home, another van drew up with 'Funeral Director' discreetly painted on its side. The younger kids gave way before the solemn terrifying undertaker who answered out-of-hours calls in person; but Penn was conscious of being grown-up, and politely asked for confirmation. Yes, Mr Jackson had indeed passed away, said the fat man in black overcoat with practised gravity, then burped, and gave her a sardonic look to remind her that her question was not really grown-up but silly, or why would he be here?

The advance of planes in even surges kept waking her all night. Kept waking everybody in the Banjo. Except Mr Jackson.

'*(a) An officer should early confer with the bereaved relatives and carefully outline his plans for the funeral. The Army seeks, by its example, (i) to protest against various undesirable practices and customs which add trouble and expense to the sorrows of bereavement, (ii) to show how it is possible for faith to triumph in sorrow.*

(b) Salvationists who 'know that if the earthly house of our tabernacle be dissolved, we have a building from God, a house not made with hands, eternal, in the heavens', should avoid wearing black clothing or other mourning on the death of relatives. They should make their friends understand their attitude in this respect. (See Orders and Regulations for Soldiers.) Salvationists while making every possible use of the grave's loud warning to the living, must be unlike the world in their expression of mourning.'

Mrs Jackson was positive that her husband had wanted an Army funeral and Brigadier Carr confirmed this from his daily prayers with the dying man. Penn and Mother looked after the little children while father explained why there would be white ribbons on the Flag and why everything about an Army funeral should have '*a thoroughly soldierly and triumphant appearance*'. The Home Call of a comrade meant that he had been Promoted to Glory and there should be no gloom about the celebration of such a victory. But the sorrow of those left behind was not to be neglected or treated heartlessly either.

'*The principal aim in everything connected with a funeral should be the salvation of souls, the increase of holiness and zeal in Salvationists, the comforting and spiritual development of the bereaved, and the glory of God.*'

Mrs Jackson said she understood and Penn looked with renewed respect at her parents and their Army: it did make sense, if you believed what all Christians professed to believe.

Alice came home for the funeral looking old-fashioned but dignified in clothes chosen by the elderly school-mistresses. She gravely accepted the Army's white arm-band stamped with red to be worn on the left arm instead of mourning and supported her mother closest to the coffin. Her longish darkish clothes, worn unself-consciously, and her long pale face with green eyes observant and unflinching, made Penn feel as frivolous as the twins in her halo-hat and lacy jumper. Alice had changed; seemed in some ways older than her former friends and in others younger. She smiled slightly at them from her place at the graveside. She seemed completely sure of herself in a nervous way as she concentrated on the service in her odd but graceful clothes. '*Above the waves of earthly strife...*' The Corps Officer led the singing with her concertina as the coffin was lowered into the earth.

Wreaths were discouraged as a waste of money but the little children threw garden flowers into the grave. Father took their hands as Mrs Jackson wept on Alice's shoulder until the song ended. Then he tenderly released the biggest boy, touched his head to keep him in place and in contact, and raised his hand. The Colour Sergeant lifted the Flag and its brave white ribbons caught the morning air as its darned blue edge dipped into the dark shadow of the grave. They had reached the last words of the funeral service.

"*God bless and comfort the bereaved!*" called father.

"*Amen,*" the Salvationists responded loudly.

"*God help us to be faithful unto death!*"

"*Amen.*"

"*God bless the Salvation Army!*"

"*Amen.*"

It was a quiet funeral as Mr Jackson's conversion had been too recent for the Band to take time off work on a week-day as they would for a warrior of longer service. All dispersed now, the allowed alternative to a march to the Hall to the striking up of a salvation war song. Mrs Carr had made refreshments in their own front room and then helped Mrs Jackson see to her house and young children while Alice and Connie and Grace and Penn talked quietly in the afternoon garden. They were all conscious of difference but tolerant because they remembered each other from so long ago and because of the seriousness of the occasion. Connie and Penn began to make a daisy chain, slipping each flower into the split stem of the next. Soon the four girls were sitting in a circle as they had when they were small, plaiting daisies idly, and passing pieces of information to each other as recently they had passed funeral biscuits. It was the thought that mattered. They recalled stitching along one side of a sheet on long-ago Empire Days while friends hemmed the other three sides. The landscape of cotton was changed as you edged along by mutual consent. Mountain peaks of snowy stuff were flattened in the turn of a wrist. Life was less simple now.

Alice was sorry in a way to have to leave her ladies but pleased to be home. She would join Penn at the mixed school next week. The allied landings had been successful a week ago; but that day there was news of a frightening new bomb which had no driver and gave no warning. When calls to tea echoed through the Banjo as dusk began, they parted with aloof, warm smiles for their own homes.

The Carrs were quiet over tea. Mother had been crying; not only for Mr Jackson. After tea she stood up from prayer and said suddenly:

"It's a great sorrow, you know."

"Shush now Mummy," said Father.

"No, I think it needs to be said. It's a great sorrow to your Father and me. I've asked for guidance but I don't understand it, I might as well confess. Penny, pet, why won't you rededicate your life and be a Soldier?"

Father said, "Now then, Mummy, it's been a difficult day."

But: "Why?" Mother insisted.

"Well..." Penn's difficulties with the doctrine seemed petty under Mother's pained and loving demand. She wished she could express her real doubt truthfully and clearly.

"Let's leave it now," said Father. "It's not good to let too much emotion cloud our judgement." But he saw that the argumentative girl was moved by Mother's too much emotion more than by his patient discussions; and wondered where his duty lay. His wife, meanwhile, had registered his firmness and went on in a tone less intense: "I'd just like to tell her a story before we leave it."

"Very well."

They took their armchair seats beneath Jesus knocking, around the empty summer grate shining with black-lead and a vase of flowers where the fire should be.

"It's kept coming back to me all day," said Mother.

Penn leaned forward willingly. "Yes?"

"The night of the fire of London, when they dropped all those incendiaries, you were in the country. It was a bad time. Just after Christmas in 1940. After Dunkirk and when we cycled down to visit you. Daddy and I and everybody in the Banjo was out. You know we don't often go out front. But it was such a sight. And you could soon tell that it wasn't the usual bombing so we didn't need to stay in our shelters. You could see this bright orange to the west; sky brighter than before the black-out, much brighter. Father thought it looked about at the City. Where Headquarters was. And soon you could smell it too, even as far away as this; and see smoke in the air above the brightness of what must be flames. So Father—I didn't like it—got his bike out and set off to see what it was and if anything could be done. I think he knew then; he'd had a Call, I felt that too. He didn't come back all night. None of us got much sleep. The noise and the smell and the worry. But of course I was worried for him. The Jacksons were very kind and so on. But I didn't know what would become of your father, out in the midst of it on his bike. And then just after dawn he got back. He was ever so dirty with smoke, tired out. He pushed his bike up the path, not saying anything. When we got in he took off his cycle clips and pushed his cap to the back of his head and I saw he'd got some cuts and bruises under the soot. And I saw he'd shed a tear too. And he said the Headquarters had gone, burned to the ground, with all the Army records and everything, and he'd stood and watched it. In case there was anything he could save; but there wasn't. They couldn't control the fire at all round there. Everything went except St Paul's. But to your father it was the International Headquarters which stood for what all our lives were dedicated to. He couldn't save anything. It was just getting light and we knelt to pray, just as he was, like that, and I was crying but he was strong then."

Penn could see that her father was shy but moved by the memory. "Go on," she asked her mother.

"Well; he asked forgiveness for setting so much store by a building and thanked God for the lesson not to put your faith in bricks and mortar. Cycling home—and think how tired he'd be—it had come to him that this was a sign and a reminder. The Kingdom of God is not made with hands. Though Headquarters were paid for with money they could ill afford from soldiers and officers all over the world, it was not the Army itself. And then he said—I've always remembered—that you, Penny, that you were a stronger vessel than the great building he had seen burn down that night. That any little child with Jesus in her heart was a fortress which would last longer than any hall. That the Army, like the City of God, was built of souls; and the Army's future was in the saved souls of its children. And he prayed that you would stand fast against temptations and that your soul would stay safe though the citadels were burning." Father was saying shush and watching with a troubled face as her mother's emotion worked on Penn; though reason until now had been all her objection. "So now you know how much it means," Mother finished.

"Yes," said Penn. "Now I can. And I do want to. I'm sorry."

Mother smoothed her skirt and stood up. She always ironed out wrinkles with firm movements of her patient, work-worn hands. She appeared satisfied to see Penn near tears, but that now it was time to tidy up. "You must pray about it," she finished, straightening the picture above the mantelpiece unnecessarily on her way into the kitchen.

Father cleared his throat. "And you must think about it too," he said. "We want you to be true to yourself."

"Whatever that may be." She pulled a face. "Is it so important?" Mother's devotion and duty made her ashamed of self-regard.

But: "Yes," said Father; "very important."

"You mean my conscience? The inner voice? Sometimes it just seems an excuse to take yourself seriously."

Father said: "It is. Used properly."

Penn looked at him with some surprise. He had changed too. His face was not soppy at all; whatever Michael might condemn about people who knocked at the door of your heart. She looked from Father's grave but stern expression to the picture between them above the mantelpiece. The lure of Jesus with his knot of thorns: his crown was a closed circle: it left out too much: it left out blood and fire as Dr Julian interpreted and even as the Army preached.

"But," said Penn. "When Headquarters burned. . . ."

"I learned something, Mummy's right. But not to put my trust in any soul doing even the right thing for the wrong reason."

Through the kitchen door they heard Mother washing up. She was singing a chorus at the top of her clear sweet voice and clattering cutlery like cymbals. The sound was both rebuke and comfort. "I don't want to let her down," said Penn.

"Then don't," said Father. "You'd do that by doing what she wanted just because she wanted it. Your mother's faith deserves better than that. Come on. Let's help her with the drying-up."